The Last Empath of Doctsland

Leah Putz

www.darkstroke.com

Discover us online:
www.darkstroke.com

Join us on instagram:
www.instagram.com/darkstrokebooks/

Include **#darkstroke** in a photo of yourself
holding this book on Instagram and
something nice will happen.

To my parents,
who always encouraged me
to keep writing.

Acknowledgements

Special thanks to Amelia for the help on the title, Karin for being my idea sounding board, to Renee (@cursedcatcus on Instagram) for her incredible work on the map, and to darkstroke for taking a chance on this debut author!

About the Author

Leah Putz has been writing for as long as she can remember. Filling notebooks in school, writing on the scrap paper stolen from her mom's desk at work, and even producing a short story in 7th grade, distributed to family and friends. She writes almost as often as she reads.

The Last Empath of Doctsland is her first novel. She set out to create a fantasy story featuring the key character types she missed when reading stories in the genre, notably strong women, people of color, and LGBTQ+ characters.

She lives and works in Minnesota, spending her free time either hanging out with her dog Frodo, or travelling as much as possible.

The Last
Empath of
Doctsland

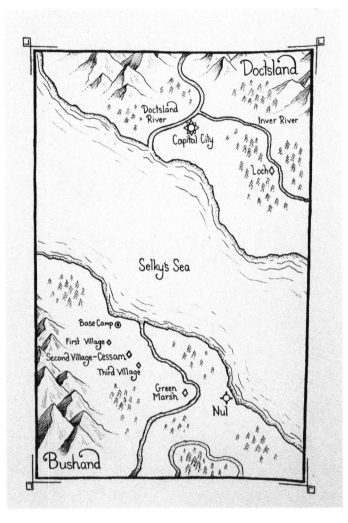

Dearest Counsellors,

Please find here the account of our journey, as written by myself and the lady Lisalya Manyeo. We hope it may offer explanation for my sudden disappearance, as well as the loss of many strong and true Doctsland soldiers. I shall accept any punishment you see fit to place upon me, including the confiscation of my crown.

Most Sincerely,
Prince Viktor of Doctsland

Chapter One

Lisalya

"Lisalya. *Lisalya!*" My mother's voice startled me awake, though I hadn't even realized I was sleeping. The excitement of the townspeople had kept me up most of last night, so I had spent the morning in an exhausted daze. I'd headed to the outskirts of the town, where a well was situated on top of a hill. Upon arrival I must have sat down and accidentally drifted off. Floating at the bottom of the well, the bucket sat waiting. "Did you fall asleep?" Ma asked, concern heavy in her voice and her strong brow. "How much sleep did you get last night?"

Standing, I swept away any grass that had stuck to my backside and cringed at how damp it was. The danger of sitting on the ground in such a rainy country - the grass is always wet. "I'm fine. Sorry, I know the water was needed."

"It's alright," she replied, pulling the bucket up. "I guess I'm just relieved you've gotten at least some rest this week."

She was right in assuming this little nap by the well is the most rest I've received since the queen died. The whole village was bubbling with nerves and excitement, so much so that it crept beyond the limits of the town center and reached me in our home on the outskirts. Though I merely felt the hysteria, I could easily predict what they were all thinking. *When will the prince be coronated? What will it be like to have such a young, seemingly debaucherous ruler? Will he tour the country, as other new rulers have done in the past? Will he come here?* None of these questions were anything I cared to know the answer to. Who ruled this country had never really affected our small, lakeside village, so why should I care if the queen died, or if her enigma of a step-son was going to be King? Why does *anyone* care?

Unfortunately, regardless of my feelings about the monarchy, I couldn't help what anyone else was feeling, or to stop their emotions from filtering into my mind. One of the biggest burdens of being an empath (and apparently the only empath in this country) was that when big events happened like this, everyone started buzzing and it would be impossible to shut their voices off. Mother would usually be hovering over me during times like these, anxiously trying to make sure I'm okay, but I'd learned to try to keep my distance from people. The farther the distance, the easier it would be to drown them out.

"When we get back, set the water by the fire. Your grandmother needs to boil it." My mother's voice stirred me out of my reverie, during which she'd already secured the bucket to her horse's reins and mounted. I hopped onto my horse and we began to make our way back towards the village.

"What is she making again?" I asked as we rode.

"Pa got nicked by a stray arrow when he was hunting. She has to disinfect and seal the wound. I'm surprised you haven't felt it yet. We must still be too far away."

As if on cue, a sharp pain began to sear through my calf, growing stronger as we approached our home. Typically, I would only feel faint senses of people's injuries. My empathic abilities weren't as strong as the empaths of old, who could feel everything from everyone, but I was thankful for that. I would have certainly lost my mind. However, I did feel, acutely, the pain of those I loved. The familial bond strengthened my mind's connection to them.

Ma must have noticed the grimace I had tried to hide. With the sympathetic gaze she often adorned, she replied, "I'm sorry, love. Hopefully it will be short lived. I don't imagine it will take your grandmother long to heal him."

I smiled, hoping to ease her mind. It was never easy for her to know I have to bear the pain of others. "No, surely not."

The rest of the journey was spent in silence, my mother choosing not to speak in an effort to allow me space to focus. As we approached, the excitement of the villagers grew louder, and I felt myself nearly vibrating with their curiosity. I shifted in my saddle uncomfortably as the feeling grew to be too much, and pain began to pierce my temples. I tried to tune them out using a technique I had developed for myself as a child to help me sleep, or to just give me some peace of mind. A deep breath, eyes closed, focusing on the tangible sounds of the world around me. The wind through the curled black and white strands of my hair, the hooves of our horses hitting the ground, the water sloshing back and forth in the bucket, the villagers greeting us. *The villagers greeting us.* My eyes snapped open as I heard real voices speaking, greeting. We had arrived back into town.

I put my head down as we rode through the village towards our home, having never been very comfortable with the level of fame, or infamy, rather that my family gained since my birth. The Manyeo women had always been known to be powerful, descended from an ancient line of witches. Magic flew through our veins as thick as blood. But when rumors began to spread of my abilities as an empath, our name became even more renowned. The empathic power was thought to have died out hundreds of years ago, when the last known empath went mad due to the force of her abilities, and she took her own life before she could pass on the trait to any children. That extinction ended with my birth, however.

I brushed my thoughts aside as we came up to the house. Ma dismounted immediately with the water and bolted inside the house, her concern for Pa's wound obvious. I wasn't as worried. Though the pain was sharp, I could feel it was probably not deep. And grandmother could fix almost anything. This would be an easy session for her. After dismounting, I grabbed the reins of both horses, leading them into the pasture behind our family's house.

Grandmother was still waiting for the water to boil by the time I strolled through the front door. Pa sat right beside her with his leg outstretched and trousers rolled up past his right knee. "How did this even happen?" I asked as I made my way towards them in the atrium. I took a seat across the small fire that was boiling the water.

Pa looked up and grinned, stretching his sun tanned face. "Ah, it's nothing. Just a scratch."

I rolled my eyes, but smiled back nonetheless, "It hurts a bit more than 'just a scratch.'"

Sighing, he leaned back on his elbows as my grandmother began to wipe the wound with a damp cloth in preparation for her healing spell. "Just a stray arrow. Kid that isn't so good at aiming tried to go for a rabbit, nicked my leg in the process. I think he probably feels worse than I do about it."

I couldn't help but widen my grin at my father's genial nature. Of course he wouldn't have held it against the person that had accidentally shot him, though plenty of others would. Closing my eyes, I let his sensations flow over me, to feel exactly how he felt about the occurrence. As suspected, I felt no hint of anger from him. There was some mild irritation and an obvious throb in his leg, but that was already beginning to soothe as Grandmother's magic and herbs worked together to heal her son.

"Hey!" My eyes snapped open to look at him at his exclamation. Though he wasn't 'gifted' with magic the way his mother and his daughter were, he was the only person that could ever sense when I was prodding into his feelings; a small glimmer of the magic that blessed the women of his blood. "I know that look. Get out of my feelings." He meant to sound affronted, but couldn't mask the glint of amusement in his voice, or in his eyes.

Grinning sheepishly, I held my hands up. "Sorry, Pa. Won't happen again."

It was his turn to roll his eyes. "We both know it will, you nosy thing."

I mirrored his exclamation. "Hey!" He didn't respond, but his shoulders shook with laughter and I couldn't help but reciprocate.

Finally Grandmother spoke, wiping a stray grey hair out of her face, clearly tired of our antics. "Are you two done? I'm

8

not finished yet and it's a little hard when you're squiggling around like a toddler." She held two boiled leaves over the wound, pushing them into his skin and painting around their edges with her reed.

He grimaced, frowning. "Sorry, Ma. It's Lis' fault." I scoffed, earning a wink and a chuckle from him.

"Really Pa, you ought to be more careful."

"She's right, you know." I turned at the sound of my mother's voice to see her strolling in from the hall, carrying a dry cloth for bandaging as soon as grandmother was done with her spell. She had piled her black hair atop her head and changed into her typical pink house dress. "You should be more careful. You're not twenty anymore. It's not as easy to heal older flesh."

"Sheesh, love, you make it sound so delicate," Pa replied sarcastically. "I'm not dying, and fifty is not *that* old."

"I know, I know." Ma took a seat beside Grandma, holding the bandage cloth close. "And I know this isn't particularly your fault."

"Finally! Someone is making some sense!" he exclaimed as I bit my lip to hold back a giggle.

"But! It could easily have been. You are a bit too reckless for your age. It's time you learned to take it easy. Why were you even out hunting today? We have plenty of food and you know it's been tough on Lisalya since the queen died."

"Ma-" I began, but Pa cut me off.

"That is true, I didn't need to be out. But it's fun to go out. And Lis can take care of herself."

Ma's gaze turned sharp at his argument. "She fell asleep at the well."

He turned to face me. "Is that true? Have you been getting that little sleep?"

Shrugging, I tried to make light of it, hoping they wouldn't get too worried about me. "It's just a little hard to sleep here, so close to everyone."

"Can't you do that 'turn off' thing you do with us sometimes?" Pa asked.

I couldn't help but roll my eyes. Twenty-three years of

knowing me and he still didn't get it sometimes. "Pa-" I started before my mother cut in.

"Really Regin. She has explained this to you possibly a hundred times. She can block out particular people, but only a handful at a time, and she has to consciously select the people she wants to silence. When the whole town is in an uproar, including visitors she doesn't know, there's nothing she can do."

"Right, right, I remember. Sorry," he said, standing and stretching his leg. Ma huffed before heading into the kitchen while Pa turned back towards Grandmother. "All finished? That was quick."

"Yes, all finished. It was not deep, as you know, so it was quick work," Grandmother replied before turning towards me as she wiped her sweating hands on her apron. "Lisalya, I do wish you would get more involved in healings." I opened my mouth to object but she silenced me. "I know the bulk of your skills lie in your empathic abilities, but that doesn't mean you cannot also heal. Healers' blood is strong in your veins, it's what our family is known for. You must learn to harness that part of your power before my time is through."

"I have a long while before that happens, Grandmother."

She sighed, clearly as fed up with having this conversation as I was. It wasn't sticking. I knew I needed to carry on with the healing practice once she passed, but somehow accepting that meant I had to face the fact that she was getting older. At some point, she wouldn't be around anymore. It was something I wasn't quite ready to acknowledge, and for some reason pushing off learning to heal felt like keeping her alive and well forever.

Ma came into the atrium from the kitchen. She was holding a large pot full of beans, peppers, and other vegetables. "As long as you already have a fire going out here, I'll just cook dinner over it." She halted, dark eyes so similar to my own widening as they flitted from face to face, trying to read the room and sensing the tension. "What were you talking about?" She asked, trying to lighten the mood, while also getting to the root of the discussion. As the only member of the family not 'blessed' with any gifts, she always was often the voice of reason and mediator.

"Ma is trying to get Lis to learn how to heal again," Pa explained.

Now it was my mother's turn to sigh. "Lis, do you want to be a healer?"

Her question startled me. I don't think anyone had ever asked me before. It had always just been assumed that was what I would do, whether I had wanted to or not. "I-" I began, but hesitated, not sure how to respond.

She knelt beside me, taking my hands in hers and looking into my eyes, searching them for truth. "If you don't want to learn to be a healer, if that isn't what you want to do with your life, you don't have to."

My heart swelled. I knew that my mother cared enough to give me the choice no one in my family had ever had, the choice to do whatever I *want*. But being now faced with the choice, I didn't know *what* I wanted. "I- I'm not sure."

"You're not sure?" Grandmother spoke up, the rage barely concealed in her voice. "Everyone in this town relies on this family. When somebody is injured or sick, we help them. We save them. And we are the only ones in these parts who can. People travel for hours, from all over the country for our help." I bit my lip, holding back tears that threatened to spill onto my cheeks.

"Ma, don't pressure her. She already has enough of that with feeling what everyone around her feels." He was right. I could feel the guilt and pity from both of my parents, as well as the fury radiating off grandmother.

"I want to help people as we always have. I do. I just… I don't know."

After a long hesitation, Grandmother spoke, her voice a bit gentler. "You don't feel ready?" she asked.

I shook my head, words seeming unnecessary when she had already articulated what I was feeling.

She paused before sighing again. "The son of one of the fishermen tripped and fell as he was playing with his friends. It seems he has a broken arm and his knees are quite scratched up."

"Um. Alright?" I said, furrowing my brow in confusion, not sure why she was telling me this.

"He's coming in an hour. Will you at least entertain the idea of assisting me with his healing? No-" she continued, before I could interject my objection. "No more than your parents do. But perhaps being present during a healing for someone other than yourself or your parents will help. Over time, you will begin to remember what you see me do. It will become natural to you."

I stared into the fire, taking my time to mull it over. "Alright. I'll do it. I'll help you heal the fisherman's boy."

She grinned, and I couldn't help but send a small smile back her way. "Wonderful, my dear." She stood, and I noticed with a slight panic for the first time that she moved a bit slower than she ever had before. Flickers of light from the fire danced across her dark skin as she made her way past it to her bundle of herbs in the corner. She picked out a few and handed them to me. "Now, go fetch me five more bundles of each of these. You'll find some at the shop in town, the berryroot and sage to be exact. The rest you'll see at the edge of the forest. People don't use those for cooking, so no one thinks they're important enough to harvest and sell."

I stared down at the collection of greens and deep purples in my hands. "What are those called?"

"They're known most commonly as dragonshearth and thimbleweed," Grandmother said absentmindedly. She'd shifted her focus to organizing the herbs she currently had and cleaning up the corner she kept all of her supplies in. She worked most often in the atrium of the house as its center location made it easy to collect something from any other room. She also felt that it focused her power, both its location in the center of the house and its lack of ceiling or roof, which strengthened her connection to the natural world. The supplies she stashed there were well organized and sturdy so that nothing would blow away in the breeziness of the open room. "What are you still standing there for? Hurry along!" She snapped me back to reality and I realized I had just been loitering, watching her tidy like a fool.

I smiled at my own foolishness. "Sorry, Grandmother. I'll be on my way!"

With that, I strolled back through the house and outside. As soon as I set foot on the emerald grass I quickened, making my way to the edge of the forest a half mile away as quickly as possible without sprinting. Grandmother had told me to hurry along, and I wasn't keen to disappoint her any more than I already had today. After a pit stop in the towns center to purchase the berryroot and sage, I was in the forest within thirty minutes.

I began my search as soon as I had reached my destination, and quickly found it to be much harder than I had anticipated. As I scanned the ground with my eyes, I felt the prickle of a foreign feeling nearby, but I pushed it aside, assuming it was one of the villagers heading to our house on some errand, and I wanted to harness my focus and turn it towards pursuit. All of the plants looked the same to me, despite having examples of the dragonshearth and thimbleweed to compare them to. "I don't know how she does this," I muttered, pacing around somewhat aimlessly.

"What are you looking for?" an unfamiliar voice asked. Startled, I jumped, whirling towards the direction of the voice to find a woman I had never seen before. *Strange,* I thought. *I know everyone in the village. Although maybe this is an out of towner come for healing.*

"Who are you?" I asked in return, rather than answering her question.

She stood, feet together, and bowed. "Siofra, captain of the prince's guard, as well as one of his personal guards."

I eyed her closely, suspiciously, trying to work out whether I was going to choose to believe her or not. Her garb matched her title. She was adorned in silver armor nearly from head to toe, in stark contrast to the simple brown riding pants and long sleeved tan shirt that I wore basically every day. She was holding a helmet at her side, and short chestnut-colored hair which framed her round face. "Why would one of the prince's bodyguards be here?"

She raised her eyebrows and took a step forward. "You haven't heard?"

I took a mirrored step back, still unsure about her and her story. "Heard what?"

"The prince is coming."

Eyes widening in shock, I forgot to be wary of this stranger and took a step forward towards her. "Coming here? Why?"

"That is a matter of royal business that only concerns the prince and those he seeks." I made no reply, waiting for her to continue as I could sense that she clearly had more to say, or perhaps more she wanted to ask. After no more than a beat, she did just as I suspected. "What are you looking for?" she asked, repeating her initial question.

I hesitated, then decided I might as well just tell the truth. Even if she wasn't who she said she was, it wasn't as if my collecting herbs in the forest was a secret. "These plants, dragonshearth and thimbleweed. I need to find them for my grandmother."

She scrunched up her nose, bunching up her freckles. I almost giggled, it was a funny look on such a previously serious face. "Why would you want dragonshearth and thimbleweed? They're fairly useless, aren't they?"

I shrugged and went back to my searching. "Most people think so. They have their benefits, though, apparently," I added as an afterthought, realizing I didn't really even know what they did, I just trusted grandmother's word that they were useful.

She raised an eyebrow, but pointed at the ground to her right, nonetheless. "Well, there's some thimbleweed right there. I can't help you with the dragonshearth, though. I don't see any around."

Without hesitation I scurried over towards the spot she pointed out and, sure enough, found a thick patch of the purple, thorny thimbleweed plant. "Thanks very much!" I exclaimed, pulling the plant carefully out of the ground so as not to prick myself on its occasional thorn.

She shrugged, and I chose to think that it was a silent

'you're welcome.' Growing curious, I tried to see if I could snuff out her purpose. I sensed her wariness and determination, but that really didn't tell me much about why she may be in Loch. "What are you doing all the way out here anyway? If the prince really is coming into town, shouldn't you be with him, you know, 'personally guarding' him as his 'personal guard'?"

She shifted her stance to put her weight on one foot and crossed her arms defiantly. "I'm securing the perimeter. We need to make sure there are no bands of thieves, vagabonds, or even rebels lurking on the outskirts of the village or even hiding-" she gestured towards the forest "-in the woods."

"I suppose that makes sense. But there aren't any. Not in Loch."

She shrugged, unconvinced. "I have to check, I can't just take the word of whoever. I best be getting back to it. Happy to help you find your thimbleweed, and good luck with the other one!" She called the last bit over her shoulder, having already begun to walk away.

"Thanks!" I called after her. "Have fun guarding the prince!" I added as an afterthought, still unsure whether I believed he was really coming here or not. It seemed too far-fetched. Why on earth would a member of the royal family, especially one immediately next in line for the throne, and for all intents and purposes already king, be coming to our small village? The only out of towners that ever visit were looking specifically for our family and the healing we may have offered, and I highly doubted the prince would be so injured as to come this far. And if that had happened, surely I would have felt a buzz like nothing before coming from the town. But I felt nothing more than what I had already been dealing with since the news of the queen's death. *If* the prince was coming, or already here, it was one hell of a well-kept secret. If even one person from town had known, surely the news would have spread like the worst of wildfires.

Finally, after a few minutes of pondering, I shrugged, deciding I didn't really care if or why the prince might be here. I re-poured all of my focus into searching for the plant, not wanting to waste any more time meandering. I weaved amongst the signature narrow, tall trees of our country, careful not to step on any moss covered rocks and slip.

Sure enough, after only a few minutes of searching without distraction, I found a patch of dragonshearth nestled up against a pine tree, almost completely hidden from view. Once this was plucked from the ground, I hurried home, all the way worrying that I had spent too much time in my collection. On my way, I made sure I had my mind blocked. If the boy had beat me there, and truly had a broken arm, I didn't want to be burdened with all that pain upon my arrival.

"Finally!" My grandmother grumbled when I strolled inside. I sighed when I saw that the fisherman and his son had already arrived, thankful that I had thought to block myself. But that also meant everyone was definitely waiting on me. "Here, I'll take those," Grandmother gently took a bundle of herbs from my arms and began inspecting them closely before making a sound of contentment. "Good job. These are in good condition. Now what took so long?" As she spoke, she made her way over to her fire and began breaking some of the herbs into small pieces before sprinkling them into the fire.

"I ran into a stranger and got distracted." She looked up sharply, alarm evident in her deep set eyes, but I shooed away any worries of danger. "It was fine. She meant no harm." I finally took stock of the guests we had, seated on cushions near the fire, but not too near. I winced as soon as I saw the boy, who could not have been more than seven or eight, cradling a mangled arm to his chest.

"Give me your arm, dear," Grandmother said gently to him, holding her hands out. Reluctantly the boy tried to move his arm, but a sob was ripped from him. He bit his lip to try to hold it in, clearly trying his damnedest to be as strong as he could. Whimpers still escaped despite his efforts. "Lisalya, will you take a cup of that?" She nodded to the water simmering on the fire. "Hand it to him."

Nodding, I ran to fetch a cup from the kitchen and did just that. I felt a little light-headed as I leaned over the bubbling pot, breathing in the warm fragrance of the boiling herbs. Whatever this was that brewed was undoubtedly very strong. As quickly as I could I scooped up the potent liquid and handed the hot cup to the boy, who took it with his slightly trembling good hand.

"We'll wait until it cools off a bit, and then I want you to take the biggest drink you can manage, okay?" The boy nodded at grandmother's words.

The next few minutes were spent in silence, waiting for the liquid to cool enough for the boy to drink it without burning his mouth. Grandmother rubbed some of the leftover herbs on her hands, along with some lavender oil. "It should be cool enough now. Drink, my dear." The boy looked nervous, and a tad skeptical. He sniffed it and hesitated. "It will help to numb your pain," Grandmother said, and with that reassurance, his eyes went wide and he immediately put his lips to the cup, draining it quickly enough that the rest of us couldn't help but chuckle as his eagerness.

"It should kick in almost instantly. When you're ready, try to extend your arm to me." She held out both hands, prepared to take the arm once the boy was ready.

Nearly as soon as the cup was empty, he passed it to his father and closed his eyes, taking a deep breath and attempting to prepare himself for the daunting task of moving his damaged arm. Once steadied, he slowly moved it a bit towards grandmother. His eyes snapped open and he grinned. "I can't feel it! It doesn't hurt anymore!" The joy in his voice made me smile, and I opened myself up a bit so I could feel how the healing process felt in his body, now that the pain was numbed and replaced with a warm, tingling sensation. Once I broke down the wall I had built around myself, I felt multiple sensations, among them the fisherman's concern for his child, and my grandmother's calmness during the act of performing a healing like so many others she had done in the past. By far the strongest sensation was the warmth and tranquility coursing through his body, which I assume stemmed from the drink.

Once he realized he had no pain, he extended his bad arm

towards Grandmother without hesitation. She took it gently and began massaging the oil and herb mixture from her hands into it. As she did this, she hummed a low, relaxing and familiar melody. I'd heard it many times, always during the mending of broken bones. I knew it from when she had repaired my own broken ankle twelve years ago, when I was a mere eleven summers old. The song, which was a soft melody that repeated itself every minute or so, lasted no more than five or six minutes. She never stopped her careful messaging of his arm, sure to cover every inch of the red and angry flesh and, as she continued, it became less red and less angry. By the time she reached the end of her song, it no longer had the mangled look it held before. In fact, it seemed as good as new.

"There you are dear," she said, releasing the arm at last. "Leave that oil on until you are finished walking home, then you may rinse it off. Your arm is fully healed now."

"Thank you, truly, Madam Manyeo. You really are a gift to this community." His father stood and bowed down to Grandmother. He grabbed a basket that I hadn't noticed sitting at his feet. "Here, please take these fish. They're the freshest catch we've got. I only brought them in from the lake two hours ago."

Grandmother took the basket, smiling and thanking him as she walked both he and his son to the door.

I sat back down near the fire and heaved a sigh, contemplating what I had just witnessed. But I was struggling to keep my eyes open, still exhausted from my lack of sleep, and the energy it took to maintain the block I had made until the boy was numb had drained me even more. Sure, I had seen Grandmother heal people before, plenty of times. But I had never paid as much attention to it as I did today, and I had certainly never before watched with the knowledge that this will be my job someday at the forefront of my mind. I still wasn't sure I could handle the pressure, and I most certainly did not feel ready to handle anything on my own, let alone being the sole healer of a full village.

Chapter Two

Viktor

I shifted foot to foot, trying to appear calm to all that saw me. All but one, my best friend and right hand man Jion, who could surely see I was agitated. Being friends since childhood meant he could easily recognize the signs. I chewed the inside of my cheek, and my hands clasped together behind my back tight enough that I was sure my knuckles were white. My eyes, hidden from view of the crowd in the hall by the long silver hair that fell past the bridge of my nose in loose waves, bore into the floor with enough intensity that I was surprised I wasn't boring a hole into it.

"Sire?" One of the councilmen spoke up, attempting to get my attention after a few minutes of being ignored. I gave no indication that I heard the man.

Taking a breath and probably hoping not to royally piss off the royal, Jion gave me a slight nudge and a whisper of, "Vik."

After a moment I lifted my head, and my pale blue eyes met the court before turning to Jion. "Hmm?"

Jion jerked his head toward the awaiting nobles, and I followed his gaze before taking a deep breath and speaking. "Yes, I know it's time for a coronation. I know it's well *past* time, and that preparations need to begin immediately." The deep baritone of my voice commanded all attention as I threw their words back at them. "I am aware of all of this."

"You must put your servants to work to begin preparing the castle," the same councilman said, confident he had my attention, and, he thought, my ear.

I cleared my throat. "What I *must* do," I began, "is to

protect our country from the threat of our neighbor, and until recently ally, Bushand."

"*Surely* King Siglind wouldn't launch an attack now, so recently after your step-mother, the Queen of Doctsland and his *mother*, died. Surely he will respect the peace of the mourning period. It is a universal custom."

Rapidly losing my patience, I waved him, and all the others, off. "Please leave. There is much for me to do as you all have mentioned, countless times," I added, the snarky tone heavy in my voice.

Jion, who had been fighting to keep his thin lips in a tight line in an attempt to thwart laughter, let loose as soon as the last courtesan left and the door shut behind him. "I'm sorry, Vik, but their cluelessness is astounding."

I shot him a glare, but there was no real threat in it, and finally I smiled, though it didn't quite reach my eyes. "Will you shut up, Jion? You look like a rabbit with that stupid grin and your teeth sticking out."

"Hey!" Jion said, only partially affronted. "My grin isn't stupid!"

I clapped him on the shoulder sympathetically as I walked past. "You keep telling yourself that. Now, are we going to figure this mess with Bushand out or what?"

"What about 'the coronation'?" Jion asked, quickening his steps to keep pace with me.

I shot him a sideways glance. "You're joking right? You know I don't give a sod about that ridiculous party."

"Time was when you would have leapt at the chance to throw a party like that."

"Yeah well." I paused, reminiscing the days when I loved any opportunity for a dance and a drink. "That was before." I hoped Jion recognized the hint of nostalgia and heartbreak in my voice. He must have, because he decided, compassionately, to change the subject.

"Alright, so we're skipping the coronation. What are you going to tell the council?"

Smirking, I stopped walking as we reached the door to the front entrance of the palace. "Nothing."

Before Jion could respond, I pushed the doors open and took a look around to make sure no one was near before continuing outside. I threw the hood of my cloak up, pulling it low over my face in the hope that I could walk through the city unrecognized. "Let's head to your house. We need to come up with some sort of plan, and we need to make sure none of the members of the court get a whiff of it. Otherwise they'll come barging down my throat with this coronation garbage again." Jion nodded, but I stopped suddenly. "Will Hope mind?"

Jion snorted and started to laugh. "Not at all. He'll either be gone attending to a patient, or he'll be reading something, paying us no mind."

I smiled, relieved, and we continued on their way. We walked through the city in silence, trying not to draw too much attention to ourselves, or to have our words picked up by the wrong ears.

We arrived fairly quickly. Jion, being one of my closest guards, lived close to the palace with his husband. That way, should anything happen when he's not on duty, he would be able to be by my side in a short amount of time. "Hope?" Jion called, pushing open the door to his cottage. "Are you home?"

Hope, seated in a comfortable chair before a small fire in their sitting room, barely looked up from his book. "You're home early. Ah, and you've brought Viktor. Hello!" He grinned widely at me before becoming flushed. "Goodness, Jion, couldn't you have told me? I would have tidied up or something before the literal prince of our nation comes visiting."

Jion merely shrugged, tugging off the formal cape he had to wear whenever he was on duty at the palace, and draping it over a coat hanger in the corner by the door.

"Don't worry, Hope. This place shines compared to my quarters," I said, smiling.

Hope barked out a laugh. "Your quarters must be disgusting. It was Jion's turn to clean up the kitchen after dinner last night and he does a terrible job."

"Hey, hey. Easy. I do my best," Jion said, strolling into the kitchen and clearing off the kitchen table. "We can sit here. There is enough space for three or four. Is Siofra coming?"

I put my palm to my forehead. "Damn, I forgot to tell her. I think it's her day off. She's probably out in the fields with her dog. I'll go grab her."

"No, no you won't," Hope said, cutting in. "Clearly the two of you are up to some serious business if you came here to talk and you also need to bring Siofra in on her day off. You can get a head start while I go fetch her. It will send far too many tongues wagging if the prince is wandering around looking for his personal guard. His only *female* personal guard. There are enough rumors without you and Siofra meandering through the city together."

I opened my mouth to object when Jion spoke up. "Great! Thanks, Hope. We'll see you back in a bit."

As soon as the door shut behind Hope I turned to Jion. "There's nothing going on between Siofra and I. You know that right?"

Jion scoffed. "Of course I know that. I'm around you two all the time. There's no way anything could be going on. Plus Siofra takes her job way too seriously. It would be forbidden, a scandal, for the prince to be sleeping with a guard. She'd never let it happen."

"Nor would I compromise her job and her status by letting it. She'd be ostracized."

Jion shrugged. "You don't have as much willpower as she does, but I believe you. People only think that because your mother was a guard when your father married her." He didn't sound as convinced as I was, but either way I was happy enough that although the whole country seemed to believe the rumors regarding me and one of my most trusted guards, at least my best friend was smart enough not to buy into the folly. I sighed, supposing it came with the territory of having a sordid past.

"Siofra and I are barely even friends. I try to joke around with her and she never laughs," I mumbled, pouting a little.

Jion, on the other hand, did laugh, his signature high-pitched cackle in fact. "I know. I see it. And it's painful. Why do you think I laugh extra hard? To try to mitigate the awkward tension that emanates from you when someone doesn't find you amusing."

"You make me sound pathetic."

"You aren't pathetic. You've just been raised around a bunch of people that will always laugh even when you're not funny. Everyone caters to you when you're the prince. I imagine it's hard when someone doesn't, even if that someone is focusing all of her energy on her duty of protecting you."

"Yeah, whatever." I shifted uncomfortably. The conversation was getting a little too deep for my comfort, not one to delve into emotional matters often, so I shifted the focus back to the matter at hand. "We need to channel our energies into Bushand."

Jion ran his fingers through the waves of his light auburn hair, growing serious, "Right. What exactly have you heard that puts you in such an urgent mood?"

"I'll wait until Siofra gets here to go into those details, but the fact of the matter is we need a plan of attack before they are able to reach our shores with an army."

Inhaling, Jion's doe-like eyes grew larger. "I didn't realize that was actually a tangible threat. If so, you're right, we do need to attack first. If they're allowed to march here with the sort of army they are able to produce, especially with King Siglind's iron fist, we won't stand a chance. Our strength now, and throughout the ages, has always almost exclusively been in naval warfare."

"You bring up something else I'd like to discuss. We need a stronger force of foot soldiers. If whatever plan we come up with doesn't work, we can't leave the city practically undefended."

"If we move to begin gathering forces, don't you think that will prompt Siglind to strike? He'll know we're weak," Jion countered.

I shrugged, staring at the table as my mind moved desperately. "He already knows we're weak. Especially since by now he'll have heard about his mother's death. It's a pretty common assumption, both in Doctsland and the rest of Lerashnaz, that as soon as I'm crowned, the country will all but fall apart. My father and stepmother ruled so well, and I've never had the reputation of being a good prince." I fell silent for a moment, ruminating on my past. Jion didn't interrupt, knowing there was nothing he could say that wouldn't be a lie. Finally, after a minute, I sighed. "I should have prepared for this day, especially after my father died. I should have known, or at least suspected, that Siglind would claim this throne as his."

Jion spoke up, encouraging, "No, Vik. There was no reason for you to suspect he'd do this. He has no legitimate claim to the throne. Your father was the rightful King of this land, and you're his only child. But anyway, how do you even know that Siglind has claimed the throne for himself?"

Before I could reply, the front door swung open, revealing Hope, and Siofra right behind him. "What could possibly be so important that you have to drag me in on my day off?" She complained, though we couldn't miss the worry thick in her voice.

"Take a seat, Siofra." I gestured to the empty chair at the table. "We've got quite a lot to discuss."

Siofra did just that, leaning her sword up against the table as she sat down. "Wow," Jion said, snickering at the fact that Siofra was in riding gear as opposed to her signature armor. "I've never seen you without your armor before."

"Oh shut up, Jion. Yes you have," Hope called, causing everyone to chuckle and lightening the mood somewhat. "Who wants a drink?"

Siofra rolled her eyes, but smiled nonetheless. "I'm not wearing my armor on my day off, idiot. And Hope, I will take one, thank you." Without another word, Hope brought out three cups and filled them with ale before handing them to Jion and Siofra, keeping one for himself. I shot him a small smile of thanks for keeping the temptation out of my reach.

"Alright, alright. Let's get down to business," I said, accepting a glass of water from Hope, ever the gracious host.

24

Jion and Siofra immediately shifted into guard mode, growing serious and focusing entirely on me. "My step-brother has issued a claim for my throne. He's threatened that if I don't step aside before the new year, he will take the crown, which he sees as rightfully his, by force. To answer your question, Jion, Siglind sent a declaration of such to the council."

Jion slammed his hands on the table, stopping himself from leaping out of his seat and sending it flying. "He what?!"

I pulled the letter in question from my pocket. It was official, sealed with the recently updated fire-and-axe emblem of Bushand, a symbol of Siglind's growing affinity for industry. Tossing it on the table, I launched into my explanation. "He sent it to the council, probably assuming I would let everything go there without looking it over first, but he underestimates me, regardless of how neglectful I may have been in the past. As soon as the queen died, I ordered any royal decrees or messages be sent to me in her stead prior to reaching the council. When the messenger from Bushand arrived with this, he was loath to give it directly to me, but he had no other choice."

Siofra inhaled sharply as she read over the letter herself. "Before the New Year... That's barely four months away."

I nodded, clenching my jaw. "Yes, it is."

"So," Jion continued as he stood and began to pace. "We need a plan. Obviously Vik isn't going to just give his throne away to this outsider, and we can't wait around for Bushand to attack. We need to make the first move, or build up our defenses, or *something*... We need to do something." He strolled into his bedroom, returning a few moments later with an old, weather worn map that he rolled out onto the table. The map focused on Doctsland and Bushand, Selky's Sea lying between them and a small land bridge at the north which connected the two opposing countries. "I saved this from my journey to Bushand with my father, who accompanied *your* father as his guard on the to meet his possible new bride. It was my first trip I was permitted to go on as an early teenager, and my last trip with my father prior to his death, so I've saved it. I'm surprised he let me go if I'm honest, going to Bushand as a Doctslandian was dangerous then. Only the marriage between your father and step-mother united the countries, though it appears that was a temporary truce now. Regardless, this map may be of use now."

The three of us sat in silence for a bit as we gazed at the map before us, each searching it as if it could provide a solution to our dilemma. The only noises in the room were the crackling of the fire and the occasional sound of Hope turning a page in his book as he tried not to eavesdrop on his husband's conversation.

"Could we lead an army to the Northern Pass? Surely that's where he'll attack. He doesn't have enough of a fleet to attack from the sea. His strength is in his army," Jion suggested, pointing to the mile wide stretch of land connecting Doctsland to Bushand.

"Our army is not strong enough to hold that pass. We could keep it for maybe a few weeks, but Siglind would break through with his thousands, and then there would be nothing blocking him from taking Capital City and the rest of Doctsland," Siofra said.

"But that's definitely our best chance. If we just wait for them to attack here we'll surely be annihilated. The pass gives us a fighting chance," Jion replied staunchly.

Hope suddenly jumped up from his seat, slamming his book. "Jion," he scolded. "Siofra just said that's basically a suicide mission. I'm sure the three of you can come up with another plan. One that doesn't end with your death and the absorption of this country into whatever Siglind is making Bushand."

"Dear, I'm a soldier. Part of my job is possibly dying for my country."

Hope put his hands on his hips, fixing his husband with a sharp gaze that had me wincing. "I know that but it doesn't mean you go off on the first bad plan you think of." Jion bristled at his plan being called 'bad,' but knew better than to argue, especially with Hope and Siofra on the same side.

"What if…" Siofra began, then hesitated.

"Go on," I prompted, eager to hear her thoughts. She'd always been the smartest of the three of us; the most tactile.

"If the rumors you mentioned about Siglind experimenting with dark magic are true, then we can't face any kind of outward attack from him. We have no defenses against such a thing. Our only chance would be to take him unawares. So what if we break them down from the inside?"

Jion, who had been standing in the corner, half leaning up against the wall, came forward and placed his hands on the table, causing the muscles in his forearms to bulge. "What do you mean, 'break them down from the inside'?"

A small smirk grew on my lips as I pondered her words. "Not everyone in Bushand is entirely happy with Siglind's reign since his mother left ten years ago. In fact, whispers have been growing of resistance, the possibility, however slight, of rebellion. Whispers strong enough for me to catch wind of them here."

"Exactly," Siofra said, nodding and returning my smirk. "If we infiltrate the country, perhaps we can feed into that growing resistance."

"Why would the people of Bushand aid us in a war to keep Siglind from taking power over Doctsland? It's not as if it has all that much to do with them. Would they risk being traitors to their own country to help ours remain independent?" Jion countered.

Siofra sighed. "I hadn't thought that far."

We grew silent once more, all deep in thought. Finally I spoke up. "Siglind won't give up. He won't surrender, possibly unless he faces total annihilation, and even then I'm not positive he'll give in. He will continue to reign as a terror to his people, and a threat to ours unless we remove him from power."

"But then who will be king of Bushand?" Jion asked the question we all wondered.

"It certainly won't be me. I don't want that kind of power. I'm not sure I'm even ready to take over my own country.

This has all just happened so quickly."

"Siglind has a sister, right? She hasn't been seen publicly much since their mother came here, but she exists. And she's next in line. Perhaps she will be able to take over."

"Yes, Lura," I said, remembering my step-sister. I had only met Lura and Siglind once, during their mother's coronation as Queen of Doctsland when I was twelve. Siglind had been fairly timid, and didn't speak to me much until we grew to know each other better, but Lura had been kind and outgoing. While the pressure of ruling a nation at a young age had turned Siglind into someone cruel, I hoped the same could not be said for Lura, and that she'd be willing to take up her brother's mantle. "We'll have to hope so," I sighed.

"Alright, so we infiltrate the country. Stoke the fire of resistance. Promise them a new leader, so long as they help us to dethrone Siglind. Will that be enough? Can we win with this secrecy and resistance alone?" Siofra spoke everyone's thoughts aloud.

"No, we can't. Even if all the people of Bushand joined us in our fight. It's a struggling, farming nation. The majority of its people are not warriors, they don't know how to fight, and their weapons will be merely the supplies of their houses, for the most part, especially since Siglind came into power. He doesn't allow the common folk to keep weapons for fear of an uprising. I am sorry to be so blunt, but we need our army," Jion said somberly.

"You're right," I said, nervously fiddling with my now empty water glass to keep my hands busy. "And don't apologize for being blunt, you never have before." I shot a sad grin to my friend before continuing. "Jion, you're the only one of us that has been to Bushand. How much time do you think it will take us to make our way to the countryside rallying people to our cause before we make it to Nul?"

"Hmm," Jion said, strong brows creased with deep thought. "It depends on where we're starting from. But I would guess two, maybe three months. That's if nothing waylays us."

Nodding, I stood and examined the map from above,

eyeing the stretch of sea between Doctsland and Bushand closely. "It will take approximately two weeks to for us to sail to Bushand. We'll need a small vessel, one that won't attract any notice. We won't be able to fit very many people on it. The three of us, certainly, but perhaps only a small crew in addition. Right before we leave, I'll issue a command for our entire naval fleet to launch exactly three months after we depart, leaving only a few hundred foot soldiers behind to protect Doctsland. With any luck they'll reach Nul around the same time we do for a join attack on the city."

"It might work," Jion said, gazing intently at the map. "But I don't think you should go, Viktor. If this were to fail, we can't afford to lose you."

"If this fails, it won't matter if I'm lost. The country will be lost anyway," I pointed out.

"We could stand a chance if you were still in Doctsland. There would still be hope."

"Jion," I said somberly. "If this mission fails, we will lose our entire fleet, not to mention two of our best fighters." I glanced between Jion and Siofra. "All that will be left for Siglind to do is set sail and arrive here. Nothing will stand in his way. My presence in the capital won't change that. I will be of more use coming with you."

Siofra bit her lip, hazel eyes burning into her ale as she spoke. "As much as it pains me to say this, I have to agree with Viktor. He knows Lura, and he may be our best shot at convincing her to join us and stand against her brother." My eyebrows shot up and I couldn't keep the shocked, yet smug smile from my face. I had somehow gotten Siofra's approval.

"It may work, but it's leaving a lot up to chance," Jion pointed out.

There was a moment of silence, each pondering the plan and how to improve it. Finally, Jion broke it. "What if we try to beat Siglind at his own game? What if we were to get magic involved as well?"

Siofra replied slowly, confusion etched on her tanned face. "What... exactly do you mean by magic? What kind of magic?"

"I've heard rumors, and if I've heard them, I'm sure you all have to, of a magical family in Doctsland, near to the Loch, far from the city."

"The Manyeo family, yeah. Everyone knows about them. They're always held together by a matriarch, usually a healer," Siofra explained.

"A healer would be helpful on our expedition, in case of any skirmishes, or accidental injuries," I said.

Jion put up his hand to still me. "Not the healer. Rumor has it the granddaughter is an empath."

Jaws dropping, both Siofra and I remained silent in shock. "The empaths are gone. There hasn't been an empath in almost a thousand years." Siofra spoke in quiet shock.

"Apparently not anymore."

"I've never heard this rumor. How do you know this?" I asked. I knew I'd been a bit out of the loop in the last few years, absorbed with women and gambling, but I didn't think I was so out of touch that I would miss a rumor like this.

Jion shrugged. "I *don't* know, that's the issue. It is but a rumor. We have to travel to their village to see for sure. But I'm not sure we can waste that trip if the rumors are unfounded."

"Do we have any other choice?" I asked, though everyone in the room knew it was rhetorical. "How long will it take to get there? I haven't traveled around the country as much and the two of you. I don't have a great concept of our geography."

"The quickest way will be the river. If we push off here in a small, quick ship, we can be there in two days. Coming back will take a bit longer as we'll be going against the current, but we can make it in three."

"That's a week wasted if we're wrong," Siofra said.

"But an empath gained if we're right," I said softly, a determined edge to my voice. "Think of what that could do for us. As it stands now, we're going to be walking into Bushand blind. Yes, we know there is unrest, but we don't know who or where that may be. We'd be wandering around with no guidance, hoping to come across someone that will help us. If we don't happen across anyone that will join us, or enough anyone's, before the fleet reaches Nul, we'll be defeated, no question. But with an empath, we will have the guidance that we need. She can tap into where there is unrest, and lead us to who may be inclined to join our cause. It could be the difference between glory and annihilation."

"Then we have to take the risk," Jion said, nodding.

"Agreed," Siofra replied.

I stood and paced a bit, never able to keep still when I'm anxious. My mind raced as I thought about how little time we had at our disposal. "We need to hurry. The sooner we get to this village, the better. If there is no empath, we may at least convince them to allow us to bring the healer back with us. Though not as valuable as an empath, a healer would still come in handy."

"Do we really even need to come back? Can we not just leave from Loch? We're closer to the sea there, anyway, that would help to speed up our timeline," Siofra suggested.

"Yes, I don't see why not." Jion replied. "How soon could we depart from Capital City?"

Siofra shrugged. "I'm not sure. I'd have to check the docks to see when a boat is available. If there's something open, we could leave as soon as tomorrow. Can you depart that soon?"

It was my turn to shrug. "The council won't have time to coronate me. They won't be happy, but when are they ever?" I crossed my arms over my broad chest and nodded definitively, making my mind up for certain. "Yes, I can leave tomorrow. I'll just have to sneak away. Otherwise they'll do everything in their power to stop me. These stupid traditions of coronation are more important to them than protecting our country and our people. It won't take them long to figure out where I may have gone, especially with my order for the fleet to set sail. My guess is they won't want to admit they let me sneak off. They might just pretend I'm still here."

"How about this. I will ask around at the docks today," Siofra replied. "If there is a ship available, I will secure it for myself for use tomorrow. If anyone asks questions, I'll say

I'm going to visit my family. They live south of the city, along the river. I've been to visit before, no one will ask any questions."

"That should work," I said. "I'll head back to the palace tonight, keep up the pretense that I'm working with the council to plan the coronation. In fact, I may as well play it up and give in to some of their more outrageous demands. That should keep them occupied and distracted enough with planning for me to slip away to the docks tomorrow without anyone noticing, or at least not noticing until I'm long gone."

"How will I inform you if I secure a boat? If everyone thinks I'm leaving and I suddenly show up at the palace to talk to you, people may get suspicious."

"People *will* get suspicious," Jion corrected.

"If you're able to find a boat, tell Hope." I nodded in Hope's direction. Hope merely shrugged and then nodded, not that he had much of a choice. "Hope and Jion live close enough to the stables that it can be assumed you're in the area to tend to your horse. It will be a lot easier to slip away here quickly to deliver a message than it would be to get to the palace. Once Hope has the information, he can easily pass it to Jion, who is always coming to and from the palace and won't seem out of place at all."

"It shall be done, Vik," Jion said.

"Don't you mean 'Your Highness'? I'm going to be king soon," I teased, fighting back a grin.

Jion stifled a laugh and, with an exaggerated bow said, "Apologies, your highness."

Hope draped an arm over Jion, and it pained me. I knew their separation would be difficult for both of them, and a felt a pang of guilt that I was taking Hope's husband from him and thrusting him into a dangerous journey. But, as Jion had said, he's a soldier, and they both understand that such sacrifices are part of his duty. "It's so strange to see you all act so serious."

"Honestly, it's quite strange for us to be so serious. Apart from Siofra," Jion replied, shooting a teasing wink towards his co-guard, who stood from the table.

"I've had about enough of all of you, especially if I'll be stuck with you all for the next few months." She moved towards the door. "Hope, I'll be around tomorrow mid-morning to deliver the message, whether I've got a boat or not. Will you be home then?"

"I'll make sure I am. Someone can surely cover for me at the infirmary so I could spend some time with my husband before he leaves."

"Alright. I'll see you then," she said, before giving a sharp nod to both Jion and me, and heading out of the house.

"I suppose I should go too, before anyone starts panicking and wondering where I am," I said, making my way towards the door.

Jion clapped me on the back. "I'm sure they're already doing that. Have fun playing your part!" I rolled my eyes, but couldn't help but grin at his teasing.

Hope, ever the well-mannered citizen, bowed, dark hair falling into his eyes as he stooped. "How many times has Jion said that you don't have to do that?"

Hope smiled a heart-shaped grin, though it didn't quite reach his eyes, his worry for his husband evident on his face despite his effort to hide it. "He can say it all he wants. I'll continue to give you the respect you deserve as the leader of our nation."

"I'm not quite the leader yet, that remains to be seen. But alas, your gesture is appreciated. I'll see you tomorrow, Jion. Goodbye Hope. Have a lovely evening."

Shutting the door gently behind me, I took a deep breath in preparation for my return journey to the palace. Not that it would be far, but I was going to have to try to make it there and sneak inside without getting caught if I wanted to avoid getting roped into another long discussion about the goddamned coronation. *I swear if I have to endure one more lecture about how important it is I'll deliver the crown to Siglind myself,* I thought, huffing as I began my walk through my beloved city.

I reached the top of the hill and paused before entering the palace, choosing instead to use the opportunity to overlook

Capital City. Its dark sandstone buildings were quiet, as they often were at this time of night, but my heart swelled as I thought of the inhabitants of its bustling streets. Though this was a rainy, noisy city, I grew up here, and had hardly been away all my life. Then I saw my beloved city aflame, embroiled in the inferno of war, its peaceful citizens cut down mercilessly by the blades of Bushand. Such it would be if Siglind and his famed brutality was not stopped. *I will do anything necessary to keep this place safe* I thought, heading inside the palace's back door.

I said a silent prayer as he snuck into my bedchamber, thanking the heavens that I had made it safely home without being trapped. I should sleep before the journey ahead of me, but so many worries weighed on my mind that I doubted I'd get a wink. Nonetheless, I stripped my shirt off and flopped down on the bed, determined to try. It wasn't long before I fell into a fitful, worried sleep.

My slumber was plagued with a series of frightful dreams, causing me to drift in and out of consciousness. One common thread was the soft, stern voice of a woman. At first I assumed it was Siofra, but it soon became apparent that it was not when she spoke in a harsh tone that Siofra, strong as she was, would never dare use with a royal. Then the distinct resonance of blades crashing together and the cries of battles drowned out any other sound.

***

I woke the next day with a start, jerked out of sleep by a loud pounding on my door that had exploded into my dreams. "Prince V, are you dressed and ready for today's events?" a muffled voice asked from the hallway outside my room.

I groaned before answering. "I'm awake," I answered, before mumbling to myself grumpily. "I'll likely never be ready."

"Shall I come in? I've got your breakfast ready, same as always."

"Yeah, yeah," I replied, scrambling around my room to get dressed. The servant I'd had since he was a child, who basically raised me, entered shortly carrying a tray full of eggs and freshly baked bread from the palace kitchens. "Thank you, Gabriel. I appreciate it."

"Of course, your Highness."

"Ah, please don't call me that. Not you too. Everyone keeps calling me that, and I'm not even officially a ruler yet."

Gabriel smiled, light amusement sparkling in his eyes, before bowing. "I apologize, young Viktor, but now that your father has passed, you've taken his place as my Master. I owe you great respect, and as a fine young man, you deserve it."

I huffed but didn't argue, knowing well enough that it wouldn't do any good. Instead, I changed the subject. "What do I need to be getting ready for this early anyway?" I glanced out my window, taking in the pinks and purples painting the sky above the cityscape. "The sun hasn't even properly risen."

"You should pay more attention to your royal agenda now that you're officially on the road to becoming king." Gabriel chastised lightly. "You've got a full day of meetings to plan the details of the coronation."

Rolling my eyes, I gently took the tray from Gabriel's wrinkled hands. "Of course I do."

"Such is the life of a king."

"Early meetings?" I questioned, digging into my breakfast.

"Sometimes." If anyone would know, it would be Gabriel. He had been by the king's side for as long as I could remember, assisting him with everything. Including raising his son for him.

"Hopefully it gets better after all this coronation business is through. There are bigger and more troublesome things to worry about, after all."

"The fact that you know this is why you will be a fine king, young Viktor." Gabriel bowed, reassuring me as he could sense my uneasiness at becoming a monarch. "I must take my leave now. There quite a few coronation preparation tasks I've been assigned by the council. Please leave the tray on your nightstand as always. I will be back to fetch it when I tidy your room."

"Thank you, Gabriel," I said, feeling slightly guilty about my plans to ditch the coronation in favor of traveling down to the Loch. I hadn't lied to Gabriel since I was knee deep in gambling debts and trying to hide them from my father. *Hopefully they will all understand in time,* I thought, swallowing my last bite.

Chapter Three

Viktor

"Valvox!" I cursed, gripping the side of the small boat tightly and leaning out over the edge. "No one ever told me I would feel like emptying every last inch of my stomach the entire time I'm on a boat. I don't remember it ever being like this before." Shortly after I had finished my breakfast, Jion met me with Siofra's message. She'd secured a boat, and they were prepared to leave as soon as possible. That was six hours ago, and we had been on the river ever since.

"That's because you weren't on a small boat before," said Siofra. "The large ships your father brought you on were more stable on the river than this one." As if to prove her right, a large wave crashed over the vessel, lurching it back and forth.

I heaved over the side once more. "It's horrible. We've got a day more of this?"

Laughing, and not known for empathy, Jion replied, "The current is strong. Hopefully it will get us there ahead of schedule."

"Do you want anything to eat?" Siofra asked, opening up one of the baskets she had prepared for the journey.

"Kelps no!" I burst.

Simultaneous to my exclamation, Jion yelled out, "Kelps yes!"

Siofra laughed, a dimple standing out on one cheek, and threw Jion a chunk of salted beef before turning to me. "Try looking out over the horizon. Or just close your eyes and try to go to sleep. If you can't handle this ride on the river, our journey across the sea to Bushand will be a walking nightmare for you."

Rolling my eyes, I took her advice nonetheless, settling into a corner of the boat and gently closing my eyes. I felt disappointment settle into his skin. Before embarking on this trip I'd somewhat looked forward to exploring more of my own country, but now I could hardly enjoy any of the rolling, forest green hills of our land without wanting to empty my guts. Though the sun was shining, the wind on the water was high and chilled, and I pulled my cloak around me to stave off the cold.

Jion sensed my melancholy. "Don't worry, Vik, you really aren't missing much. Along the river is mostly just trees and thickets. It's nothing different from what we've seen at home."

After giving a very small nod, I drifted into an uneasy, sloshing sleep.

I woke after only a few hours, and spent the duration of the trip leaning my head against the ship, and admiring the scenery. "It truly is beautiful, this country."

"It is," Siofra replied. "It will be such a shame if Siglind gets ahold of it. With his love of industry, our forests and clean water would not last long in his hands."

Looking out over the green of the trees and catching glimpses of the wildlife within, Jion set his jaw, determined. "He won't."

We passed a few riverside villages, which paid no heed to the small boat with what looked like three insignificant passengers. The majority of them had never been out of their village, must less traveled to Capital City and caught a glimpse of the prince, so they had no inkling as to the importance of those who were drifting passed.

"We're coming up to the Loch soon," Siofra warned. It was near dusk, and we had spent almost twelve hours on the water. I for one was eager to step foot on solid ground once more.

"We shouldn't approach the Manyeo family at this hour. Let's find an inn to stay in for the night," Siofra offered as a suggestion.

"Agreed. I'd like to sleep in a nice bed before worrying about the next portion of our journey. Also, Vik is much more convincing when he didn't spend the bulk of the day vomiting and passing out."

I huffed out a laugh. "Jion's got a point. And we will need to be as convincing as possible. Have either of you been to this village before? Do you know where an inn is?"

"I haven't been to *this* village before," Siofra said. "But for the most part they all follow a similar structure. We can tie the boat up at the docks. Usually there is a road from there that leads directly into the town centre. Once we're in the town centre, an inn will certainly not be hard to find."

Jion and I nodded, and I looked out over the water as the river bank on both sides widened in the dark. The stars above sparkled in the reflection of the water, and even with the bright moon and stars I couldn't make out the other side of the Loch as we floated in. Drifting into calmer waters, the harsh, swift current of the river steadied and slowed. Jion grabbed an oar and began steering over towards the left.

After about twenty minutes of slow passage we reached the small marina. The three of us worked together to tie the boat up to a small and empty section of one of the docks. As soon as the last rope was tied, I practically leapt from the boat onto the dock. "Ahh," I exclaimed. "It feels so nice to be on solid…" I looked down at the swaying dock beneath my feet. "Well, semi-solid ground."

"It will feel even nicer to be in a bed," Jion said, yawning and stretching.

"Yes, that's very true," I said, chuckling. I turned to Siofra. "How far of a walk do you think we have before we reach the inn?"

Siofra shrugged. "I can't say. Most likely not far. The fisherman probably make the walk to the docks and back multiple times a day. It's probably not too strenuous a journey. I don't know that I've ever seen a town center more than half a kelpstep from the docks."

"Great," Jion replied, shouldering a large pack of food. "Let's get going then. The sooner we walk, the sooner we sleep."

Most of the walk was spent in silence. All members of our small company were exhausted from the journey and pent up with nerves about the longer trip ahead of us. Pulling my hood over my head, I said a silent prayer to the Kelps that I would not be recognized. That would put the secrecy of our mission at jeopardy. The sounds of crickets singing echoed in the night, and the only other sound that could be heard was the squish of mud against our feet on the road. Soon, however, we began to hear the distant, but distinct, sounds of music and people. "We must be coming up to the town centre now. That's the sound of a gathering at an inn if I've ever heard it."

"You would certainly know," Jion laughed. "Let's hurry. I'm tired. Some of us weren't able to sleep the whole boat ride."

I elbowed him lightly in response and laughed. "Better sleeping than vomiting, surely."

"I can't argue with that," Jion said before looking ahead and seeing Siofra far in front. "Hey! Wait up!"

She turned to look back at them. "If you two would pick up the pace instead of goofing around we'd probably already be there by now."

Jion and I glanced at each other, laughing and rolling our eyes, but jogged to catch up to our comrade, nonetheless. Quickly, we began to see the glow of light as the trees around them thinned and before we knew it, the road had widened into a large square surrounding a village green. The center of the green held a small well, encompassed on three sides by public and private buildings. The public buildings were illuminated by lanterns that highlighted the hanging signs and murals which identified each building. It wasn't difficult to pick out the inn, though we couldn't quite make out the sign marking it as such, people were coming and going from the central building and it was clear that the music they'd heard was sourced there. We all exchanged grins before making our way towards the source of the revelry. Before moving forward, I adjusted my hood, making sure it was pulled low enough to cover most of my face. Though I wasn't well traveled, I knew the silver of my hair could likely give me away as the prince, and I wasn't sure I wanted to attract that kind of attention, especially since I didn't have the greatest of reputations.

Once we had circled around the green, we eagerly pushed open the door of the Empath's Arms Inn. As soon as we stepped over the threshold a silence suddenly blanketed the room. The common area was packed full of patrons there to drink, and to enjoy the singing and strumming of the traveling bards, or, most commonly, both. Each person turned to gape at the newcomers.

"Is this a common response outside Capital City?" I whispered to Siofra.

"Not particularly," she replied. "Though it's not unheard of in small, close knit towns to be wary of a band of strangers."

"Fair enough," I said, shifting uncomfortably. I wasn't typically a shy man, but the combination of the sudden silence and all eyes on us made me extremely nervous, that feeling heightened by my need for anonymity.

Siofra cleared her throat before speaking loudly. "Good evening everyone. We are travelers from Capital City, hoping to explore the small villages in Doctsland. We hope you may welcome us with open arms!"

There was a beat of silence before a welcoming cheer echoed throughout the room, causing me to breathe a sigh of relief. They seemed to be quite excited at the prospect of visitors from the city. Jion clapped me on the back. "I'm grabbing an ale. Or three. Would you like to join me?"

"Yes, please."

"I'll sort out some rooms while you two are drinking," Siofra said before heading over to the man who hunched over a large book, taking notes and counting bills, marking him clearly as the innkeeper.

"Does she ever just relax?" I said as Jion and I moved towards the bar.

Jion laughed heartily. "No."

As we leaned up against the bar side by side, the bartender rushed over. "What can I get for you two?" he asked through this burly beard.

"An ale my comrade, please," I answered cheerily. Socializing with the people of my country outside of Capital City, especially incognito like this, was a new and exciting experience, and I found it hard to wipe the grin from my face.

"Of course. Right away," he replied. "And anything for yourself?" I shook my head and as the bartender scurried away to pour the drink, I took a minute to glance around the room. Since the pause upon our arrival, everything had gone back to as it had been before they walked in. Perhaps there was even more of an air of celebration and excitement amongst the folk, many of whom were sparing not so subtle glances at the company of strangers. The room itself was small in comparison to those I was used to in Capital City, but its size presented an aspect of coziness that I had not before experienced. I decided I loved it immediately, and admired the small stone fireplace, the plain and dark wooden beams, and the candles that hung on each to light the room, which seemed to lack an overhead chandelier. Its simplicity enamored me, and when I turned to pay for Jion's ale, I had a half smile on my face.

"How much do we owe you, sir?" Jion asked.

"We don't often get strangers at the inn. You've brought some excitement here with you. The ale is on the house!"

In response, Jion lifted his drink to cheer the man. I leaned toward him to whisper, "Surely we must pay."

Jion scoffed. "Of course, but I know he will try not to accept. I'll leave two silvers on the counter when we head to our rooms."

I pulled a couple of coins from my pocket and handed them to Jion. "Make it two golds."

Jion's eyes scrunched up as he grinned widely, accepting the coins before taking a hearty drink from his ale. By this point Siofra had reappeared and stood beside them at the bar. "I secured two rooms for the night. You two are sharing." Jion and I groaned in unison, while Siofra glared at us, less than impressed. "Don't be children. It's only for a little while. And it's safer this way."

"Fine," I said, yawning. "Let's go then. I'm exhausted. Show me where this room is."

Jion made a noise in the back of his throat, as he often did when he was irritated, but drained his drink and followed, nonetheless. "Exhausted," he mocked. "Says the man who slept the entire way here."

I chuckled and sent my friend an elbow to the side but felt too tired to argue further. Siofra led us through the common room and down a narrow hallway with two doors. "That," she pointed towards the door on the left, "is your room. And this is mine. You know I'm a light sleeper. I'm close enough that I will wake up to come to your aid immediately if anything should happen."

"Yes, thank you, Siofra." I was about to open my door, but stopped and turned back to her. "What is our plan for tomorrow?"

"You may sleep in if you'd like. I plan to scout the town for a bit, and possibly locate the whereabouts of this Maneyo family we're looking for. I'll meet the two of you back here when I'm finished. If you aren't awake by midday, I'll simply pound on your door until you are."

"Ugh. So subtle," Jion groaned, opening the door to our room and heading inside.

"Thank you again, Siofra. I'll see you tomorrow," I said.

"Good night, Prince Viktor." She spoke in a hushed tone. There was no one to be seen in earshot, but Siofra was always the cautious, paranoid one of us.

I had barely shut and locked the door before Jion had collapsed onto the smaller of the two beds and fallen asleep, still in his traveling gear. My lips quirked into a small smile as I kicked off my shoes and got undressed. I crawled into the bed and noticed it wasn't nearly as comfortable as my large feather bed at home. Despite that, I drifted to sleep almost immediately after resting my head on the scratchy pillow.

***

After what felt like a mere five minutes, the loud sound of pounding at my door pulled my from my slumber. Looking blearily at Jion, I saw that he was already lunging out of bed and grabbing his sword. "Who is it?" Jion boomed, his voice startlingly lower than I was used to hearing it, and very much like the sound of the threatening guard he could be when he wasn't goofing off with his friends or his husband.

"It's me," Siofra called back from behind the door. Jion visibly relaxed as he pulled the door open. Siofra was dressed in full gear and, frankly, looked less than thrilled. "I cannot believe you two were still sleeping."

"What time is it?" I croaked, my voice rough with sleep.

"Later than it should be. Most have already eaten lunch. I've been out all morning, scouting the perimeter of the town," she explained.

"Did you locate the residence of that family we're looking for?"

She nodded, hands on her petite armored hips. "I haven't gone yet, but I asked around town and nearly every person I spoke to knew of the family and where they reside. They seem to be almost revered by the townspeople. Apparently even this pub is named after the Manyeo empath's of old. They live a bit outside the town center. It would take some time to walk there, which would have been fine had you two not slept in so late. If we want to be there and back by nightfall, we will need to leave soon and we will need horses."

"Alright," Jion said as we both stumbled around the room getting dressed and gathering our belongings. "Let's go then. I'm sure the inn has horses we can pay to use for the day. I'll go talk to the keeper."

"Already done," Siofra said. "Three horses are waiting for us out front."

"Great. Let's be on our way," I said, tightening my belt around my slender waist and slinging my pack over my shoulder. *That's got to be the quickest I've ever gotten ready in the morning.* I thought, wryly, *Thanks, Siofra.*

As soon as we exited the inn, three horses were presented

to them by a young boy whom Vik assumed was probably the apprentice to the stable master. "Here you are, my Lords and Lady," he said, bowing. He handed the reins of a small, yet formidable looking brown horse (which seemed to match her exactly) to Siofra, introducing him as "Seanigh."

Next he led a butterscotch horse to me and said, "This is Butter. She will treat you well. She is rather large, but very sweet and eager to please." I smiled as I took the reins.

Lastly he presented, "Cat," a massive black horse, to Jion, who laughed loudly at the name and subsequent explanation. "He is friends with all the stray cats in the neighborhood. They sleep at the stables in his stall with him."

Jion smiled at the boy. "Thank you very much. They are fine horses indeed. We'll take great care of them and return them by nightfall."

I quickly mounted Butter, and Jion and Siofra did the same.

"I wish you safe travels," the young boy said, grinning and bowing once more. The warm smile on his rosy face proved he was immensely proud of the beasts, and of his duty in presenting them. "The horses will serve you well."

I grinned down at him. "I'm sure they will. We look forward to our return. Thank you."

After blushing with pride, the boy scurried off, causing Jion and I to share a grin. His excitement was infectious, and just what we needed to distract us from our nerves and get us through the journey of the day.

"We're off," Siofra said, digging her heels into her mount and taking off at a trot.

"I guess we are," Jion replied, doing the same. I followed and sped to a gallop to catch up.

"How far of a ride is this?" I asked once I was side by side with my companions.

"A half an hour at most. I expect we will make it in less time, if we keep up this pace, which I'm sure these horses can manage."

The sun shone brightly as we wove through rich green forests and clearings on a small gravel road. It made me sweat in my armor, though I didn't mind it in the least. Not much could dampen my spirits as I admired the beauty of the countryside I rode through, especially not some sweat. Birds chirped, and we even came across a waterdog, which I had never seen before in the city. I gasped, pointing to its small, fury form as it rushed along the foliage.

"There must be a pond nearby," Siofra answered with a smile. I gazed in awe, trying to memorize everything about it, from its wide brown eyes and thick copper fur to its webbed and hoofed feet. I stared at it until it was out of sight, and then allowed my eyes to wander more around the peace of the wilderness.

The loud voices, clanking of metal from the barracks, and other noises I was accustomed to in the city, had disappeared. In their place was a sweet silence, interrupted only by the footfalls of their horses and occasional bird song. Missing also were the distinct smells of the city, something I was more than happy to get away from. I took a deep breath, closed my eyes, and smiled as the floral, grassy scent filled my nostrils.

True to Siofra's estimate, little more than half an hour had gone by before we came into a large clearing with a white stone house in the center. "Here we are," Siofra said, pulling Seanigh to a stop as Jion and I followed her lead. "I'll go first, introduce myself, make an announcement that the prince is here. We won't be able to hide your identity *and* convince them to join us, so it's best to reveal you to them. I'll also sus out any potential threats. Jion, you stay here with Vik."

Jion gave her a sharp nod, and she moved forward leaving us behind. "And we wait," he said once she was out of earshot. "Kelps, I hope this goes well."

"It will," I said. "It has to. The best case scenario is that we leave her today with a healer and an empath on our side. The worst case is that we only have a healer *or* an empath. Anything else is not an option."

Jion glanced at me. "Will we take them by force if they do not agree to come willingly?" he asked, his voice stiff.

I hesitated, then let out a defeated sigh. "No, of course not. Then we wouldn't be any better than Siglind. We just..." I paused. "We need to be convincing. We need to win them over."

Jion shrugged his wide shoulders. "Then we will," he said simply.

We watched anxiously as Siofra disappeared into the home. "We shouldn't have to wait long. She's fairly quick when she scouts."

"Quick but thorough. I don't know how she does it."

"Maybe you should have her teach you."

"I'd never give her the satisfaction," Jion cracked, causing a fit of laughter to envelope us both. We quickly regained control of themselves, knowing Siofra would be less than impressed if she came out to signal us and we had dissolved in laughter.

Our timing was excellent. Shortly after mastering ourselves and replacing our smiles with stoic stares, Siofra stepped out and called to us. "Prince Viktor," she said, using my formal title for the first time in days. "Please enter the Manyeo residence."

Jion and I shared a glance and a nod before dismounting and moving forward. After reaching the entrance, we tied Butter and Cat on a post next to where Siofra had tied Seanigh. The animals immediately turned to the trough full of water. Feeling my nerves start to rise, I paused before heading inside. I closed my eyes and took a deep breath before I stepped over the threshold.

Jion turned on his booming announcement voice. "We thank you greatly for welcoming us into your home. May I present to you, Prince Viktor." I bowed, and the members of the household followed suit. As I came forward, I threw my hood back to reveal my hair and face. My silver hair, an emblem from my father, was famed, and there was no doubting the legitimacy of the title I claimed. I took the opportunity to survey all those that were in the room. It was a very small crowd. An elderly woman sat beside a small fire, her white hair tied into a knot atop her head. Behind her stood a couple, or at least what I assumed was a couple. The man had a bandage around his leg, and his arm was wrapped around the shoulders of the woman next to him. Lastly, my eyes fell upon a young woman. She stood on the other side of the fire, almost as if shielding the elderly woman. Her jet black hair was streaked with a large chunk of white blonde at the front, full lips set in a fearsome line, her grey eyes seeming to pierce me.

The man stepped forward. "You do us a great honor, Prince V. My name is Yeoman, and this is my wife Alicen." He gestured towards the girl that I couldn't seem to take my eyes off. "My daughter Lisalya." She bowed stiffly. "And the matriarch of the Manyeo household, my mother, Isotta, the great healer."

I bowed once more. "A pleasure to meet you all," he started to say, only to be cut off by the youngest.

"Why are you here?" Lisalya asked. "And you..." She gestured at Siofra. "Why didn't you tell me earlier the prince was coming to my family's home?" Her father immediately scolded her under his breath, and her grandmother held up a hand to silence her.

"I was merely out scouting, and was not aware that you belonged to the very family we were searching for. My apologies if I have caused you any distress or confusion," Siofra explained.

I saw the panic in their eyes at the possible offense from Lisalya and sought to reassure them. "I understand this visit is abrupt. We will explain everything shortly. It is a rather long story, though, and we've been riding for an hour. Do you perhaps have somewhere we could sit?"

"Of course. Let us head to the Peristyle," Isotta said, using a cane and her granddaughter's arm to stand. "Alicen, could you prepare some food and drink for us and our guests? We will have dinner together after we hear this long story of yours." Alicen nodded and scurried off, I assumed in the direction of the kitchen. All that remained followed Isotta as she strode through the atrium and into the opening of the Peristyle. All along the walls were plants and flowers, and in the center was a large round table with eight seats. Isotta took a seat and the rest of us followed suit.

A moment of awkward silence ensued before I cleared my throat and anxiously twiddling my thumbs. "Well, I suppose I should begin. Our country faces a great threat. You may not yet know, but my step-brother Siglind, King of Bushand, has claimed the throne of Doctsland now that my step-mother has passed away. He plans to send his army here to take the crown by force. If they are able to set foot on our soil, they will destroy everything. He and his army are not known for mercy. In fact, their reputation is quite ruthless. I cannot let it come to that. If it does, we truly don't stand a chance." I glanced up and met their terror stricken eyes. "Now, I do not wish for you to despair. In fact, please feel assured." He gestured to his comrades. "For we have a plan that we will need your help with."

"What is it?" Lisalya asked, her low voice steady despite the worried crease in her dark brow.

Taking a deep breath, I began. I did my best to lay the plan out before the family, trying to keep my tone hopeful and to remain positive that they would succeed in an effort to reassure the family and ensure they're assistance. Siofra and Jion chimed in occasionally to add their own thoughts and to assist me in my explanation. Gathering that Isotta was the leader, I carefully scanned her face as I spoke, hoping to discern her thoughts on the matter, but she remained frustratingly stoic. It took time and, as I spoke, Alicen began to emerge with drinks and trays of fruit, vegetables, and meat. By the time I had finished, a feast was laid out before us. Frankly, I was starving.

"And how *exactly* do we factor in here?" Lisalya was the first to speak, defiance in her voice. It was already clear to me that she for one was not eager to join us. I dearly hoped she was not the rumored empath, though from the information Jion had heard it seemed that was an unlikely wish.

"Well," Jion spoke up. "We know you have a great healer among you. Bringing a healer along on this quest would help to protect our lives should anything befall one of us. It would be a great advantage to have that reassurance. And..." he hesitated.

"And...?" she repeated, a rounded eyebrow raised.

"We have heard rumors," I finished.

"What kind of rumors?" she asked.

I flashed her the smile I'd often used to disarm anyone I was trying to win over. "You certainly don't want to make it easy on us, do you?" To my dismay, she didn't seem affected in the least. That had usually worked on the young women of Capital City. "We hear rumors that you may have an empath among you."

Yeoman drew in a sharp breath before he could stop himself, and Jion smirked at the involuntary response. That in and of itself was an indication that the rumors had some truth.

"And how, pray tell, would an empath be of service on this mission?" Isotta said.

"Gathering enough of the people of Bushand to our side is absolutely imperative to our mission. However, we're going in blind. We have no idea where to find or how to pick out those that are most likely to be sympathetic to our cause. Approaching the wrong people could, and most likely would, prove disastrous. If we had an empath with us, on our side, we could drastically lower our margin for error. Truth be told, it may very well prove essential to the success of the mission as a whole." I did my best to emphasize how critical the matter was- to stress how desperately we needed their help.

The family before them had all turned their gazes to Isotta, who sat silent and pensive. Feeling the crisp tension in the room caused me to stiffen; I wasn't accustomed to this kind of intense anticipation. I felt as if he was standing on the edge of a cliff, hanging on whatever words would come out of this old woman's mouth next. I didn't have to wait particularly long before she opened her mouth and spoke, though it wasn't what I was hoping for. "I'm famished. Let us eat. We can discuss further after we've finished."

Though hungry, I struggled to hide my disappointment. I

shared a glance with Jion and Siofra, and saw my own emotions reflected in their eyes. But I buried my feelings and smiled. "Of course," I replied. "What a wonderful feast you've prepared, Alicen. Thank you very much."

The three guests all bowed our heads to our hosts in thanks. As the custom in Doctsland was for the guest to break bread, I felt it appropriate for me to take the lead. Picking up a knife, I cut into the steak in front of me before popping the delicious piece of meat into my mouth. After swallowing, I lifted my glass, smiled, and nodded- signaling it was time for the feast to begin. The others all followed in my footsteps eagerly, digging into the meal almost ferociously (at least in Jion's case who, like me, had slept through breakfast).

The meal, though impeccable, lacked small talk, and I took the opportunity to glance around the table. All seemed deep in thought, pondering everything that had just been laid before them. Isotta remained unreadable, but Yeoman, Alicen, and Lisalya all looked troubled. To my surprise, this encouraged me rather than the opposite. *If they're worried, perhaps it's because they know they'll have to say goodbye to one of their own because they're coming on the mission,* I thought- or rather, hoped.

The somewhat awkward meal came to a close after each person set down their utensils. After a beat, Isotta spoke. "The rumors you've heard have truth. While I am the sole healer in this house, my granddaughter here is, in fact, the empath you seek."

I held my breath, anticipating her words as she continued. "Unfortunately my health is failing me. I simply would not survive this mission you seek to go on, and would certainly hold you back, and it appears speed is of the essence. I will stay here, and attend to the villagers who need my help." Jion sighed in disappointment at my side, but I wasn't so quick to give up hope. After all, the empath was more imperative to the mission than the healer. "I cannot speak for my granddaughter." She turned her gaze to the young woman in question. "However, I can encourage her to assist you."

Lisalya stared at her, shock and dismay etched on her

rather beautiful face. "Grandmother?" Her argument fell dead in her mouth as Isotta lifted her hand to silence her.

"Lisalya," she said gently, turning towards her granddaughter and taking her hands. "What have I always told you is the purpose of this family, our purpose?"

Struggling to meet her grandmother's searching eyes, Lisalya looked down at her feet. "Helping people."

"Yes, helping people. If this quest were to fail, it would bring insurmountable pain and suffering upon the very people we've spent our lives healing and helping, not to mention countless others throughout Doctsland. We cannot allow our beautiful country and its people to fall into the hands of King Siglind."

"I know," Lisalya said, sharply. "I agree. But don't you think I could do more here, helping to protect our home and our town?"

Isotta shook her head. "There is no home, no town. Not as it has been. Not if Siglind's forces are able to land here. I know you don't wish to leave. Truth be told I don't wish you to leave either, I'm sure none of us do," she gestured to her son and his wife. "But I agree with our prince. Having an empath on this mission is imperative to its success. And you know as well as anyone that there are no other empaths left."

Lisalya sat completely still. It seemed to me that there were words frozen in her mouth that she couldn't manage to thaw. It also appeared that the matter was now out of our hands. I stood. "We have made our case. The decision lies in your hands, and we will give you privacy to discuss and make an informed one." I glanced at Jion and Siofra, signaling them to follow my lead. "We are staying at the inn in town tonight, The Empath's Arms. We are on a rather tight schedule, so we'll be leaving in the morning," I turned my gaze to Lisalya, who sat biting the nails of one hand, and I tried to implore her with a simple look. "If you choose to join us, meet us there before dawn." Bowing, I finished my speech, and prayed they would make the right decision. "Thank you again for your hospitality."

Chapter Four

Lisalya

After the prince and his entourage departed, I couldn't quieten my thoughts. I felt certain that my place was here, at home, with my family. It certainly wasn't with the prince, whom I'd only ever heard of as an irresponsible, negligent person. My mind buzzed with uncertainties, and with the intrusion of my parents feelings. Though they were practiced in keeping their thoughts inside their heads, or at least a lot quieter than the untrained mind, I could sense the distress pouring from my parents and, to be frank, it heightened my own. Grandmother, as always, was unreadable to me. Somehow she had managed to keep her emotions under lock and key, though she hid very little from me verbally. In this particular predicament, she had made herself clear. She wished for me to go with Prince Viktor, but nearly every fiber of my being screamed not to.

When I could no longer take the swirling in my head, I slipped out of the house, hoping to go unnoticed. "Lisalya!" my mother called after me, but I ignored her, having neither the words nor the energy at the moment. Just the need to escape to quiet solitude, if only for a little. As quickly as I could, and before my parents could stop me, I hopped onto my horse and galloped to the well.

I breathed a sigh of relief when I was out of the range of the house and closed my eyes, basking in the sweetness of the silence.

Everything that had been said throughout the day raced through my mind, as well as what I felt from the prince and his companions. They all seemed swaddled in a terrifying combination of fear, tension, and desperation. In his speech, the prince tried his best to convey the dire need of this quest, but none of his words could portray this the way his feelings did. Frankly, it shook me to my core, and increased my desire to stay at home curled up in my bed, rather than the opposite. *If the country is on the brink of such disaster, wouldn't I rather be at home?* was the thought that kept circling in my mind.

After tying my horse to the post nearby, I took a seat by the well, resting my head against the cool stone. I closed my eyes, with the intention of just resting them as I thought over my choices, but I slipped into a light sleep.

***

The sound of footsteps jerked me out of my uneasy slumber and I hopped to my feet, defensive. I listened acutely with my mind, but to my horror heard nothing. "Relax dear." My shoulders dropped as I heard my grandmother's voice. "It's just me. I knew I'd find you here."

I reclaimed my seat on the ground beside the well. "It's the only place I can feel my own feelings sometimes."

"I know," she said, taking a seat on the ledge of the well beside me. She let the silence grow, and I started to fidget.

"I know what you think. I know you want me to go off, gallivanting on this quest with the prince and his lackeys," I huffed.

"I made my wishes clear, yes. Though gallivanting is not quite the word I would use," she said, not even attempting to keep the smile from her voice. After another minute or two of silence, she spoke again, this time with no hint of a grin. Her voice wobbled, and I wanted nothing more than to lay down and rest my head in her lap like I had as a child. Pride had me remaining upright, however. "Are you upset simply because you don't wish to go? Or, are you upset because you don't wish to go, but you know that it's the right thing to do?"

I sighed, running my fingers through the soft grass beside me. "I'm not certain. I don't know what to think, or what to feel. All I know is that I don't want to leave our home, our family. It's all I've ever known. It will be dangerous… I'm scared." I spoke the last words quietly.

She rested her hand on my shoulder in a comforting gesture. "I understand. I wish I could go in your stead, or at least accompany you. You have to do what you feel is right. I can't make the choice for you. No-one can. But something tells me that in your heart you've already decided."

"I'll miss you," I said, wiping at my eyes before the tears that threatened could fall.

"We'll miss you too," she replied softly. "Now, do you really want to spend your last night at home curled up on the ground, alone next to a well?"

I stood. "No. I do not."

"Then come. Let's go home."

The ride home felt a lot shorter with Grandmother's company. We talked the whole way, though what about I couldn't say. It seemed we spoke about nothing in particular, empty conversations to fill the silence, but that's what I needed. Speaking about such light, seemingly meaningless topics kept my mind from wandering down the dark path of what the future could hold.

In typical fashion, my parents were waiting up for me at home, though they seemed more distressed than they had when I'd left. I was met with red-rimmed eyes and sniffling noses, making it achingly hard not to break down and cry along with them. However, I knew it would not serve me to give in to the sadness in my heart. "Come on," I said. "There's no need to cry. I'm sure I'll be home before you know it."

"So you're certain? You're going? Lisalya, this is going to be very dangerous. You've heard about Bushand, King Siglind. He rules with an iron fist, killing anyone who opposes him. If you're caught on this mission…" She choked, her voice trembling in a way that made me squeeze my eyes shut.

"Yes," I replied, doing my best to keep my voice strong. "I know the dangers. I know the risks. I'm going."

"Are you sure? Absolutely sure?" It was my father's voice now that trembled, something I had rarely heard. It was difficult to bear.

I closed my eyes and steadied myself. "Absolutely sure." Repeating his words, I smiled through the tears that swam in my eyes, feeling relieved that the decision was made, and nodded. "It's the right thing to do. I know that. We've helped the people in Loch for generations. It's time to help the rest of Doctsland now."

My parents shared a glance before pulling me into their arms. My mother spoke. "I don't want you to go. I'm terrified. But I also know that there's no arguing with you once you've set your mind to something."

Sniffling, I smiled. "Let's stop talking about it. I'll make my way to the inn tomorrow morning, and that's that. Let's just... enjoy this night together for a while." And we did just that.

***

Before the sun had a chance to even think of rising, I was out of bed and packing. I pulled my thick hair from my face and tied it back before getting dressed. Initially I wasn't sure where to start when packing. Sure, I'd been away from home before, but only on short trips. I had no clue how to pack for such an endeavor as the one I now faced. I shrugged my shoulders and took my best guess. I grabbed my riding gear, a few spare clothes, and what little travel wear I had acquired throughout the years. Afterwards, I snuck into the kitchen and threw some food in my bag — bread, fruit, and some salted meat that my father had prepared. *I don't think this was necessarily meant for me,* I thought, thinking of his frequent long fishing expeditions. *But oh well.*

As soon as I had everything in order I crept through the house and out the front door, careful not to make a sound and wake anyone. Making the decision to leave was hard enough, I couldn't bear the thought of having to say a proper goodbye. For some reason saying goodbye felt like it meant goodbye for goods though saying those words would mean that I was not coming home and wouldn't see my family again.

I felt a pang of guilt as I hopped onto my horse in the chilly darkness of the early morning. Turning around, I spared one last glance at my childhood home before blinking back my tears and urging my horse forward.

Leaving hours before the sunrise meant that I could take my time, which was very much needed. I didn't know when I'd see this land again, this town, which had always belonged to my heart, and as I led my horse slowly through the forest I tried to commit as much of it to memory as possible - the lanky trees, the soft crunch of the earth beneath my horses feet, the hills and valleys that I knew like the back of my hand. But even with the unhurried pace I maintained, it felt as though the journey was far too short. Before I knew it, or felt even a little prepared, I found myself approaching the town centre of Loch.

"Well, here we go," I muttered to myself, urging my horse forward towards the inn. No matter how short the journey had seemed to me, there was no question I had taken my time. The sky had already begun to paint itself vibrant hues of purples and pinks with the sunrise, and I knew as I approached the front door that I was just in time.

I felt everyone, scattered and worried, before they even opened the door and stepped outside. As soon as their eyes fell upon me they froze, both physically and emotionally, it felt like their very minds were holding their breath, trying to figure out if I was real or if my sudden appearance was too good to be true. I dismounted, bowing to address the prince and his companions. "Prince Viktor."

This seemed to snap them out of their stupor, and I felt a semblance of relief flood over me through all three of them. The prince flashed a somewhat rectangular, though unquestionably charming, smile I recognized from yesterday. "Miss Manyeo. I'm very pleased to see you. Does this mean you'll be joining us?"

"Please call me Lisalya," I replied. "And yes, it does. As

much as I don't want to, it's our best shot at saving our country, is it not?"

He grew solemn. It appears that it is."

The woman I had met in the glade, Siofra, stepped forward, though rather than the armor I had seen her in previously she wore tanned trousers, a white shirt, and a cloak the same deep green that was the signature of many Doctsland uniforms. "Thank you for your assistance."

I smiled grimly. "Don't thank me yet. We don't know how this will all turn out."

"Nevertheless," Prince Viktor said, and I noticed both he and their third companion bore matching cloaks, "we truly appreciate your willingness to accompany us. And to use your gifts to help Doctsland."

"I know," I said.

The third spoke. "That settles it. We've gained an empath." He cracked a buck-toothed smile in my direction, and despite his cavalier demeanor, I felt the relief that was washing over him. "Now, let's be off."

"Off where, exactly?" I asked. The prince and the other man, Jion, I believed, both turned to Siofra with questioning looks.

"Right, where do we go from here, Siofra?" Prince V asked.

I gaped at them, choosing not to bother hiding my growing irritation. "You don't know? You've had all night to plan. I left early to meet you here and you don't know?"

Siofra ignored me, fixing the prince in her gaze. "That's up to you, I suppose. Now that we know the empath is joining us." She shot a glance my way. "We know we don't necessarily have to go back to the city to formulate a backup plan. But we still can if you'd like, to re-group before we head out on our next endeavor…" She trailed off and the prince picked up where she left.

"But then we'll probably run into the coronation issue again. They'll all be furious with me for having left. I can't imagine it will be as easy to sneak away again. Can we use the ship we have to get all the way to Bushand?" he asked.

Jion shook his head. "No, we need something larger. We should also pick up a few more supplies, to re-stock and to prepare for the new journey. We've got another mouth to feed and a much longer ride ahead of us."

"Miss Manyeo," Siofra started, but I held up my hand to stop her.

"Please, all of you, just call me Lisalya."

She nodded and gave me a friendly smile. "Lisalya. Do you know where we may inquire after a larger boat?"

I shrugged, not entirely familiar with the shipping industry, but I knew the town well enough to guess. "I would probably start with the docks. Occasionally they've got ships for purchase or hire. It's not terribly often. We are a smaller town after all. But it happens."

"Great," she said. "I will head to the docks to see if we can find a ship for us. Lisalya and Vik, you will make your way to the market to grab provisions. Jion, go with them, please. It doesn't seem anyone knows the prince is here, but it's best to be cautious in case he is discovered."

The prince shifted, feeling unsure of himself. "I'm not sure where the markets are."

I sighed, feeling annoyed at his inability to pick up on the obvious. I'd always heard of him as an inept young man, incapable of doing much for himself beside pouring a drink, and he was certainly living up to those expectations. Plus, it was strange being surrounded by so many unknown people. I felt their emotions in a heightened sense, and I wasn't sure why. It was overwhelming me, and making me moody. "I know where they are. I live here."

The prince seemed to sense my irritability, and was beginning to match it. "Thank you for the reminder," he snapped back. "Lead the way."

Our party split as Siofra had directed, and I started making my way towards the market, trying to ignore the fact that I had the prince and Jion following me. They seemed to have picked up on the fact that I wasn't interested in small talk, so they trailed behind silently. As we walked, I worked on the exercises Grandmother had been telling me to practice;

building up the walls in my head to protect myself from everything that everyone else was feeling. If I was going to be traveling with these people for months, I was going to have to learn how to shield myself from the onslaught of their emotions, otherwise it would simply grow to be too much.

We didn't spend too much time at the market, thankfully. Flutters of excitement grew louder and more persistent the longer we were there, and I could only imagine what the townspeople thought. *What is the Manyeo empath doing with those strange men?* As quickly as possible, we stocked up on as much food as we could carry in our packs, and were given a mule to help us carry a few more packfulls, at least as far as the boat, at which point we would send it back.

"This should be enough, right?" I asked as we started heading towards the docks.

Prince Viktor nodded, the hood covering his long silver hair bouncing with the movement, and cracked a crooked smile. "It *should* be. Jion can seem to have a bottomless appetite sometimes. But I imagine he'll be on his best behavior. We'll make certain none of us go hungry." Jion snickered behind me, and I wondered briefly if he was always so informal with his guards. It didn't line up with my image of 'royal behavior.'

"I suppose this won't be as exciting to eat as the grand meals you're used to at the palace," I said.

"No," he said quietly. "You're right. It won't be. I grew up with a fairly lavish lifestyle. Wandering through the wilderness of another country will be quite an adjustment. But, it's one I'm willing to make."

As we approached the docks, Jion went ahead to find Siofra. The prince and I stood in awkward silence until he returned. "Any luck on finding that boat?" the prince asked, and Jion jogged back.

Jion scoffed. "Of course. And it's quite a nice one, at that. Siofra seems to be getting everything situated onboard. Come on, I'll lead you to it."

As soon as we arrived, my gaze wandered over the

massive boat. *Lady of the Loch* was painted on the side of the bow and to the left of a row of nine oars. The deck wasn't visible from my vantage point on the road, but I could see two large masts, each of which held a massive off-white sail. Siofra leaned over the railing from the deck and immediately launched into an explanation of the plans for the trip. "We should be able to set sail as soon as this evening, provided we can get organized and ensure we have everything we need. First we will head back out of the Loch and into Inver River, heading upstream for a bit. Then we can connect to Doctsland River from there and start to head towards the sea."

"How long will we be on this boat?" I asked.

"It's tough to say. But I imagine it will be close to two weeks or more."

"And will we be stopping at all?" I could sense apprehension growing in the prince and had to admit I was feeling it myself.

"Not unless we have to," Siofra said. "Come up along the dock. There's a bridge here to allow you onboard," Siofra called.

Following her instructions, we crossed the front of the ship to reach the dock on the other side. Sure enough, a plank of dark wood connected the deck of the Lady of the Loch to the dock.

"Shall we start bringing the supplies onboard?" The prince called, shielding his eyes from the sun with a long slender hand.

"Please do. Once you're here I'll show you around and Jion can introduce you to the crew since they're all already best friends."

"Great," I said, grabbing one of the packs off the donkey and heading up the plank and onto the deck of the boat.

"Welcome aboard," Siofra said with a friendly smile. While I appreciated that she wanted me to feel welcome, black spots were beginning to circle my vision, a surefire signal that a migraine was on its way, likely due to all the people surrounding me. Coupled with my sour feelings towards the journey as a whole, I was feeling quite glacial towards her and everything else.

"Thanks," I murmured, trying to focus my vision in an attempt to stave off the growing pain in the base of my skull.

"Go ahead and throw that on the deck for now. I'll show you where the supplies are stored once we've relieved that donkey of its burden." Following her instruction, I tossed the pack I was carrying and the pack I wore on my back on the deck and waited for the prince to join us with the rest of the supplies.

"How was your excursion?" Siofra asked him once he'd met us onboard.

"Well we got the supplies, so I suppose it was successful." he shot me a glance that I couldn't help but roll my eyes at.

Siofra looked confused but seemed to brush it off in favor of being productive. "Follow me. I'll show you the supply room." She grabbed one of the packs I had discarded and led us towards a small set of stairs going down towards a plain looking door. She opened it to reveal a dark room full of crates of food and wine. "Here is where you can come if you need any food or drink. Please use discretion. We do have a rather long journey ahead of us, and a small, but full, crew to feed at least until we reach the shores of Bushand."

"Yes, save some of the wine for the rest of us, please," I quipped, glancing pointedly at prince Viktor.

Siofra intervened before the prince could snark back. "Despite what rumors there may be floating around, Prince Viktor has left his days of revelry behind him. He has greater responsibilities that he has taken on dutifully."

"I can speak for myself, Siofra," he said, staring at me with venom in his light blue eyes. "I'll leave enough wine for everyone else. I'll just drink your share." He turned away out of the supply area and back onto the deck, where I heard him greet Jion.

"Come," Siofra said, a bit awkwardly. "I'll show you to your quarters."

"Are they separated at all, from other people? It's rather painful for me to be in close quarters with others for long," I said, pushing on my eyebrows, trying to relieve some of the building pressure.

"You and I are set to bunk together. The prince will be given the cabin, of course. However, I can simply bunk with Jion rather, if it's a problem. Are you able to control them at all, your empathic abilities?"

I began to shake my head, then winced and stopped, the movement triggering mounting nausea. "Not much. My grandmother was trying to help me learn to close my mind, but I haven't mastered it yet. It only works in short bursts, and not at all if there are more than a few people in close quarters with me."

"And it's painful for you?" she asked, curiosity and concern in her gaze.

"It tends to lead to migraines."

Wincing, Siofra shook her head, "That sounds awful. I will bunk with Jion for the meantime, until you're able to gain more control. I'm not certain what the situation will be once we arrive in Bushand, but being on the ship will make it difficult to avoid being in close quarters with anyone. I suggest you keep practicing what you were working on with your grandmother. It may very well come in handy, especially onboard."

I nodded, taking her words to heart as we walked through the narrow passageways of the ship. "Here we are," Siofra said, opening a slim door into a, frankly, tiny room.

"Was this initially for us to share?" I asked, incredulous as I looked around the room. It contained one set of bunk beds, a small closet, and a desk that had to be even smaller than the one I had used as a child in school.

"And will be again, once you have a bit more control of your powers. I won't be able to stomach bunking with Jion for long. He's dreadfully annoying. Believe it or not, this is one of the larger rooms on the ship. The majority of the crew all sleep below deck. We're lucky to have our own space." I frowned, glancing around the room and trying to think of where I was even going to fit my belongings. "I'll give you some time to get settled. We're pushing off in about an hour, and we'll have dinner in the cabin to celebrate the trip and pray to the Kelps for success at dusk. Do you remember how to get back to the deck? The cabin is just off it."

"Yes, I remember. Thank you Siofra." She gave me another friendly smile and a nod before leaving and, thankfully, closing the door behind her.

Once she left, I tried to relax my mind a bit, and closed my eyes, reveling in the silence. The crew aboard were present, but they existed merely as a distant buzz. I threw my pack on the bed and quickly tried to dig through it, organizing what I could into the closet while leaving some room for Siofra. I bit my lip as I worked, holding back tears, both at the pain in my head and the feeling my heart tugging towards a home I had barely even left yet. *This is going to be a long road*, I thought. Once finished, I laid down on the bed to rest my eyes before quickly sinking into a deep, much needed sleep.

***

I awoke to knocking at my door. Disoriented, I hadn't realized I had fallen asleep, or even meant to. "Lisalya," I heard Siofra's voice calling. "Dinner is prepared. Are you ready to join us?"

Scrambling out of bed, I began to tear through my belongings in the closet to try to find something decent to wear to dinner, silently thanking the Kelps that sleep had dulled the threat of a migraine to a small headache. "Give me a moment please." I called back.

"Don't worry. It won't be a formal ball by any means. Just Prince Viktor, Jion, the captain, and the two of us," she spoke reassurance.

"In that case, will my riding gear do?" I joked, knowing such garb would be entirely inappropriate for a scheduled dinner with the prince, no matter how 'informal.'

"Uhhh," Siofra hesitated, and I burst out laughing as I pulled a light blue dress over my head, thankful that I had thought to throw it in my pack that morning.

"I'm only kidding, Siofra. Will you come in and fasten this

for me, please?"

"Absolutely," she replied, slipping into the room quickly and with a welcoming smile on her face. Again, she wasn't in her usual armor, but this time she donned a lilac dress in a similar style to mine, corseted at the waist, and flowing in gilded layers until it kissed the floorboards of the ship. Her cropped hair was pulled half up, and the red tones were complimented by the purple of her dress. "Wow," I said. "You look so pretty!"

Her grin widened. "Thank you. I have to get out of the armor every once in a while. Now let's get you ready." She tightened the corset for me until it felt as though I couldn't breathe, and helped me brush my hair, which had become wild during my nap, into submission. "How did you get this blonde streak?" she asked as she began to style my hair.

I shrugged. "I'm not sure. It came when I was too young to remember, around the time my parents began to suspect I had powers other than the typical healing of my family. My grandmother thinks that maybe it was the stress of feeling what everyone else was feeling and having no way to control it due to my age."

"It must have been difficult growing up with such a strong ability. Especially without anyone to understand what it's like," Siofra said, gently pulling my hair back.

I hummed. "It was. For a while, my parents managed to keep my powers secret. For my own protection, they didn't want anyone knowing or seeking me out with their troubles, especially when I was a child. It was hard, though. Grandmother is a well-known healer- the most well-known in this region of the country, in fact- so people of all sorts, with all sorts of injuries, were coming and going from our house daily. Folks started to notice that when someone came in with a torn knee, the little girl who lived there would begin cradling her knee to her chest, tears streaming down her face. In a last ditch effort to keep my powers concealed, my parents built a house apart from my grandmother's." Siofra gasped. It was fairly taboo for a family to live in separate houses, no matter how large or how many generations the family contained. "What my parents did for me, in their attempt to protect me, made us stand out all the more. Once I was old enough to handle my abilities more and conceal them on my own, I asked that we move back in. I knew I could help grandmother with her patients, and I wanted to put my power to use, rather than just letting it smother me all the time."

"That was very brave of you," she said, putting some final touches on my hair which consisted of pulling a few waved strands out to frame my long face. She gestured for me to stand. "Let's go." She held her hand out towards the door and, following her gesture, I exited the room and followed her towards the prince's cabin. While I was a bit nervous, I wouldn't be able to find my way around the ship, it was surprisingly easy to navigate, and soon we found ourselves back on the upper deck. Bustling and voices could be heard clearly from within the cabin, and in the dim light of the glowing sunset I could make out the flickering flames of candles through the window.

I felt a sudden shyness come over me and halted, looking back at Siofra who had been following close behind. "Can you go in first?" I asked, preparing my mental blockades from the certain rush of emotions I would feel upon stepping into what was sure to be a crowded room.

"Of course," she replied As soon as she opened the door I felt a pressure in my head. The room was full, containing not only the prince, Jion, Siofra, and me, but several crew members that were setting the table and arranging the meal as well.

"There you are! Siofra, did it take you awhile to remember how to put on a dress?" Jion snickered as soon as we stepped through the threshold. Siofra punched his muscled bicep in response.

The prince, who had been giggling at their exchange, regained control of his features as he stood to bow. "Siofra and Lisalya, it's lovely to have you." After introducing us to the captain and the few members of the crew present, he continued addressing the room. "Thank you all for joining us, not only for dinner this evening, but for this endeavor as a whole. We are a small team, on a covert mission, but hope and determination is in our hearts, and I cannot do enough to express my gratitude."

A small cheer rose as we moved to take our seat. Jion had kindly pulled mine out for me and I thanked him. After sitting, I gripped the table tightly and focused, which helped to relax my mind. The prince seemed to notice, looking slightly concerned as he eyed my hands, though I released the table quickly. He leaned closer, lowering his voice to avoid attracting attention. "Are you okay, Lisalya?"

I blushed at his concern, and at the small part of my mind that was marvelling at how good he smelled, a combination of mint and pine that was creating a tantalizing musk, and brushed him off, not willing yet to show any sign of weakness. "Yes, I'm alright. Thank you for asking." Thankfully, all of the recent practice I had been doing with grandmother was starting to pay off. The blockages were getting a bit easier to maintain, and were becoming more effective at keeping the minds of others out of my own.

Once the crew members were finished with their tasks and had left the four of us alone, Prince Viktor raised a tall glass of wine. "I know I already said thank you, but I want to reiterate it, especially to this small group. I wouldn't be able to attempt this road without the three of you by my side. May this journey be Kelps-blessed," he said with a nervous smile and a pink hue in his cheeks. We raised our glasses to match his in a toast.

"Now that that's settled, let's feast." Jion spoke after draining his glass in one gulp. "This will probably be our last big meal for a long while, so enjoy it."

I took a sip of the dark red wine, trying desperately not to make a face at the bitter taste, though my blanching did not go unnoticed. "Are you not a wine drinker?" Jion asked, chuckling slightly at the scrunch in my face.

"We have wine occasionally, but it's usually light, and sweet. This is good, but…" I trailed off, not wanting to accidentally cause offense.

"This is sailor's wine. It's stronger, harsher. Good isn't a word I would use to describe it, but it's drinkable." Prince Viktor smiled as Siofra and Jion both laughed, nodding at his words in agreement. "The food, however," he continued after taking a bite of the roasted chicken before him, "is delectable."

Once the head of the table had broken bread, we were free to dig in. Prince Viktor was right, the meal was delicious, consisting of roast chicken, apples, potatoes and onions. "I didn't realize there was such a good chef to be found in Loch."

"The employees at the inn in town generously prepared it for us," Siofra explained.

Jion jumped in. "Vik dramatically overpaid for my ale last night, so they made it as a thank you."

"Vik?" I asked, puzzled, having not heard that name before.

"Jion and I have been friends since we were children. His father was my father's closest guard, so we grew up side by side, though Jion has some years on me. Vik is a childhood nickname of mine," the prince explained, mirth dancing in his eyes.

Ignoring him, Jion continued gushing about the food. "They said this meal is an ancient local delicacy."

"That's true. I've never had it, though the recipe is known to my family. Chicken is hard to come by this far from the city, so it is only prepared for very special occasions. My mother probably would have prepared it for you if we had known in advance you'd be arriving. It is a treat to finally try it."

"The meal your mother prepared was very good, and it was very kind and generous of your family to provide a meal for us even though we arrived without notice," the prince replied.

I smiled at his praise, bowing my head slightly. "So, Siofra, are you also an old friend of the prince?" I asked, hoping to get to know my companions a little better.

"Kelps, no. If I had known the two of them all my life I

wouldn't have this job." Despite her harsh words, I could hear the jest in her voice and see the hint of a fond smile on her full lips. "I started as a simple soldier as soon as I was old enough to join the Doctsland navy."

"She worked her way up to personal guard of the prince in just five years, through sheer determination and intimidation tactics," Jion interjected.

Siofra's hazel eyes rolled in an exaggerated fashion. "Shut *up* for *once*, Jion! She doesn't know us yet. You're making me sound scary."

"Contrary to popular belief, Sifora isn't scary," the prince said, shooting a pointed glance at Jion though he was biting back a smile with his slightly crooked front teeth. "She worked her way up to personal guard through hard work."

Laughing, I nodded, slowly getting a sense of their camaraderie as a group, and appreciative of their efforts to include me in that. The rest of the meal was spent in idle chatter, all of us doing our best to enjoy the delicious food and trying not to think too much on the road ahead. While it was surely fraught with perils and there would need to be much planning and discussion before we landed, this was not the time. We celebrated the Doctsland custom of a great feast party the evening before a journey, to bless it. Given the circumstances, the party wasn't very feasible, but the feast was present, and we were determined to make the most of it. As Jion said, it was likely we wouldn't have another for a long while.

After the meal, and a few more drinks, my barricade was beginning to get weak. The drunken happiness but underlying unease of my companions (with the exception of the prince, who appeared to be drinking only water), and of those members of the crew in close proximity began to seep into the edges of my mind. Yawning, I took that as a sign to retire and stood. "I'm going to head to bed. Thank you for the meal," I announced. The others stood and bowed to bid me off.

"Goodnight. When you awake tomorrow, meet me on deck. We've got some training to do," Jion said, sitting back down and pouring himself another glass of wine.

I nodded before leaving the cabin and making my way back to my bunk. I had barely managed to disrobe before I fell into bed and drifted off to sleep, wondering briefly what kind of training Jion was referring to.

Chapter Five

Lisalya

The next morning was disorienting, to say the least. As I opened my eyes, I expected for a moment to see the familiar ceiling of my bedroom at home. When I saw the mattress of the top bunk above me instead I blearily rubbed my eyes, confused, before everything came swirling back in a rush. The last thing I remembered from the previous evening was Jion requesting me on deck for some sort of training. With a groan and a stretch, I stood from my bed, careful not to knock my head on the top bunk. The movement of the boat, last nights' drinks, and the relative proximity to everyone else on the ship already had me feeling slightly woozy. The last thing I needed was a knock to the head. After pulling on my trousers and an off-white blouse and vest, I braced myself and prepared to face the day. Before exiting the room, I did my best to put up mental blockades. *I'll need to use this time on the ship to learn how to better put up blocks, as well as learn how to search people out if that's what my purpose on this mission will be,* I thought, exiting the room.

It was easier to navigate the ship and make my way to the deck. I was growing accustomed to the twists and turns of the narrow ship hallways. It also helped that the closer I got the louder the voices and noises from the crew were, both physically and mentally. When I finally crested the stairs, I held my hand up to shield my eyes. It had to be close to noon, the sun was high and bright. There were numerous crew members around, all busy with their own tasks, and I glanced about me, wondering if Jion was awake yet or if I had beat him. It was as good a time as any to practice, so I

71

closed my eyes and quested out, searching for the unique voice that made up his mind. Scrunching up my face, I tried to focus on opening a crack in my walls to allow Jion to slip through but no one else. I grinned when I sensed him, just a flicker through my blocks, but coming from the left. I closed up the crack and opened my eyes just as he began to approach.

"Ahh, there she is!" His voice broke out amongst the crowd. I turned towards the sound to see him walking towards me from the direction of the prince's cabin. "You certainly enjoy your sleep, don't you?" he said, keeping a good-natured tone.

I rubbed my eyes, finally adjusting to the brightness of the daylight. "What time is it?"

"After noon, I'd say. Siofra and I have been up for hours, helping the crew and waiting for you to arrive. I wanted to go wake you, but Siofra wouldn't let me. She said sometimes being around people makes your head hurt? Anyway, she thought you might need the time to rest," he answered, gesturing to Siofra, who was assisting one of the crew members with a sail.

"I'm sorry for my delay. Siofra is right, sometimes it is painful for me to be around people. This morning, though, I think I just overslept. Where is the prince?" I asked, unaccustomed to seeing Jion without Prince V by his side.

He nodded towards the cabin. "The prince does not take well to sea journeys. He is resting in his cabin."

I wondered briefly if that were true, or if he was just hiding in his cabin instead of helping the crew, or assisting with training. *That seems more likely, if any of the rumors about his spoiled nature are true,* I thought. What esteem I had gained of the prince during last night's dinner was starting to slip away.

Jion reached a veiny arm towards a sword that had to be longer than my torso and thrust it towards me. My eyes grew wide, and I stared at him in shock. "What do you want me to do with *that?*" I asked, bewildered.

A smirk spread across his handsome face. "Your training."

"I've never wielded a sword before," I said, staring at the weapon skeptically.

"Neither had I," Siofra said, stepping up beside Jion, her own sword firm in her grasp. Her hair was pinned back, and she looked ready for battle somehow. Even without her armor, she was an intimidating force. "Until my mother handed one to me and taught me to use it effectively." She nodded her head towards the sword that Jion held out to me. "Take it, and we will begin."

Gingerly I reached out with both hands and took the sword from him, lurching forward with the weight in my hands. His smirk grew into a grin. "First we'll work on how to hold it. One handed. Are you stronger with your right or left?"

"My right. But even so, I don't understand how I can hold this with one hand. It weighs as much as I do!" I exclaimed, letting go with my left hand and trying, and failing, to lift the sword off the ground.

Jion laughed heartily, eyes scrunching up with his wide grin. "It doesn't weigh as much as you do, that much I can assure you. But you are right, it is heavy. Learning to wield it properly with one hand will take time, and practice, but you will grow strength. Soon it won't be any trouble to get it off the ground."

"Whose sword is this anyway?" I asked, lifting it with both hands once more to examine the detailed handle.

"It was my mother's." My head snapped up at the unexpected sound of the prince's voice. I saw him, his normally olive-toned skin appearing pale and his face worn, (perhaps Jion was right about his sea sickness) making his way slowly towards us.

"The queen? The one who just passed?" I asked, eyes widening with wonder at the sword in my hand once more.

Prince Viktor shook his head. "No, that was my step-mother. My birth mother died when I was small, and my father remarried a widowed princess from Bushand. That is the queen who recently died. This sword belonged to my real mother, and has been sitting unused since her death, locked away in my father's bedchambers. I took it into my own keeping after his death." He hesitated, eyes locked onto the weapon in my hands.

Jion spoke up during the prince's pause. "There weren't many weapons we could sneak away from the barracks without being noticed. We took as much as we could and brought as many of our own as we could manage. I imagine we'll need them if all goes well and we're able to gather people to our cause. I know the smallfolk in Doctsland don't have access to weapons, nor do they need to, being a safe country. Perhaps the people of Bushand will be in a similar situation."

"Clearly it was the right choice, bringing it along. It's already coming in handy," the prince said, a small smile on his lips before he suddenly blanched, his face turning green. Despite my barricades, I felt a wave of nausea rush over me as well.

"Perhaps. You should go back to the cabin. We can handle teaching Lisalya how to fight." Siofra said gently. The prince nodded before turning and doing just that.

"He looks... unwell," I said, watching as he ducked back into his cabin hurriedly. The more distance he put between us the more his illness receded from my mind. I breathed a sigh of relief when he shut the door.

"Yeah, he's a mess on a ship. We learned that on the journey to Loch," Jion said. "Now enough distractions. Time for you to learn to fight like a Doctsland soldier!"

"First you need to pick the sword up off the ground," Siofra said, looking at where the end of the sword kissed the deck with raised eyebrows.

Groaning with the effort, but also with a bit of a dramatic flair that I won't deny, I heaved the weapon upright. "Pointy end towards the sky?" I joked.

Jion laughed and nodded. "Pointy end toward the sky. See, you're a natural. You already know which end is up."

From her place by my side, Siofra reached towards the hilt. "Now let's adjust your hands. There is a proper way to hold a sword, it will help balance the weight and make it easier for you to handle. We'll start with two hands. You said your right hand is dominant, yes?" she asked. I nodded and she continued. "Okay, so with your right hand, grasp the hilt up here, closer to the blade. Then place your left beneath it, here." As she spoke, she guided my hands to the proper position on the leather-wrapped hilt. "This part here," Siofra continued, pointing towards the golden top of the handle, which held an ornate design of twisting vines and leaves, "will protect your hands from the blade." Once my hands were in place she let go and stepped back. "Now hold it up and move it around a bit."

I followed her instructions and found that the new placement of my hands made it a lot easier to lift the blade, though it's weight still made it difficult considering my arms weren't used to exhibiting this kind of strength. "That feels a bit better, right?" Jion asked.

"Yes," I replied, feeling a bit powerful with the blade firmly in my grasp.

"Alright, your hands are in the right spots. Let's work on your stance," Jion said.

"Stance?" I asked. "Won't I be moving all over if I'm in a fight?"

"Yes, but you've got to have a foundation before you get to that. Otherwise you'll be flailing around with no purpose."

I nodded, trying to mirror his position. Feet hip width apart, knees bent slightly. "Like this?"

"Good," Jion said. "Keep a bend in your knees, it will help with your balance. It'll also keep them from locking, which can make you pass out. Try to stay light on your feet to increase your speed." As he spoke, he began to circle me slowly. "Keep me in your line of sight. Don't let me get behind you, or in any blind spots."

I turned, rotating my feet to keep him in my vision. Jion smiled. "That's great, Lis. Good job. You've pretty much nailed the standing position. So now comes the hard part. Footwork."

Siofra stepped in. "The quick footwork in the heat of battle will come naturally with time and practice. Everyone develops their own style. As we practice you'll begin to develop yours. Until then, try to move in a way that feels most natural. Like Jion said, stay light on your feet. Don't dig your heels in and stand in one spot, try to keep moving."

"Siofra and I will duel for a minute. Pay special attention to how and where we move our feet."

I watched in amazement as they began to move. They were so quick it was hard to focus, but I took Jion's instruction to heart and tried to follow their feet with my eyes as best I could. It proved difficult, the distraction of the blades clanging together made it hard not glance up at their swords, but I was determined not to tear my eyes off their quick moving feet. I watched as they danced back and forth, moving lightly and swiftly across the deck of the ship, and somehow maintaining enough control as they moved to not strike each other accidentally. My eyes widened, and I wondered how this would ever come naturally to me the way Siofra had described it.

"Do you want to try?" Siofra asked, and I blinked up at them, terrified.

"Don't worry, we won't go so quickly on your first try. We'll help you build up to that," Jion said.

Nodding slowly, I lifted the sword in my grasp. "Alright, I'll try." True to his word, Jion approached slowly. He explained what he intended to do before he did it, ensuring I knew where and when to lift the blade to parry his blows.

We continued until it felt like I was going to pass out. The fatigue coursing through my veins grew heavy, a weight that seemed to be pulling my arms downwards whenever I tried to lift them to block. As I weakened physically, so did the barricade in my mind begin to break. By the time we stopped, it had nearly crumbled completely, and I felt the emotions of everyone nearby churning in my head. I tried to push them back to focus on the task at hand, but when I failed to raise the sword high enough and Jion nicked my arm with his, he declared it was time to be done for the day. "We'll pick up again tomorrow. I reckon if we do a bit each day, you'll be a skilled enough fighter by the time we reach Bushand."

"Okay," I said, breathing heavily and examining the small cut on my right arm.

"I think Vik has some bandages in the cabin." He gestured in that direction. "You can get that cleaned and wrapped up. We'll meet here tomorrow after you wake, just like today."

With a soft smile of thanks, I nodded before making my way towards the cabin. I took the blade with me, thinking I should return his mother's sword back to the prince, at least for the day. I knocked lightly at first, feeling nervous about entering the prince's space, especially while he was sick.

"You may enter," I heard him call from within.

Pushing the door open, I was met by darkness and again nausea poured over me. The prince had pulled all the curtains shut, and the only light source was a sole candle on the table. Though I couldn't see him, I could make out his form beneath the covers on a cot in the corner. "I brought your mother's sword. Thank you for allowing me to train with it." When he didn't reply, I asked, "Are you alright?"

With a groan, he pushed himself upright. His hair, which had always been tied back up to this point, flowed freely over his shoulders. "I'm fine, just dizzy. Can you place the sword in that cabinet please?" He gestured with his hand to a cabinet along the wall near the door.

"Yes," I said, gently resting the weapon in the cabinet and shutting the door. "Um, Jion mentioned you may have a bandage in here. Is that correct?"

He cocked his head, curious. "Why do you need a bandage?"

Lifting my elbow, I showed him my wound. "I may have sustained a slight injury at the end of that training Jion and Sifora gave me."

The prince smiled, and I was surprised to find that it dazzled me a little. "A cut during your very first sparing lesson? That's basically a rite of passage." He peeled his covers off and crawled out of bed and over to the cabinet. "Here," he said, pulling out a long bandage. "I'll help you wrap that up."

"Thanks," I replied.

77

"So, how exactly did you get this?" he asked, gently wiping the wound with a cloth before applying the bandage.

"My arms were getting tired. I wasn't able to raise the sword up quickly enough, so I couldn't block Jion's blow. Thankfully it only nicked my arm."

"Jion usually has pretty good control of his blade. It could have been much worse if it had been someone else. The sword does get pretty heavy after a while. How long was the training? An hour?"

I shrugged. "Around there, maybe two." I glanced back down at the sword resting in the cabinet. "I don't even remember a queen before your step-mother. I was too young."

A pang of sadness struck through the nausea, and I glanced at him to see it written on his face as well. His eyes were downcast, focusing on the bandage he was applying, but a frown had settled on his lips, "I hardly remember her either. She died when I was very young, killed in a skirmish with Bushand. We've never had a great relationship with them, something my father tried to remedy when he took their princess to wife. But we're seeing how that turned out," he said with a humorless chuckle, bitterness thick in his voice and heart. "That sword is one of my only keepsakes from my mother."

"The soldiers in Loch always named their blades before they went off the Capital City to join the military. Does this sword have a name?"

The prince nodded. "Mother named it after my grandmother, Gaisgea. They were both warriors- each had served in the royal guard. That's how my parents met."

I glanced up at him in confusion, though he seemed to be focused on wrapping my wound, "Your father married a soldier? Not a princess?"

A small smile broke the furrow in his brow slightly. "I'm surprised you don't know. Though Loch is a long way from Capital City, and nearly thirty years have passed. But yes, he married a soldier rather than a princess. It was quite a scandal, or so I've heard. And my parents, particularly my father, always worried that my legitimacy as an heir would be questioned because my mother was a commoner. I never thought that would happen, but now I see that they were right to be concerned. There," he said, his somber tone lifting. "You're all set. Try to take it a little easier while that's healing."

I bowed. "I'll take it as easy as Jion allows me too. He said we're to do lessons every morning until we arrive."

"Really?" he said, eyebrows raised. "And how long did they say this journey would be? Two weeks? You'll be the best fighter of us all with practice every day!"

I laughed incredulously. "I doubt that. I need all the practice I can get right now, I just hope I don't have to put it to use for a while. I'm not sure I'm ready for that."

"Yeah, me neither. But we've got time to prepare ourselves."

I felt the ship rock beneath my feet, and saw the prince's face pale. "I will let you get back to sleep. Thank you again, Prince Viktor."

"Please," he said, "Just call me Viktor. Or even Vik, as Jion and Siofra do. There's no need for formalities out here."

I smiled and bowed once more before exiting the cabin and shutting the door gently behind me, feeling a little odd about the pleasant interaction with the prince.

"All wrapped up?" Jion asked when he saw me step out into the broad sunlight on the deck, shielding his dark eyes with his hand.

"Yes, Prince Viktor assisted, well, actually, he did all the cleaning and wrapping. He told me a bit about the history of the blade I'm working with as well, Gaisgea."

Jion cocked his head, and a surprised look came over his face. "Did he really? How is he doing in there?"

I shrugged. "He seems okay. He got up and moved around a bit, but when the ship lurched a few minutes ago he went pale and had to lay back down. He almost looked green-ish."

"Well, he must be feeling a little better if he was helping to bandage you up. I'm surprised he told you the name of the sword. It's something he holds dear to his heart, and I don't think he shares it with many."

I wrung my hands, feeling awkward and unsure how to respond. "I feel honored."

Jion smiled, sensing my unease. "As you should. Now, ready for lunch?"

At the mention of food I brightened, realizing just how hungry I was after hours of sword fighting without any breakfast. I also hoped some food in my stomach would give me the strength needed to reinstate my walls before a migraine came on. "Kelps, yes. I'm starved. What's for lunch?"

"Nothing as glamorous as what we had last night, that's for sure. Biscuits, salted meat, and a little bit of cheese, at least until it goes bad. But on an empty stomach it can taste like heaven," Siofra came up from below deck carrying three small packs. She handed one to each Jion and I, keeping another for herself. "Well," she said. "Let's dig in!"

"Does the prince need one as well?" I asked.

"He's got food in his cabin, though I doubt he'll eat it for a little while. It's hard to eat much when you've got travel sickness," Jion explained, taking a big bite out of a piece of bread.

"Hopefully he will adjust. It would be a shame to have to spend the entire voyage abed sick," I said. I was also hoping he'd adjust so I wouldn't have to stomach his illness whenever I was in his presence.

Jion and Siofra both shrugged.

"He's resilient," Siofra said. "He'll get tired of being cabin-bound and will power through it. I'm sure it's driving him crazy to hear all the excitement out here on the deck without being able to join in."

"I give him until end of day tomorrow. He'll be out here with us," Jion added.

We continued chatting quite aimlessly until we had all finished with our lunch. Jion left to help the crew- apparently he knew a bit about sailing and enjoyed the work. I was beginning to succumb to the overwhelming emotions of everyone around me. My head swam painfully, and the brightness of the sun was making it difficult to keep my eyes open. "Is it alright if I go lie down for a bit? Just to rest my head?" I asked.

"Certainly. You're done with your fighting lesson for the day. The rest of the day is yours to do with as you wish," Siofra replied. "Are you feeling unwell?"

"No, but I think I need some time away from all these people." I gestured around the deck, where about a dozen crew members were scattered about doing various tasks.

"Ah, I understand. Rest well!"

I smiled and headed back into my small room.

Chapter Six

Viktor

I slept through the afternoon and straight on til the next morning, waking just as the sun was beginning to peak over the horizon, it streamed in through the windows of my cabin. Though nausea was still clouding my head, I couldn't stand being cooped up in the cabin any longer, so I got dressed and stepped out onto the deck. Closing my eyes, I revelled in the feeling of the cool, sea-salt air as it hit my face and soothed me.

"I *knew* you'd be out of there today." Jion's voice had me snapping my eyes open. I was surprised to see him up and about so early.

"What are you doing awake? You're not an early riser."

"I'm not usually. It's hard for me to sleep without Hope. Five years of sharing a bed with my husband makes an empty one feel foreign," he said, and though I knew he was fighting it, I noticed his brows knit together and a sense of longing on his typically jovial face. I opened my mouth to reply when Lisalya stepped out from below deck. Her black and white hair was pulled back, and she wore the riding clothes she'd had on when she first met us at the inn. Sleep was cloudy in her brown eyes, though she smiled as soon as she spotted us, and I noticed that as she did so the slight cleft in her chin disappeared.

"Good Morning," she said. I handed her my Gaisgea, and as she held my mother's sword I was struck by how lovely she was. I felt a little dazed, and shook the thought from my head, trying to remember how mean she could be when in a foul mood to distract myself from her beauty. I also remembered her ability to sense others' feelings, and shifted uncomfortably, a blush rising to my cheeks that I couldn't fight. *I need to learn how to protect my mind from her somehow.* The idea that there could be someone out there that could sense my thoughts and feelings was unsettling, be they friend or foe. If I really wanted to be the best king I could be, I had to acknowledge and ward myself against anything that could be a threat. Taking a seat near the edge of the deck, I decided to observe the day's fighting practice.

"Good morning, Lis. I want to focus on your footwork today, and your ability to block. Are you ready?" Jion asked.

She nodded, then winced as she raised her blade and said, "Your husband. What is he like?"

"The tenderness in your muscles will dissipate as we begin. They're stiff right now," he said, grinning. "So you heard that, did you? Yes, my husband, Hope. He's a surgeon in Capital City. He married me, so you know he's handsome and has great taste. He's also brilliant. We met when I became injured during my training to become a guard. I was only seventeen then, but I knew right away that he was the one. He, on the other hand, took some convincing." He chuckled, eyes dreamy with the memory. I couldn't help but smile, remembering Jion rushing to the palace immediately after and gushing about the 'entrancing' student he'd just met.

"What do you mean?" she replied as she parried his first blow.

"He was still studying at that time. When we met, he was shadowing the surgeon in the infirmary. He was so focused on learning, on becoming the best medical professional he could be, he saw me as a distraction. We became friends, but he had no room for anything more until he was finished with his schooling. I was in love, so I waited." Those were a long couple of years, listening to Jion pine after Hope on the daily. I'd considered asking my father to extradite Hope's medical badge in an effort to cure my friend's heartsickness, but I'm glad I didn't. Knowing Hope as I do now, he never would have accepted. He had to earn that badge fair and square.

They pranced around the deck, and I admired how quickly

Lisalya was learning the craft. I'd had several years' worth of lessons from expensive tutors, and she was picking it up easier than I ever did, her movements lithe and swift. She stumbled occasionally, biting into her plush bottom lip in concentration. *She's overthinking her footwork*, I thought. I jumped into the conversation though I knew the story well, hoping it would distract her enough to allow her footwork to come naturally. "How long did you wait?"

Lisalya shot me a relieved smile as Jion answered, speaking to her even though I asked the question. His father being my own father's personal guard meant we'd known each other since we were toddlers. That length of friendship lends itself to some sort of psychic connection. He knew I knew the answer to the question, and was asking for her benefit. "Almost two years. They felt like the longest two years ever, but the night that he received his badge of qualification was the best night of my life, and he's well worth the wait. We were married only six months later. Good footwork! You're already improving and it's only day two!"

Color rose to her dark cheeks at the praise, and she swept Gaisgea to the side, blocking another hit. They continued like that until it was clear that Lisalya could hardly lift the blade any further. The sun had fully risen and was now high in the sky, beating down on us mercilessly. Siofra, who had come up from below deck at some unknown time during our training, tutted at Jion's russet hair, which was sopping wet with sweat and clinging to his face. "You sweat too much. You're disgusting. Go bathe."

He cackled, mirth dancing in his eyes. "How? We're on a boat." He turned back to Lisalya. "We can be done now. That was about three hours, which I think is plenty for today. I'm getting hot."

"Thank Kelps," she said, breathless. Her chest was heaving, and her hair had come undone, falling in loose waves around her face. She lifted her hand to her head, pressing onto her eyebrows as she murmured, "I'm going to go lie down." Briefly I wondered if I should ask if she was okay, but she was gone before I could get the words out of my mouth.

"Feeling better?" Jion asked, taking a seat beside me.

Shielding my eyes from the sun, I replied, "As better as I can while we're on this god-forsaken vessel. I hope she's alright." I nodded to where Lisalya had stood moments before. "She seemed as though her head hurt."

Siofra joined us, leaning against the side of the ship. "She isn't used to being in such close quarters with so many people, and she doesn't really know yet how to control her powers."

"And they hurt her?" I asked.

Siofra nodded. "She gets migraines."

"How do you know?"

"I asked." Siofra shrugged. "She told me."

'Well," I said. "How can we help with that?"

She shrugged again. "From what I gather, being separated from everyone as much as possible helps. But, I think that's a question you should ask her, not me."

"I don't think she likes me," I said, trying to keep the pout from my voice.

Jion laughed. "Tons of people don't like you. You don't usually care."

I socked his shoulder, frowning as I tried not to laugh. "Thanks for the encouragement, Jion."

Siofra ignored us and continued. "You might consider learning to hide your mind from her, Vik. I know she's on our side, but I don't think it's safe for anyone to be able to read your mind."

"Yes, I had thought of that this morning, actually. I'm not sure where to start to be honest. I don't fully understand her power, let alone how to mask myself from it."

"She said she can block people out by building walls in her mind. I don't know if that would work in the reverse, but it may be somewhere to start…"

I stood and stretched. "I'll work on that. Jion, did you bring your father's map?"

He leaned on his sword, huffing and sweating, "Yeah, it's down in my bunk."

"Will you grab it and meet Siofra and I in the cabin in a few minutes? I want to try to pinpoint where to land, and what areas or towns we should try to hit. I know we won't be able to make a rigid plan without knowing how the people feel in those areas, but it's a start."

"I'll be there," he replied as Siofra and I turned to head towards the cabin.

We heaved a collective sigh of relief as soon as we were inside and out of the scorching rays of the sun. I sat down at the table, my leg bouncing anxiously as I began to think about everything we needed to accomplish in order for this journey to be a success. The weight of it all was crushing, and my fingers danced along the table.

"We've been onboard for two full days now, which means we've got over a week and a half still to prepare," Siofra said gently, joining me at the table and trying to talk me out of the hole I was falling into.

I shot her a small smile of gratitude. "There's just so much I don't have control over. We've gained the empath, which is fantastic, but it appears even she doesn't understand fully how to use or control her powers. What if she can't do what we need her to do? What if we can't find anyone sympathetic to our cause? We could be offering ourselves up to Siglind by going to Bushand."

Siofra shrugged. "You're right, we could be. That is the risk in any mission of stealth such as this. But do you really think the whispers of discontent with Siglind could have reached us in Doctsland without having any truth to them? On the contrary. It must be truly widespread to have reached our ears. And Lisalya, she is trying. Just as we all are. If she uses this time on the ship to strengthen both her mind and body, which I know she will, I believe she will gain control over her abilities. I have faith in her."

I raised my eyebrows. It wasn't often Siofra had so quickly grown to trust and care for a person as she had Lisalya. Her faith, and her words, were a great comfort, and I was just about to tell her such when Jion entered.

"Thank Kelps you cleaned yourself off a bit before

86

coming," Siofra said as he plopped into a chair beside her, rolling the map out onto the table. He seemed to have dried off a bit and had changed into a fresh tunic.

He grinned at her wickedly and leaned towards her a bit. "My hair is still wet with sweat. Do you want to smell it?"

"No!" she screeched, causing a burst of laughter from him. "Can we just focus?"

Jion had a knack for switching from goofing around to becoming serious in a startling amount of time. He put that skill to use now. "If I remember correctly, when we came all those years ago we went directly to the port in Nul. Obviously, that's not an option in this case."

Siofra leaned forward, examining the map with her brows scrunched together. "Green Marsh is a rather large city, correct? Second to Nul? Perhaps it would be best to try to land somewhat near there, close enough that we can easily ask for their help if Lisalya gives the okay, but not close enough to be easily caught by them should they be loyal to Siglind."

"It's also near enough to Nul. We don't have much time to try to rally troops. I think we should try to stay as close to Nul as we can whilst remaining secret. The longer we have to march, the more likely we're caught, and the longer it will take to reach the city. If the fleet arrives and we aren't there, it could prove disastrous. We have to stick to the timeline," I said.

"I agree," Jion said. "It's best if we can land somewhere between Green Marsh and Nul. It looks like there's forest and the river, we may be able to make a camp somewhere hidden in the woods and with the sound of the water hiding up somewhat."

"That's provided Siglind hasn't cut down the woods, yet," Siofra pointed out. "It may be difficult to hide the boat, and ourselves. But those are issues we can deal with when they come. That is most definitely the best place to land to stick to our timeline and give us access to the most people."

"Great," I said, happy with the decision and the fact that we were able to come to it so quickly. "It's a plan."

Chapter Seven

Lisalya

As the journey progressed, both the prince and I seemed to be growing accustomed to the sea voyage and the close quarters of everyone onboard. The journey itself was easy, though long, and I used the time to continue to practice building and maintaining my mental walls, as well as becoming familiar with each person I was traveling with to ensure I could recognize their mind compared to someone else's should the need arrive. That is, until the storm hit.

We were only a day or two from reaching our destination when it began, overnight, though the crew had been expecting it all day, sensing it in the thick, still air and the darkening sky. I woke up when the ship lurched so hard I was thrown from my bed. Sore already from the training I'd been doing daily with Jion, I winced as I pushed myself to standing. I stumbled around my room, pulling on my trousers and running out to see what was going on.

When I arrived on deck, fear doused me. Waves larger than anything I could ever have imagined barreled into the ship, nearly knocking it on its side. I held on to the railing near the stairs to anchor myself and avoid getting swept into the sea. In my terror, I allowed the barricade on my mind to slip, and I was instantly overwhelmed with the unique mixture of fear and determination that was swarming throughout all of the crew members, including Jion, Siofra, and even the prince, who I saw attempting to secure a sail by tying it to a mast, with the help of another crew member. Another wave crashed into us, and I saw a man tumble over the edge of the ship. Despite the devastating influx of emotions mingled with my own fear, I rushed over to where he'd fallen and found him gripping the side of the ship and trying to pull himself back onboard. Grabbing his hand, I braced myself against the side of the ship and tried to heave him back up. It was difficult to keep my footing on the slippery wood of the deck, and just as I was about to stumble forward and be pulled down with the man I was trying to save, I felt a steadying pair of arms grab me. Without looking, I knew it was the prince due to the proximity of his mind and my lack of mental walls. After helping me get back onto my feet, he grabbed the man's other arm and helped me haul him up.

"Thank you!" I yelled, hoping he could hear over the wind and rain.

"What are you doing out here?" he hollered back. His light eyes burned between tendrils of silver hair that whipped around his face in the wind. "It's dangerous!"

"I could say the same about you! I'm trying to help!"

"Both of you should go into the cabin!" Siofra intervened.

"Why? I can help!" the prince countered, a stubborn fire in his eyes.

She shook her head. "Vik, it's too dangerous! We can't afford to lose either of you. I know you want to help, but your safety is imperative. So stop arguing and just do it!" she shouted, pointing to the cabin.

The prince glared at her for half a moment before wheeling around and stalking to the cabin. The look on Siofra's face warned me not to argue with her, so despite my desire to stay and assist to the best of my abilities, I instead turned on my heel and followed after the prince.

The roaring of the wind and the rain lessened significantly when I closed the door behind me and shut my eyes. Leaning against the door, I steadied myself and took the opportunity to reinstate my mental barricades, then sighed at the relief it brought. When I opened my eyes, I found the prince pacing back and forth. "Prince V, are you alright?" I asked tentatively, guessing that his pacing was indicative of how upset he was.

"I'm fine," he said dismissively. "And *please* just call me Vik."

Deciding it was best to leave him alone, I crossed the room and sat at the table we had had our kick off dinner at almost two weeks prior. Thankfully it seemed to be secured to the floor so it wasn't lurching around the room as the ship did. "Doesn't it drive you crazy?" The prince, *Vik,* I corrected in my mind, spoke. "Being cooped up in here when we should be out there helping?"

I turned towards him. "Do you know much about sailing?" I asked.

He looked up, confused. "What?"

I repeated the question pointedly.

"I mean, no," he answered. "Not much. Capital City is landlocked. I've been out on the warships before to christen them with my father, but that's about it."

"Me neither. I've been on boats on the Loch, but I've never been sailing in open water on a vessel such as this. It seems like in this scenario, people with seafaring experience are needed. I'm not sure how much we could help. It seems more likely we would just get in the way. And Siofra is right, the two of us are indispensable."

Rather than reply, he threw himself onto his bed in a huff, reminding me of a petulant child. My instinct was to say as much, but I held my tongue, and reminded myself that this wasn't the common annoying fisherman's son I was used to in Loch. This was the future king of Doctsland.

The struggle of withholding my thoughts was soon the least of my worries, when the entire ship was thrown sideways. Water burst in, breaking the window above the prince's bed, and showering him in shattered glass and seawater. Releasing my grip on the table, I allowed myself to slide across the room over to him. "Are you okay? We need to get out of here!" I yelled over the rushing water.

He nodded, blood running down his face, and grabbed the hand I offered to him. I glanced around the room, panicked, trying to figure out a way out. Panicked, I saw that the cabinet containing Gaisgea and other items of the prince's had been thrown across the door, blocking it from being opened. My eyes scanned the room, searching for another exit. "That window!" The prince shouted, gesturing to the window on the other side of the room, now almost directly above us. "I'll boost you up so you can grab onto the table. Once you get to the window, throw the curtain down to me."

I couldn't come up with anything better under the circumstances, so I agreed, stepping up onto his clasped hands. Reaching my arms out, I stretched as he lifted me until I could finally get a tight hold on one of the table's legs. I thanked the Kelps for his height. If he was any less than six feet this would not have worked, and we would have been stuck. Using all of my strength, including some I didn't even know I had, I pulled myself up and around the table until I could reach the curtain and yank it down. After quickly fastening it to the table leg closest to me, I threw it down to the prince. I watched to make sure he was able to grab a hold, then turned my attention to the window. It was fastened shut, and I stood on my toes using the table for balance as I reached for the latch to open it. My height was so disadvantageous that I could barely brush my fingers against it. Grimacing with frustration, I tried to push myself higher, reaching, and in the process lost my balance.

Thankfully the prince had reached me, and snatched my arm to hold me steady before I could tumble back down into the swirling water below. I glanced up, not bothering to take the time or spend the energy shouting it when it was doubtful he'd hear over the storm and the wreckage anyway. He nodded and reached up to undo the latch and open the window. Clasping his hands, he motioned for me to step into them again for a boost. I did so, and he lifted me until I could reach the window sill and pull myself up and out of it.

As soon as I breached the side of the ship, the wind and rain began whipping around me. When I realized the Prince had not followed me, I turned, looking back through the window and searched for him. "Prince Viktor!" I screamed as I saw him heading back down into the room. "You need to get out of there!"

"Just wait! I need my mother's sword!" he called back, pulling it from the cabinet near the door and fastening its belt around his waist before crawling back up and out of the ship. I grabbed to help him get steady on his feet, though it was difficult for either of us to maintain because of the strength of the storm swirling around us. "What do we do now?" I yelled over the noise.

The prince looked at me and then at the sea around us wildly, clearly unsure, until he suddenly seemed to brighten. I followed his gaze and saw a small life boat, holding Jion, Siofra, and several members of the crew. They were beckoning to us, and yelling something, though we could not hear them from the distance.

"We jump!" Prince Viktor replied, leaping off the ship after grabbing my hand and pulling me along with him.

Though it had seemed a long way down, the fall happened quickly, and before I knew it I was plunging into the deep, cold water of the sea. It filled my nose and I tasted salt on my lips as I began to fight my way upwards against the current, my connection with the prince sundered due to the violent churning of the sea.

Once I broke the surface, I looked around frantically, trying to locate the position of the boat. It was difficult to see anything in the darkness of the night, but a sudden flash of lighting brightened the world around me. I thanked the Kelps for growing up in Loch, as all citizens of the town spend a significant amount of their childhood swimming in the Loch, making nearly all of us exceptional swimmers. The life boat became visible, a mere ten or fifteen feet in front of me, but the prince was nowhere to be seen. *Maybe he got to the boat already,* I thought. The flash had been bright but swift. I'd seen the boat but couldn't make out any of the figures inside of it. It seems they'd been able to make me out as well, because suddenly a life saver attached to a rope was thrown my way. I grasped onto it immediately, and was pulled towards the boat and into it. As soon as I climbed aboard I glanced at each person, searching. "Where is the prince?!" I asked, panicked.

Siofra stood, a look of horror spreading on her face. "We thought he was with you!"

"He was, but we lost each other when we jumped," I explained, rushing to lean over the side of the boat and search the water. It was too dark, and the rain was too heavy. I couldn't see.

"I'm going in," Jion said, standing up and preparing to jump into the sea.

"Wait!" I yelled, stopping him. "It's too dangerous for anyone to jump in. We can't see anything. The chances of you getting lost are too high."

"It's better for me to get lost than for us to lose Vik. We're losing time." He moved to jump.

"No! I think I can locate him. Just give me one moment," I said, opening up my mind. It had been a long time since I'd searched for a person this way, and I prayed it would work. I focused an image of the prince in my mind, zoning in on his unique voice, trying to push all the others to the side. I found him, almost directly below the boat, only two or three feet beneath the surface, but the heavy blade strapped to his waist was pulling him deeper. "I know where he is," I said. Once I had him in my mind I held on tight and, not wanting to waste a moment more, leapt into the water to find him.

He was right where I thought he was, near the boat but too far under for us to have seen him from there. Floating, the wound in his head from the window still gushing. I grabbed him and pushed him up, breaking the surface and hollering for a rope right away. Whether or not they heard me or just saw us pop above the water is a mystery, but regardless the rope was thrown, and I latched on to it immediately. They began reeling us in at once, and it didn't take long before I was once again being pulled up over the side and into the boat, this time along with the prince.

"Is he breathing?" Siofra asked, and I saw Jion laying the prince on his back and leaning down to listen to his breath.

"I can't tell. The storm is too loud!" Jion yelled back.

I focused again on the flicker of life that came from him. "He's still alive!" I exclaimed. "I can feel him. He's weak, but alive."

Jion began to pump his chest, counting the compressions and watching closely for any signs of life. It was only a matter of seconds before the prince began coughing up water. We breathed a collective sigh of relief as he opened his eyes and appeared to regain his senses. "Where are we?" he asked when he awoke.

"We don't know," Siofra replied, clearly worried. "We have to be getting close to Bushand, considering how long we've been on the water. But there's no telling how close, or how far."

"Hopefully the shore isn't far. We've got very few supplies, all of our food either went down with the ship, or became soaked when we jumped. Thankfully Siofra had the mind to grab as many water skins as she could before the ship went down, but those won't last long," Jion said.

Everyone remained silent, fear and concern growing and I put up my walls to ensure that I was only burdened with my own. As soon as I felt I was the only one occupying my own mind, I drifted off into a fitful sleep.

Chapter Eight

Viktor

For the first time in two long weeks I felt earth beneath me. Sand, to be exact, was cushioning my body and sticking to my damp clothes as I lay face down among it. Blinking, I pushed myself upright and looked around. I had to squint and shield my eyes with my hand due to the brightness of the sun, but once my eyes adjusted I could see the beauty before me. Jade colored sand as far as the eye could see, dipping seamlessly into turquoise blue water, which contrasted drastically from the sea I remembered from the previous evening. I turned, looking behind me and was met with a bright green jungle, with tall trees the like of which I had never seen before. My eyes followed up the long trunks to the large lanceolate leaves, which had to have been bigger than my torso.

"Where are we?" I said, not knowing if anyone was even around to hear me.

Suddenly a familiar face poked out amongst the trees. "Bushand, I hope," Lisalya said, emerging from the foliage.

Brushing as much sand off myself as possible, I grinned up at her as I briefly remembered being hauled aboard the lifeboat. "I think I may owe you my life. Thank you."

She bowed her head, black hair falling into her gaze. "You're welcome, Viktor. We all have a duty to each other, I was merely upholding mine. Is everyone else alright? I don't remember landing here…"

I began to panic as I realized we were separated from the rest of our crew. Where were my friends? "All of us that were on the life boat survived the wreck." I let out a breath I didn't even realize I was holding as I heard Siofra's voice. "Thankfully, most of the crew managed to lower a second life boat and escape in it. There were very few casualties. We were incredibly lucky. The waves crashed us onto the beach after dawn, but no one was injured. I just came to wake you up, the others are a few years into the jungle. We're trying to stay under its cover while we figure out where exactly we are."

"We are in Bushand at least?" I asked.

Siofra nodded. "Jion recognized the sand. He said all the beaches here have this strange color."

"Well I'd like to help as much as I can. Lead the way, please."

When she turned and strolled back into the thick grove of trees Lisalya and I followed closely.

"It's not a far walk," Siofra explained as we trudged through the jungle. "We're all exhausted. We didn't want to trek too far into the jungle. But we needed to get off the beach, out of sight."

"The beach looked empty..." Lisalya said, confusion evident in her stormy eyes.

"For now," I spoke up. "But if I know Siglind, he's going to be anticipating an attack. He's paranoid. He will have guards patrolling all his borders, especially those on the sea. He knows our strength is in our navy." I said, coming to a sudden stop behind Siofra as I saw the bustling friendly faces of our Doctsland crew.

"I lost the map." Jion said, strolling out from among the crew to meet us. "It was in my bunk, and went down with the ship. I've no idea where we've landed, and without it it's going to be damn hard to find out."

I tried to hold off the panic that was building in me. We were stuck in enemy territory with no map and no clue where we were, or how far we were from Nul. Lisalya must have sensed my growing agitation and rested a comforting hand on my forearm which, to my surprise, helped to steady me slightly. I turned to Siofra, putting my faith in her to come up with a plan as I often had before. "What do we do?" I asked, trying to keep my voice steady.

Siofra turned to Lisalya. "Can you sense anyone nearby? Maybe if we can find someone to approach, we can ask for a map and discern our location as well as gaining some people to our cause."

Lisalya closed her large eyes, a look of deep concentration settling over her features. "I can only sense us. There is no one else anywhere nearby."

"Kelps," Jion grumbled, turning and kicking a log. He pinched the bridge of his nose, trying to gather himself, and sighed before speaking again. "We need to get moving. It's hot in Bushand, and we've only got a few water skins Siofra managed to grab. Not to mention the fact that we've got no food. We'll need to make a camp as soon as possible, but we should try to get oriented first. It has to be before noon, and the sun is in the east and on our left. We were going to head south to land near Green Marsh before the ship wrecked, and I also don't remember there being any forests like this in the south when I was here as a child. I think we're too far north."

"Then let's start heading south. I think we should move further inland and try to find the river. I remember a bit of the map, and Waterford River runs along the length of the east coast of Bushand. If we can find it, we can follow it all the way to Green Marsh," Siofra said, and I thanked the Kelps for her wisdom and gift of memory.

"Lisalya, is it possible for you to keep searching as we move and let us know if we are approaching anyone?" I asked as we began to collectively head further into the jungle, keeping the sound of the ocean in range and on the left to ensure we had a sense of our direction.

She chewed her lip. "I'm not sure. I haven't done that before, but I will try."

I nodded. It wasn't exactly the answer I was looking for, but I prayed to the Kelps that she'd be successful, accepting that that was all I could do. "Well, let's start moving."

Taking the lead, Siofra and Jion hacked a path through the jungle with their swords and we moved forward, following in their footsteps. *I hope we don't have to go very far* I thought.

They'll burn out hacking through this thick brush before long, but they'll both be too stubborn to say anything until I call for us to halt.

We had moved perhaps only a Kelpstep inland when we found the river, and we all shared relieved grins. "Let's get some water and rest a bit, then move on."

"We cannot rest for too long this close to the water. Waterford River is likely a large source of transportation. We don't want to be seen by anyone unless it's on our terms," Siofra said.

After spending a few minutes catching our breath and refilling the water skins Siofra had saved, we were ready to be on the move again when Lisalya stopped short, grabbing my arm. "Someone is coming."

My eyes widened. "Where? Can you tell from where?"

Her eyes seemed glassy as she spoke. "From the other side of the river, but moving closer. Moving towards us."

Siofra took the lead, speaking in a low and quiet voice. "Quick! Everyone, back into the trees. Hide yourselves and remain silent."

We had only just finished following her orders when voices began to rise up over the sound of the river. "Captain Carthoc! It is just his father's sword, a keepsake. He gave his life for Bushand!" an old woman howled.

They came into view, a pale man dressed head to toe in black Bushanian armor, dragging a young man behind him. A flock of soldiers followed him, along with the wailing woman.

"The law is clear. There is no reason to have any weapons under any circumstances. Having one in your possession is proof that you are conspiring against the king. The punishment for treason is death."

"He's my baby! He's only a boy!" she sobbed, reaching out for what I could only assume was her son. I gripped a branch in front of me in frustration, wanting to intervene and save him. But we had no way to cross the rushing river, and were sorely outnumbered by this Captain Carthoc and his men. All we could do is watch and wait.

"There are no exceptions to the law. King Siglind does not care how old a traitor is." The Captain spat before turning to the soldiers around him. "Mark him as a traitor and hang him over the river as a warning to others that may think of rising up against our beloved king."

We watched in horror as they tore open the tunic of the boy, who could not have been more than fifteen, and carved a large, deep 'T' into his chest as he screamed in pain. Lisalya, who was crouched between Siofra and me, winced with tears streaming down her face. Siofra put an arm over her shoulders and a hand over her mouth to silence her, and Lisalya turned into her embrace. I hoped she was able to build her walls up enough to protect herself from his pain, though that wouldn't protect her from the torment of witnessing such an event without being able to do anything to intervene.

Once they were finished marking him, they strung him up over the river, hanging him by his neck. The only solace provided was that they had dropped him from a great height, and it appears his neck snapped at once. He was no longer suffering.

The woman continued to scream, fighting vehemently against the soldiers that held her back. They laughed, pushing her into the river after forcing her to watch her son be murdered. The water rushed and swirled, the current pulling her under immediately. Even the strongest swimmer would not survive. I closed my eyes tightly and clenched my jaw, the rage flowing through me so strong it was all I could do to contain it. This was the kind of thing that would happen in Doctsland should we fail. Determination hardened in me. *We have to succeed.*

Siofra waited until we could no longer see or hear the soldiers to speak, but she kept her voice quiet. "We need to keep moving. Lisalya, can you tell if they're moving away from us?"

Lisalya sniffled, wiping her nose with the back of her hand, and choked on her words as she answered. "They've moved away. I can no longer sense them."

Siofra gave her a comforting squeeze as she nodded. "Okay. Let's go."

Trying to keep the image of the boy and the sound of his mother's screams out of my head, I marched. We moved for hours, but the jungle didn't appear to change and it felt as though we were making no progress. If it hadn't been for the river, I would have thought we were going in circles. Light was failing, and I knew we needed rest. It could be dangerous to try to move in the dark with no sense of where we were or where we were going. When we came to a small clearing, I called for a halt.

"Let's sleep here tonight. We've crossed a lot of ground today, and there's no sense in moving forward in the black of the night."

The rest of the party agreed, and I sent off two members of the crew to hunt and find something to eat. "Be as swift and as quiet as you can be. And don't stray too far," I warned as they headed off.

By the time they returned Jion had a small fire going, and we were able to eat and rest for the night.

***

I rose as soon as the sun began to trickle over the horizon. The night had been restless, the events of the day playing out over and over in my head, and I was eager to begin moving again. Lisalya sat awake, poking at the fire, tears shining on her face. "Are you okay?" I asked, my voice raspy with sleep.

She shook her head. "Not really. I didn't have time to put my walls up before…" She stopped, containing a sob that tried to escape. "And it's been hard being so near to everyone for so long. I'm usually able to get some time to myself to repair my energy. My head is killing me."

I hung my head. "I'm sorry. I wish we hadn't witnessed what we saw yesterday. Or I wish we would have been able to do something about it. My hope is we will find somewhere to make a more permanent base today. Then we can build you a shelter separate from the rest of the camp to give you the isolation that you need."

It seemed luck was finally on our side for the first time since the wreck because my hope came true. We were only a few hours into our third march when Lisalya suddenly stopped. "I can sense someone. More than one someone. A village, I think. Not far from here."

"Here would be as good a place as any to set up a camp, even if it be a temporary one depending on where we find our location to be. There's a slight clearing here, it's close enough to the river but hidden by that thicket of trees," Jion said, surveying the surroundings in a circle. "There's not much further we can go today anyway, it's getting dark already."

"Okay, let's get started then," Siofra said. "The sooner it is, the sooner we can rest for a while before we begin our first mission. Jion, will you start working on a small shelter? We'll need to go hunting as well."

"What can I help with? I'm not much for hunting, but I can start a fire easy enough. We often use them in my grandmother's healing rituals," Lisalya said.

"As soon as Jion is finished with the shelter he and I are going hunting. If you could start a fire that would be fantastic," Siofra replied.

Lisalya grinned. "Absolutely. I'm on it." She immediately sat in the center of the clearing and began to dig out a makeshift fire pit.

Wanting to help in some way, I asked. "Is there anything I can grab for you, to help?"

"Yes, actually. We need a large source of dry materials, leaves, branches, anything really."

Siofra and I both nodded, and she turned and headed out into the trees to search. I began to gather as much as I could in the area surrounding me and piled it all into the pit as Lisalya grabbed a couple of rocks that looked sharp enough to make a spark and set to work.

By the time Siofra came back with her arms full of crisping leaves and sticks, the pile was smoking.

"Great," Lisalya said as she set down her load. "Now we just need to blow on the embers and slowly keep adding more leaves and twigs."

Siofra left to assist Jion on his hunt, leaving Lisalya and me in the center of the camp together.

"Now what?" I asked, once the fire began to pick up.

"Now we need to keep it going. Rather than the smaller sticks and twigs, we need large pieces of wood. But they still need to be dry," Lisalya explained.

"Okay, I've got it," I said, rushing back out.

When Jion and Siofra returned from their hunt with a steer on their backs, the fire was roaring and large. Once they finished skinning their kill, they began to place it over the blaze to cook. "Dinner is nearly served. Thank you for making the fire," Jion said, smiling as he rotated one of the cooking pieces of meat.

"Thank you for hunting to feed us all," I replied. "And the fire was a joint effort, though Lisalya did most of the work. Even Siofra helped a bit before she left with you."

"Ah, she's good at something besides fighting? Good to know." He laughed as she lightly punched his shoulder.

"I'm good at plenty of other things!" she exclaimed.

"Oh, damn, you're right, I'm sorry. You're also good at planning. Meticulous, precise, infuriating planning."

"Speaking of planning," I said. "We need to make a plan for tomorrow."

"Tomorrow?" Lisalya asked, glancing at the sky, which was already beginning to dim with the setting of the sun. "Already? But we just got here, and we've been walking for two days. Don't we need to give everybody some time to rest first?"

I sighed and stared into the fire. "I know. But we can't afford to waste any time."

Lisalya rolled her eyes. Typically I would have been shocked by such treatment as the Prince, but I was beginning to expect it from her. *She really hates me*, I thought, and wondered why that caused such a strange pang in my gut.

"We were just in a shipwreck for god's sake. I know we're

on a tight timeline but what is one day? One day can't set us back that much," she replied.

"It can set us back enough," I said firmly, and she blanched at the harshness of my tone. Feeling guilty, I tried to lighten it as much as possible given the nature of the topic. "And it's not up for debate. So," I turned towards Siofra. "We need to make a plan for the morning."

"Yes, I came up with some plans while we were sailing," Siofra immediately launched into her plans. "We'll need Lisalya to help us locate where the rebels may be. Lis, how did you know how to locate Viktor in the water?"

Lisalya shrugged her narrow shoulders. "I've done it before, though only once. A few years ago, when I was around sixteen, my father was injured while hunting alone. When he didn't come home, we knew something was wrong. It was easier with him, even though I was less experienced, because I am so accustomed to him and his mind. I've known it all my life. I just closed my eyes and focused on him as much as I could until I found him. I did the same with Viktor last night."

I gazed at her, amazed at the abilities she had that I simply could not comprehend. Siofra continued, seemingly unfazed in her determination to craft a foolproof plan. "Do you think you can do that again, but focusing on a feeling rather than a person?"

Lisalya's dark eyebrows scrunched together in thought for a moment before she nodded. "Yes, I think I can."

"Great," Siofra said, grinning. "Then I think we should start with those closest to us, we can begin to spread out from there once we have more people on our side. We can operate from here as a base camp, provided it's close enough to Green Marsh to not throw off the timeline of our original plan too much." Jion and I nodded, encouraging Sifora to continue. "I think we should start with a small crew. If we can manage that while still being safe. Lisalya, Prince Viktor, Jion, and I should go out first, leaving the rest of the crew behind. That way, they can keep working on building and improving the shelter. We'll be growing in number, so we need to make sure we have adequate space at the camp, including multiple shelters. We should also have them build some lookout stations. One close to the beach, at least, to make sure we stay hidden."

I nodded. "I think the lookout spots should be a top priority. If we're found by the wrong people, the whole thing will have been for naught."

Jion spoke up. "Agreed. We should also build a cellar of some sort, something to keep our food in to try to make it last. We don't have much now due to the wreck, but hopefully as our party grows we can have a dedicated group of hunters to make sure we all have enough to eat. We need to make sure we build up and maintain a decent supply of food stores."

"Absolutely. Siofra, anything we're missing? What time should we head out?"

"As soon as we have daylight. Until we gain more of a sense of the land and how to get around, we should make sure we're back to camp before dark. That will help prevent any of us getting lost. We don't know how much time we may need to convince people to join our cause, leaving early will ensure we have as much time as daylight allows. We'll need to work out how far we'll have to travel…"

"Lisalya?" I said, and she turned to face me. "That's where you come in."

"I really think we should just give people a day to rest. We're all exhausted."

"I'm sorry, but it doesn't matter what you think. This is what's happening," I said, growing frustrated with her inability to understand how tight of a timeline we were on. "Yes we're all exhausted, but our lives, and the lives of our countrymen back home in Doctsland, and our freedom, are all at stake. If we don't win this war, the people at home that we love could end up like that boy we saw yesterday."

"Viktor, calm down," Siofra said. "Arguing isn't going to help anything, and if we all push too hard and burn out that could jeopardize the mission just as much as losing a day could."

I huffed, feeling irritated and antsy. Now that we were here, I wanted so badly to rush out at once and try to find people, it was hard to see reason in any other course of action. Even waiting one night was difficult, but I suddenly remembered the brief conversation Siofra, Jion, and I had had onboard regarding Lisalya's condition due to her powers.

"One day," I said, clenching my teeth as I unhappily agreed. "We will wait one day. Tomorrow, can you please try to find someone who may be sympathetic to our cause, so we can approach them come the next morning? We will need to iron out all plan details in advance so we can make an early start."

Pursing her lips, she nodded.

I stood, wanting to busy myself. "Let's get this camp finished up so we can go to bed." I moved away from the area of the fire and began working with Jion, drawing up a cursory camp layout in some dirt, including a cabin for myself, a large shelter for the current crew, and a separate shelter for Lisalya.

"Do you think that will help, with her migraines?" I asked Siofra, remembering what she said about remaining separate from other people.

Siofra nodded. "Yes, it will." Without another word, we got to work, determined to finish the build before the setting of the sun.

We made Lisalya's shelter first, and as soon I was finished I approached her, trying to be delicate as I wasn't sure if she was still angry with me. "Lisalya, your shelter is ready. It's still within the confines of the protected area of the camp, but a bit separated from where the rest of us are. I'm not sure if that will help you, or how much, but I hoped it may be somewhat of a relief."

Surprise washed over her face. "Thank you," she said, standing from her place still near the fire. "It will help, and I very much appreciate the thought and effort." I merely gave her a small smile in response and led her to her quarters. It was only twenty or thirty feet away from the main camp, and the size was drastically different than the central shelter Jion

105

was working on, which would be made to house approximately twenty people. Though the distance wasn't great, I hoped it would ease her mind.

"Thank you," she said again. "This is perfect."

"You're welcome," I replied. "I'll send Siofra to wake you tomorrow. Have a good night."

I spent the rest of the evening completing the camp with the crew, and by the time the sun set I felt like I was on the verge of collapsing with exhaustion. After entering the shelter, I collapsed on the bed made of wood and leaves and fell asleep immediately.

Chapter Nine

Viktor

Lisalya and Siofra were already awake and having breakfast near the fire when I woke and exited my cabin the next morning. I strolled up to ask if Lisalya's shelter had worked, only to find they were in the middle of a conversation.

"We'll have to make more waterskins," Siofra said.

"Make them? How?"

Jion hopped into the conversation as we resumed our places beside the fire. "You must not have much experience hunting."

She glanced at him quizzically. "Not really, no. What does that have to do with making water skins?"

"It's simple actually," I said, poking the fire with a long stick and gazing into the flames. "We've already accomplished the most difficult part, which is finding and securing the kill. Jion and Siofra have also already skinned it, and Bear and Bird." I gestured to two of the men we had traveled on the ship with "stripped it of the hair and fat while we were preparing the meat for dinner. So, frankly more than half the work is done. Do you see how the skin is stretched over there?" I gestured behind me, where the hide had been stretched and secured between two trees.

Two more members of the crew, ones I hadn't become particularly familiar with on the journey, were running large sticks back and forth across the skin.

I continued. "That's going to soften it, make it pliable. Once that's done, we'll be able to sew it into water skins. We should get at least three or four out of that one deer. We'll continue the process with each kill until we've replaced all the bags, water skins, and clothing we lost in the wreck. You can pretty much make anything out of animal skin."

"I'm surprised you didn't know. It's a very common practice in Doctsland, especially in the countryside," Jion said.

Lisalya shrugged. "We don't really have to do anything like that. We spend most of our time making medicines and performing healings. As payment, those we help provide us with goods and food. What we don't receive as payment, my father hunts and provides. I'm always helping Grandmother, so I haven't learned his craft from him."

"I suppose that makes sense. I'm sure you'll learn a fair share of new skills and crafts throughout our journey. If you ever want a lesson, you need only ask one of us. Surely we'd be happy to teach you," Jion replied.

We continued doing necessary tasks around the camp until it was close to dinner time, then I decided it was time to focus on the most important task at hand. I gathered Jion, Siofra, and Lisalya, and we sat together around the fire, ready to plan for the next day's mission.

"Lisalya, are you ready?" Siofra asked gently as Lisalya prepared to try to locate our first targets. Lisalya nodded before squeezing her eyes shut. Several moments passed as I gazed intently on her face, trying hopefully to locate any signal of success.

"Are you alright?" I asked, my concern evident in my voice when she winced.

"I'm fine," she replied tersely, not opening her eyes.

Several minutes passed in silence, and I was beginning to worry when she finally spoke again. "I can pinpoint the village I mentioned yesterday," she said. "Whether they may be with us remains to be seen."

"How far?" Jion asked.

She shook her head. "I'm not sure yet. Give me a minute." Shortly thereafter a small smile formed on her lips. "They are with us," she murmured, and relief mingled with hope flooded over me. "And not far away. Within a mile, though I can't tell the distance exactly."

"Can you tell what direction?" Jion asked.

"East," she said. "To our left."

"Great," Jion said. "That should be enough information, don't you think, Vik?"

I hummed my assent, and Lisalya blinked her eyes open. "If you need nothing more, I'm going to put my walls back up."

I nodded. "Go ahead. We have all that we need." Just as she was about to close her eyes to do so, I spoke again. "And Lisalya," I said. "Thank you." I could only hope my words could help to express the depth of the gratitude I felt.

She gave me a single nod in answer before closing her eyes. When she re-opened them, she stared into the fire for a moment before speaking. "I need some water," she said. "And then to go to sleep."

I nodded and stood. "There's a stream nearby; we found it when we were scouting the area. It's fresh water, nice and cold, clean as well. Better than the river. This way."

"Thank you," she said, standing and following me.

"Are you alright?" I asked as we strolled through the wilderness. I kept my eyes down, staring at my feet and trying to see the ground through the darkness to avoid tripping on a root or fallen branch.

"I'm exhausted," she replied. "And I'm expecting a migraine at any second. It's difficult, taxing, maintaining all these walls all the time. Breaking them down and building them back up over and over. I'm not used to it. Growing up I accepted that most everyone knew of me and my abilities, as well as the power of our family, but that has never made it any easier for me to be around people."

"Can you tell me what it was like?" I asked, eager to know as much as possible about her life, and her struggles.

"My grandmother is so outgoing, she yearns to be around people, new people especially, and of course she always helps them in whatever way she can. My parents assist her as well, gathering whatever supplies she needs and requests, and running any errands she suggests. Her son, my father, obviously didn't inherit the magic that for some reason flows so strongly in the women of his family. His wife holds no magic in her veins either. Ironically, grandmother was worried that the magic of her line would die out. When I was born that worry died instead. Though my parents and my grandparents enjoy the stream of visitors that come through our house, and even to our village, to see us, I am not so keen on it. I do want to help them, I tell my grandmother always what they're feeling, where their pain is, as soon as I can sense it before they arrive. She has found my way of describing their ailments is more clear to her than their own words, in many cases. But most often by the time they do arrive, I am in my room or away on an errand. I enjoy spending time with my family, with those closest to me. Being around strangers is exhausting, especially when I can feel everything they feel. I'm burdened with their pain, physical, mental, and emotional. Their fears, their struggles, everything. It's especially difficult when I'm operating, we're all operating, on very little rest. This day has been helpful, yes, but more time to rest would have been ideal."

"I understand," I said. "We're all exhausted, me included."

She scoffed. "And yet you're pushing us on."

"I'm scared," I murmured, my voice small with my admission. "We all are. We don't have much time. And there's so much at stake. I can barely sleep, I'm so worried about our outcome- the possibility of failure. Each of us has something weighing us down, but it's important not to let that halt our progress."

She remained silent until we reached the creek. Bending, we scooped up some water with our hands and drank. I savored the cool feeling of the water trickling down my throat.

"We know where to head, what needs to be done. If it will help, you can stay behind tomorrow. You can take the time to rest."

Standing, she shook her head. "No. I know you'll need my guidance. Maybe you could make it without me, but it will certainly be easier with me in tow. As long as I can get a decent night of rest I should be fine by the morrow."

"Well, then, let's head back so we can both get a good night's rest. Have you had your fill?" I asked, gesturing to the stream before us. Once she signalled that she had, we began the short trek back to the camp. Upon our arrival, we made ready to go our separate ways.

"I'll send Siofra to wake you in the morning," I said, bowing slightly as we parted. "Have a good night."

She smiled softly, and I thought maybe it was the first time she'd really looked at me in kindness. "Thank you, Viktor. Good night."

***

A light knocking on the side of the shelter lured me from my slumber the next morning. I had spent the night tossing and turning, my mind racing with every possible outcome the morrow would bring, until finally falling into a restless sleep. "One minute," I called to whoever was knocking before sitting up with a groan. Digging the heels of my palms into my eye sockets, I tried to rub the sleep from them unsuccessfully before huffing in frustration. I peeled the blanket back, crawling out of bed and peeking around the makeshift shelter wall of leaves.

To my shock, it was still dark out. "What time is it?" I asked, making out Siofra's form.

"Just before dawn. We've made some breakfast. It's by the fire. We're expecting to leave soon, but we wanted to make sure everyone has a chance to eat," she explained.

I nodded. "Thanks. I'll be right there."

"Are you alright?" she asked.

"Sure. I didn't get much sleep, but I expected as much. I'll be right there." She shrugged before turning and heading back in the direction of the main camp. Quickly, I grabbed my pack, my sword, and Gaisgea, and headed out after her.

Jion and Lisalya were already up and sitting beside the fire when we arrived. "Morning," Jion said, handing me a stick with a chunk of meat speared on it. He smiled through a full mouth, causing Siofra and I to grimace.

"You're disgusting," Siofra scoffed, taking the stick he offered to her.

"Thank you," he replied, grinning even larger.

"We should eat quickly, and leave soon," I said, standing. "It's starting to get light out, and I don't want to waste any bit of daylight."

Following my own advice, I ate as quickly as I could. As much as I wanted to be resting and didn't want to feel rushed, I was engulfed with the need for speed. We had no idea how long this would take, and we couldn't afford to risk being out after dark in enemy territory.

"I'm finished," I said, wiping my hands on a patch of grass, which was damp with morning dew. "You said they were east, right?" I asked. "Does that stand true still? They haven't moved?"

She closed her eyes for a moment before speaking. "I'm not sure, I think most of them must be asleep. I can sense something, but it isn't strong. It seems to be coming from that area still, though."

"We'll start heading that way then. Will there be any way to know if the status or location changes?" I asked.

She bit her lip, seeming to ponder for a moment. "I'll leave my walls down and try to keep my focus on them. If they wake or move, I should be able to sense it," she replied.

"Thank you. Alright, let's go."

I handed her Giasgea and we made our start. Lisalya led the way, letting her mind pull us in the direction we needed to go. Training my eyes on my feet, I stepped carefully through the thick wilderness. Following close behind me were Jion and Siofra. We had made it about halfway in silence before anyone spoke. "Let us know if you sense any hostility nearby," Jion said. "We need to be prepared enough to have time to draw our weapons."

She stopped short, turning to look back at us as she reached for her sword. "Should I just have mine drawn now?"

Shaking my head, I replied. "No, I don't think we should approach with our weapons drawn unless we have to. That may set the tone for this meeting in a negative way and could lead to violence. We want to avoid that at all costs."

She signalled her understanding with a brief okay and continued forward. We didn't move far before she stopped again, this time so abruptly that I nearly ran into her from behind. "We're getting close," she murmured, her eyes shut. "And people are waking up."

"Now that we're closer, can you sense how many there are?" Siofra asked.

"Not quite," she replied. "I can tell it's not many. A small village, perhaps? But I cannot discern the exact number."

"They're just beyond those trees." She pointed straight ahead, passed a patch of trees so thick we couldn't see beyond it.

I took a deep breath and struggled to calm my nerves. "Are you sure?" I asked, speaking softly. I'm not sure even Siofra or Jion heard me.

"Positive."

"Okay." I faced them all and they gathered around me, forming a circle. "Here's the plan. One of us should go out first."

Siofra cut in. "I'll do it. I'm a woman. It will be less threatening to see a lone woman entering your village than a strong, armed man. If they attack, you know I can handle myself."

"Alright, Siofra will go out first. Remember, don't draw your blade unless you absolutely have to. Introduce yourself, and say you're with an envoy from Doctsland. I don't want to let them know my true identity until we know without a doubt we have their loyalty. Once you feel it's safe, and Lisalya confirms, give a signal and the rest of us will come out."

I gave Siofra a look of encouragement and a small smile. She returned it before turning and heading out into the clearing. Taking a deep breath, I closed my eyes and prayed to the Kelps for success.

I heard the low timbre of Siofra's voice, but it was too far and too muffled by the brambles between us to make out what she was saying. A few agonizing minutes of uncertainty passed before I heard the telltale sign and spoke. "She's giving us the signal." Lisalya opened her eyes and looked at me questioningly.

"She tapped three times on her armor. It was muffled, but I heard it. It's a distinct pattern we use between the three of us. Lisalya, is it safe for us to go out?"

"Yes. I sensed confusion and a bit of nervousness, but nothing aggressive. We're safe."

After a swift moment of attempting to calm my nerves, I followed Siofra's steps out through the hedges and into the clearing. We moved rather slowly, trying to ensure that we didn't appear too threatening. As soon as we stepped out we found Siofra, standing close by and speaking to a small group of men and women. I glance around taking in the village before me. I thought Loch was a small town, but this paled in comparison. There were around ten buildings, all bungalows colored the same light brown shade, with thatched roofing. Between them was the clearing Siofra and the others occupied. As we approached, Siofra began our introductions as instructed. She must have found someone who spoke the common tongue, for she continued in the language we all understood. "These are my comrades. Viktor, a peaceful envoy from Capital City in Doctsland, Jion, his bodyguard, and Lisalya, a healer from a small town quite like yours."

We bowed, and I spoke. "Thank you for your willingness to hear what we have to say."

One of the women, tall and fierce in appearance, returned my bow. "I am Ailee, the chieftain of this village. Siofra mentioned you may have a plan to halt this tyrant that is currently ruling Bushand. We would like to hear more. But first, we will give you a proper welcome to our village. Connor." She addressed a young man standing beside her. "Please lead them to the feast hall."

Nodding, Connor turned and began to walk towards the largest of the buildings, gesturing for us to follow. The hall he brought us to was taller than the other buildings, and once we stepped inside I could easily see why. Large, ornate, pillars held up a vaulted ceiling. The intricate reliefs that decorated each pillar took my breath away, and I paused to examine one as we walked inside. The images of soldiers marched upwards towards the ceiling. "Bushand has always been a military nation. Our soldiers are our pride," Connor explained, watching as I traced my fingers over the sculptures.

Placed in the center of the hall was a roaring fire, and seating was arranged around it. "Please take a seat. The leaders of our village will hear what you have to say, and then we will discuss amongst ourselves our course of action."

I bowed, thanking him, and Connor left to fetch the others. While we waited, we aligned ourselves on some of the logs closest to the fire, sitting in the order of myself, Lisalya, Jion, and Siofra. I huddled close, holding out my hands towards the flame. The damp morning air had a chill to it that even our march was not able to dissipate.

We didn't have to wait long, only a few minutes before about five people, that I assumed were the village leaders after Connor's statement, began to file in following Ailee. They took seats directly across the fire from our party, and Ailee began to speak. "We are all very curious as to why we have an envoy from Doctsland in our village, especially considering the recent declarations from our king. Please, enlighten us."

I opened my mouth, beginning the long spiel I had given to Lisalya and her family previously, as well as answering a few questions the villagers had, with Jion and Siofra chiming in every so often.

"So you have only one envoy, a few guards, and a healer to challenge the might of Bushand?" Ailee asked.

"So far, yes. The key to our mission so far has been stealth, and the hope that there are many within Bushand willing to join our cause, and raise arms against King Siglind. I know he has not been a kind leader thus far," I said, thinking of the woman that lost her son.

"And what happens after? Let's say that this works, and Siglind is overthrown. Do we then become a part of

Doctsland?"

"I can assure you that the current ruler in Doctsland does not have any interest in conquering Bushand. His plan is to work with the King's sister, Lura, in the hopes that she will take over rule of Bushand once he is deposed."

Ailee seemed to mull over my words before glancing at the other leaders near her. "We will need some time to discuss. Give us a few moments. Food will be brought to you and we will return momentarily."

I stood and bowed. "Thank you for your consideration. I do have one question before you leave." Ailee paused on her way out to look back questioningly. "Can you tell us where exactly we are in Bushand? Our ship sank, and we washed up on a beach nearby. We aren't entirely sure of our whereabouts."

"Of course!" she replied. "I will have a map sent with the meal."

Shortly after the leaders left, a group came in with plates of hot meals they gave to each of us. I picked through the dish, wondering at the difference in cuisine. In Doctsland we ate mostly stew, bread, and meat. This plate was full of rice, which I had only ever had before at my stepmother's coronation, and chunks of beef. We ate, a cloud of silent tension hanging over our heads.

"Can you tell what they're thinking? What they're going to do?" Jion asked Lisalya earnestly.

She shook her head. "No, I can't tell what they're thinking, it doesn't work that way. I can only tell what they're feeling, and even then it's not always clear. I feel uncertainty rolling off them, but that cannot tell me what course of action they may decide to take."

"We just have to wait," I said.

"Hopefully not for long. The suspense is killing me," Jion said, fidgeting anxiously. The level of stress and anticipation swirling within me had taken my appetite completely, but I made an effort to eat as much as I could stomach so as not to offend our hosts. Once I was finished, I examined the map with Jion. The village was too small to have its name on the map, but a hand-drawn 'X' marked its location a mile and a half inland. We were able to identify our arrival site, and the location of our current camp, which placed us closer to Nul than we had expected. I sighed. We could operate from our current camp location. We wouldn't have to waste time moving it.

Thankfully, Jion's wishes came true and we didn't have to wait for long. We had barely finished eating when Ailee and the other village leaders came back into the hall.

"We have taken a vote, and decided to assist you in your quest." I immediately felt a wave of relief and joy wash over me as Ailee continued. "We are a very small village, as you can see, so we aren't able to contribute many soldiers to your cause. We also don't wish to send anyone who is unwilling. We have relayed the information and the plan to the rest of the village, and there have been fifteen volunteers to join you. We will send with them some of our secret store of weapons. They are forbidden, but we keep some in the village center to protect ourselves if needed."

I bowed. "We are honored to accept your assistance, and we deeply appreciate it. We have a camp set up nearby, the volunteers are welcome to join us there. It is small, but we plan to expand it as needed as we grow."

After I gave Ailee a detailed description of the camp's location, she assured us that the volunteer soldiers would meet us there the following morning, to give them one last evening with their families and friends before joining our cause. Graciously thanking them once more, we took our leave, heading back to the camp before sundown, pleased with our small victory.

Chapter Ten

Lisalya

The journey back to camp was much different than our journey that morning. It felt as though a weight had been lifted off our shoulders, and we laughed and were merry all through the short walk. We arrived an hour or two before sundown, and split up to try to make the best use of the remaining daylight. The members of our troupe we had left behind had made a fair share of progress building the camp as well as hunting. Jion went back to work making the replacement water skins, Viktor went into the shelter to begin planning what tomorrow would look like, and Siofra and I did some more fight training.

"You've gotten much better!" Jion commented, watching as he worked.

I grinned back. "Thank you." Over the course of the time onboard I had grown more comfortable handling Gaisgea, and was growing confidence in my abilities with each sparing session. Though I still hoped to never have to put them to the test.

After a short while Viktor emerged and beckoned us to join him as he took a seat next to the fire.

"Today went well," he began after we all got comfortable near the flames. "But I don't want us to get over confident or hopeful. We've gained members, but only a small number. Fifteen more people are not going to help in the fight against Bushand, especially fifteen soldiers from such a small village. Surely they are not as skilled as the soldiers from Bushand's capital, those loyal to Siglind. Hopefully Ailee was correct, and they will join us on the morrow. I think it is imperative that we take the day to get to know them. We need to know how practiced they are in fighting. Who needs tutoring, who is able to assist with what tasks, and so on. Lisalya, as soon as they arrive, can you please do your best to get a read on each of them and report to me?" he said. I nodded and he continued. "Jion and Siofra, you work on assessing each of their fighting abilities. Once that's done, interview them. What kind of work do they do at home? With that knowledge, Siofra can assign them tasks to do throughout the camp. Once you've each had time with each person, send them to me one by one. I would still like to operate under the guise of an envoy, but I would like to get to know each and every one of them, and to thank them face to face for joining our cause."

"You've got it," Jion replied.

"Thank you all."

"Now, when is dinner?"

I couldn't help but laugh. "Did we not just eat at the village?"

"That was at least three hours ago, come on!" Jion complained, standing and tossing Siofra and I each a brand new water skin.

"You're right, you're wasting away," the Prince joked. "We'll get started on dinner."

The rest of the evening was spent in good spirits. We ate, joked, laughed, and felt ever so slightly lighter. With this first victory, though small, came the feeling that maybe what we were setting out to do really was possible.

As soon as we had arrived back at the camp I had put my walls up, but it was getting less strenuous to maintain them, so I didn't even have to worry about a possible migraine.

Shortly after the sun went down, we went our separate ways to head to bed. Though Ailee had assured us the volunteers would arrive in the morning, we were unsure of the exact time. I wanted to make certain I was awake prior to their arrival so I could give the rest of the camp a heads up of when to expect them, as well as try to get a read on them as soon as they were in range. After making a quick stop at the creek to grab a drink and fill up my water skin, I made my way to my small shelter and prepared for bed.

As I drifted off to sleep, thoughts of the prince clouded my mind. Though he still filled me with annoyance at moments, I was starting to understand his mindset and his drive. Part of me even felt a little guilty for the way I had treated him, especially in Loch prior to our departure. As my eyes fluttered shut, I thought that I should set aside some time tomorrow to apologize.

Anything but restful, my sleep was plagued with unnerving nightmares. When I awoke, I had no memory of exactly what had transpired in them, but I was left with a strong feeling of unease. Shivering, I tried to shake it off as I got ready for the day. Before leaving my personal shelter, I double checked my walls, making sure I was prepared to go into the heart of camp. Knowing I would have to probe each new member of our party after their arrival, I wanted to make sure I preserved as much of my energy as possible prior. Once I felt confident that I was prepared, I headed out of my isolation and into the camp.

As I entered camp, I noticed that the sun was already high in the sky. "What time is it?" I asked, thinking of how long I must have been sleeping.

"I'd imagine it's nearing noon," Viktor replied. He was in the process of gutting a deer that I assumed he and Jion had killed this morning. "I thought about sending Siofra to wake you, but I figured you may need your rest. I imagine it's fairly taxing to have your mind open as long as it was yesterday."

"Yes, it is," I said. "Thank you for not waking me."

He gave me a small smile and nodded. After a moment, I gathered up my courage and continued, "I want to apologize."

He paused in his work, brow furrowing in confusion. "For…?"

"For the way I treated you in Loch. It's difficult leaving home. I think I took out a lot of that stress on you, especially when I didn't agree with you or understand your motives or purpose. I understand a bit more now, and I just want you to know that despite the way I may act sometimes, I respect you as our leader. And our future king." I felt the blush creeping into my cheeks as I spoke. It's not easy for me to set aside my pride to apologize, and I felt a bit embarrassed to be opening myself up in such a way.

His eyes widened in what I assumed was surprise, but he didn't answer right away. Briefly, I wished I had opened my mind before having this conversation, just so I could get a better read on him, though deep down I knew that would have been an invasion of privacy. Finally, after what seemed like ages, he replied. "Thank you very much, Lisalya," he said in answer, before ducking his head and returning to his work. I smiled in relief, thankful that the weight had been listed off my shoulders, but also that Viktor accepted the apology so easily and we were able to move on from the uncomfortable conversation.

"Where are the new soldiers?" I asked looking around the camp and seeing it empty apart from Vik and me. "Have they not arrived yet?"

"They have," he answered, standing and strolling over towards me. "Breakfast?" he said when he reached me, handing out a piece of meat and gesturing to the fire.

I took it with a smile and a thanks. "So if they've arrived, where are they?!"

"They're with Jion and Siofra and a few other members of the crew. They took them to a clearing nearby to test their fighting abilities. I imagine they should be back fairly soon, they left a while ago. I did tell Siofra to send them back one at a time; I was hoping you may be awake by then and thought it may help to have them enter one by one for you to get a reading on them, rather than all coming back at once."

"That will help," I said, cooking the piece of meat he gave me. "It's a lot easier for me to get a sense of one person than a group of them. How many turned up?"

Vik grinned brightly. "Sixteen. More than we anticipated. It's a very encouraging turn out. Hopefully they will all be assets to our team."

"Fantastic! And do you know when we will be going out on another excursion?"

He shrugged. "I'm not positive, but I think we should stay put for a few days. I want to make sure our new team members are comfortable, and we feel confident in them, before we go out and try to gather more people. We can use this time to grow the camp and get a bit more settled. However, if you could, in your spare time, try to search and find the next group we will target." He trailed off, seeming unsure if what he was asking was being conveyed properly with his words.

I couldn't help but chuckle at his lost expression. "Yes. I understand what you mean, and yes, I will check. I'm not sure, but I think we'll have to go further afoot to find the next group. When I reached out and found the last village, I didn't sense anyone else in a similar vicinity."

"I imagine we'll have to go further and further each time. Based on the map Ailee showed us, this base camp is within a few days march from Nul, so I don't want to move it. Plus that would be a waste of valuable time. We may have to venture out on overnight trips as needed."

"How many trips do you anticipate we'll need?" I asked, examining my meal and deciding it was done cooking and ready to eat.

"I'm not sure to be honest. I think we'll have to play it by ear as we go. We don't know how much we'll grow each time. I want to continue until we've amassed a few hundred people at least."

I made a noise of affirmation, too intent on my meal to speak until I finished. "That was delicious," I said, wiping my mouth with my hand.

Viktor laughed, and for the first time as I gazed at his boxy smile it struck me how handsome he was, with his long silver hair pulled back and his blue eyes shining. "One of the new recruits is a chef, and he brought with him a box of seasoning. With his permission, I seasoned that before I gave it to you."

"Ah, that explains it. Thank you," I said, just as a stranger emerged from the forest and strolled up to the fire.

"Normisle, welcome back!" Viktor said, standing and bowing to the young man. He glanced at me, hinting that this was my opportunity to begin my task. Nodding in acknowledgement, I bowed my head and closed my eyes. Focusing, I broke down the barriers I had built up last night, and honed in on the young man who had taken a seat near Vik at the fire. I didn't probe too deeply, not wanting to invade his privacy, but I dipped in enough to get a sense of where he was at. I felt apprehension, but also pride. He believed in the cause he had joined, and was willing and eager to see it through to the end, even though that came with a sense of melancholy at the thought of leaving home and uncertainty for what the future may hold. Not to mention fear of retaliation should the mission fail.

When I opened my eyes, I glanced at Viktor. He was embroiled in a conversation with Normisle, but when he got a chance he snuck a look at me, and I gave him a small nod of approval.

This process continued as each of the sixteen new members of the company approached camp one by one. There was a relatively even mix of male and female, and most seemed to be between the ages of nineteen to forty. Though each person was slightly different in personality and feel, the overwhelming sense of all of them was quite similar, and I didn't feel concerned that any were there for the wrong reasons, or were in danger of betraying us. The woman were especially eager to join us, for I got the sense that sometime in recent years Siglind had put in place some sort of laws restricting their rights. When the prince pulled me aside for a report, I relayed this information to him.

"Yes, I heard tell of that," he said. "A few years ago he released a proclamation stating that women were the property of their father until marriage, at which point they would become property of their husband. It's barbaric, honestly." My jaw dropped. I was shocked at the idea women could be reduced to 'property.' Each new thing I heard about Siglind reinforced the idea that we were doing the right thing in protecting our country from such a man.

"I'm very glad to hear that they're all with us undoubtedly," he said, relief flowing off him in billows. "Jion and Siofra reported that though they aren't quite at the level of the Doctsland soldiers we're used to, they are decent fighters. Most are farmers, but there is a sense of constant danger in Bushand that Nulian soldiers will show up and try to drag people off to the city for work, so they've learned to protect themselves, despite Siglind's law banning weapons."

"How awful," I said. "That they live in fear of their own countrymen."

"Yes, it is awful. But hopefully we're able to do something about that," the prince replied with an encouraging smile.

The next few days were spent just as Viktor had intended. We focused on the camp, and making sure we had provisions for our growing numbers. I took the opportunity to learn as many new skills as I could during this time, going on a hunting trip with Jion, helping to finish the rest of the replacement water skins, and even assisting in building a second, and larger, shelter, as well as a small individual shelter for Viktor. And, of course, I kept up on fighting practice with Jion and Siofra when there was time. Once, when they both were busy, I even had a sparring lesson with the Prince.

"I'm not as good as Jion or Siofra, so go easy on me, please," he said, brandishing his blade out in front of him with a smile.

I raised Gaisgea with my right hand, proud that I could now lift it single handedly, and an eyebrow. "Who shall make the first blow?" I asked, attempting to distract him. I was pleased when it worked.

"Who do you wa- Hey!" he said, scrambling to block me as I swiftly moved forward to strike. "Distraction techniques should be off limits!"

"No they shouldn't! What does Siofra always say? Battle holds nothing but distraction. That's the only way to practice that will teach you anything."

"Siofra isn't always right," he complained, keeping up

effortlessly with my attacks despite what he said about not being a great fighter like his guards.

I raised my eyebrows.

"Okay, okay. Maybe she is," he acquiesced with a laugh. We moved throughout the camp, taking turns working on offense and defense, until it was time for dinner. Our chests heaved as we finished, and Prince Viktor clapped me lightly on the back as we returned to the fire. "You've greatly progressed. I'd say you're now a soldier of Doctsland." I couldn't help but beam at his praise.

***

It only took a few days for us to begin to get restless and a bit uneasy. We had grown comfortable at camp, and I felt confident that we had done enough to ensure the new volunteers felt comfortable as well. We had also expanded the camp area to accommodate more individuals. The time had come.

When Viktor asked Jion, Siofra, and I to gather together near my shelter, we all sensed what was coming. "Alright," he began. "I asked you here because it's one of the only remaining spots in the camp separate from everyone else. We can have some privacy. Lisalya, thanks for donating your space, sort of."

I stifled a laugh at his word choice. "Not a worry. Is it time for another excursion?"

"Yes," he answered. "I feel that we've spent enough time here, making sure the new team members assimilate and expanding the camp to allow for growing numbers. We can't waste any additional time here. We've got to get back out there." He turned to me. "Have you had a chance to locate our next targets?"

I had tried previously, but wanted to make sure of the position of those I had found. Squeezing my eyes tightly closed, I focused all of my energy into my task. One at a time, I closed out each of those I recognized. Once that was done, I began to spread my awareness, opening the boundaries of my mind to try to reach out and locate someone new nearby. It was slow work, and work that I was only recently growing accustomed to. At home I had no need for such a skill, and though I practiced as much as I could on the journey, there was no one else to find on the open water, despite how large I tried to cast my nets.

Here, though, there was someone else to find. I had to reach further than before, but eventually I began to feel the tendrils of another consciousness, multiple to be exact.

"I have," I affirmed. "They're a bit further away, it will take more time to get to them than the previous group."

"How far?" Jion chimed in.

"I'd say about a two or three hour walk."

Viktor nodded, mulling this information over. "I think we should still try to do it in one day. An overnight trip is dangerous, and I wish to avoid it if at all possible. This will make for a long day, but I believe it's manageable."

"I agree," Siofra added. "Lis, can you tell how large this group is?"

"No, not exactly. I believe it to be a larger pocket of people. A small town, perhaps? I cannot be too sure."

"Let's plan for an average size town, then we can be prepared for anything," Viktor said.

"We need to bring more soldiers with us." Siofra asserted. "If we're looking at a town this time, we can't rely only on the four of us in case things go sideways. We need some backup."

"I hear you, but I'm concerned about appearing threatening," Viktor said.

"So we bring a handful of backup soldiers and have them wait outside the town while we negotiate. We can call them in with a signal if need be, but we won't be showing up to their door with an army," suggested Jion.

"I don't love it. There may be a delay when they're trying to get to us to help us," Siofra expressed.

"I don't love it either. What if the townspeople catch wind and feel threatened?" Viktor countered.

"Great. If you're both unhappy, that means I've found a

reasonable compromise. We'll go with this plan. Are we done now?" Jion said.

Viktor laughed, though it was a bit humorless. "Yeah, we can be done now. We'll leave a bit before sunrise tomorrow. Does that work for everyone?"

When we all nodded, he stood. "Wonderful. Now let's all get a good night's sleep, and pray that tomorrow's journey goes as well as our previous one. Jion, before bed can you rally up that handful of soldiers you were talking about? Preferably a mix of our original crew from Doctsland and Bushand soldiers. You can pick whoever you want, but no more than fifteen soldiers, please."

I went to bed feeling slightly uneasy, though I was unsure why. I felt confident in our plan, and I couldn't discern the source of my tension. For some reason I took comfort in the fact that I would be once again carrying Gaisgea with me tomorrow.

***

Siofra's polite knock woke me from what had been a restless sleep. It was still dark out, but that was to be expected. In a very similar fashion to the previous excursion, we ate a light breakfast together by the fire, and then set off. The main difference being that this time the regular crew was accompanied by thirteen additional soldiers. True to Viktor's request, Jion had grouped together a mixture of the new volunteers and our original crew, though our Doctsland crew made up the majority. I thought this was a smart move, in case things go sour and the Bushand soldiers decided to side with their countrymen.

Before our departure, Viktor ran through the plan once more with everyone involved, ensuring that each understood his or her place in today's journey. Those left behind at the camp were instructed to continue making room for expansion, and to spar with each other to increase their fighting potential. Once he felt assured everyone was in accordance, we left the camp.

Viktor and I made up the front of the party so I could guide him in the right direction, while Jion and Siofra made up the rear. I closed my eyes and opened my walls, focusing on the minds of those I had identified yesterday, and then we were off. I kept my mind trained on the thin wisps of consciousness I had snagged, letting them pull me in the right direction. I noticed that as we traveled deeper into Bushand, the forest I'd grown used to near our camp lessened. The chopped stumps of former trees sprinkled the landscape, and the earth seemed somewhat trampled and scorched. "What is this?" I asked Viktor as we walked.

He chewed his lip in concerned consideration. "I'm not sure exactly what this is or why it has happened, but I can tell you it's Siglind's doing. He's so hellbent on advancement in Nul, new weapons, new tools, he is plowing through the forest of the countryside to grow his army. I had heard tell of it from Bushanean envoys sent to update my step-mother on her son and her country, but I didn't really understand what it meant. Seeing it, especially after seeing the beauty of the beach where we landed, is quite heartbreaking," he explained, and the sorrow rippling off of him confirmed his words.

Though the distance was further, the journey seemed to fly by fairly quickly. As we got closer the nervousness that had plagued me the night before returned, and it did not go unnoticed.

"What's wrong?" Viktor asked, glancing at my worried expression.

"I'm not sure. The majority of what I sense is good, but I feel a slight dissension," I explained.

"How slight?"

"Very slight. Before I could not detect it even at all, but as we get closer it grows a bit stronger."

"How concerned should we be?" he asked soberly.

I stopped walking, knowing that we were very close. "I can't answer that. Make sure to station the backup soldiers as close as possible. We're almost there."

He gave me a curt nod before gesturing above the group to

Jion and Siofra. As soon as they joined us up front, he explained the situation to them. Siofra argued for keeping the soldiers with us the whole time, but the Prince overruled her. I described the location and distance of the destination to Jion, who then scouted a location to leave the troops. Once that was complete, we were ready to enact the plan.

Again, Siofra went out first. I trained my mind on the town, which seemed to be about the same size as Loch. It was bustling, and it seemed as though no one noticed the lone female warrior in their midst. "The town center is busy. They don't even know she's there," I whispered, offering an update to the Prince by my side.

"She'll figure something out," Viktor replied with a full sense of confidence in Siofra that I shared. We waited in a silence choked with tension until we heard the distinct signal from Siofra, at which point we breathed a collective sigh of relief.

When we entered the town I was shocked to find it looked fairly empty, despite how full it had seemed in my mind. Siofra stood speaking with a tall man surrounded by a small group of people. When Jion, Viktor, and I joined her, she introduced him as Merek, the town leader, and the group of men surrounding them as his personal guard. Viktor was introduced as an envoy once more, and Merek let us to a small tavern nearby.

Once inside, Viktor paid for a round of ales for us, Merek, and the guards in his company. As soon as we were seated and settled, Vik launched into his pitch. Merek seemed engaged the whole time, and I sensed that the prospect of rebellion excited and encouraged him. His guards for the most part shared his sentiment, though I felt some discord from one or two of them that concerned me. Being much less hesitant to commit than Ailee, Merek agreed at once to assist us. "I, and most of the townspeople of Cessam, are very unhappy with Siglind's rule thus far. As you probably saw on your journey, his soldiers and his crews from Nul have been destroying our countryside, the farmlands that many of our people rely on. We would be happy to join your cause. I will have one of the members of my guard distribute a call to action to the townspeople to gather as many to your cause as possible. We are no Nul, but we are a rather large village. I'd imagine you could get at least a hundred soldiers on your side."

Viktor grinned widely. "I am so happy to hear that, thank you. We will wait here while you spread the word, and in an hour or two we will lead those who wish to join us back to our camp."

Merek agreed to this plan, and he and his guards departed the brewhouse, leaving Jion, Siofra, Viktor, and me on our own for the moment.

"This seems to be going just as well as the last trip. I couldn't be happier," Jion said, grinning with relief.

"Yes, I agree," said Vik. "However, I'd like to hear how Lisalya feels. What sort of read did you get from Merek?"

"Merek spoke with absolute sincerity," I said. "And the majority of his guards shared his sentiments."

"The majority?" Vik asked.

"There was a hint of dissention that concerned me. I fear one or more of his guards may side more with the King."

"One or more? Do you have any idea of how high that number could be?" Siofra asked.

I shrugged. "One at the least, no more than three or four, though I doubt it is that many. What I felt was only a small hint."

"I don't really think we have anything to worry about, then. We're bound to run into loyalists eventually, one or two in a group of fifteen that are willing to fight for us is not so bad. It could be worse. Most likely they will just choose to not join our cause, or attempt to fight us, in which case they will be grossly outnumbered."

Viktor seemed deep in thought, mulling over the information I had presented as well as Jion's words of dismissal. After a while, he spoke. "I agree with Jion. The vast majority here are on our side, we needn't worry about such a small number of king's men."

Siofra shifted uneasily, clearly uncomfortable with the

verdict. "All it takes is one person to reveal our location and our goal to Siglind. I think we should proceed with caution, if not outwardly trying to identify these dissenters and let Merek decide what to do with them."

"I don't want to disrupt the bond we've already begun to form with Merek by immediately accusing his men. We'll proceed like normal. As Jion said, they will be outnumbered. We don't need to worry," Vik said, too thrilled with the possibility of success to want to head Siofra or I's warnings.

Siofra huffed but stayed quiet, not inclined to argue with her leader. Instead, she stood. "I'm going to order some food. Does anybody want anything?"

I shook my head, still feeling too uneasy to eat, but Viktor and Jion both supplied orders. We sat in relative silence as they ate, and it wasn't long after they finished that Merek returned. "We were able to amass a rather large group for you. They are currently waiting in the town's square for you to lead them to your camp.

Viktor immediately stood and bowed. Merek then led us through Cessam to a large square that was filled to the brim with men and women, all seemingly dressed for battle. "Soldiers!" Merek spoke with a booming voice. "This is the envoy I spoke to you about, Viktor." He gestured to Vik, who stood tall and regal beside him.

Suddenly I felt a sharp twinge of alarm. I yelled Viktor's name in warning, grabbing his arm and pulling him towards me all at once. Just as he was yanked in my direction, an arrow whistled right past where his head had been only a moment prior.

Chaos erupted. The crowd raged, and made such a booming noise that it almost drowned out the anarchy in my mind. I couldn't make sense of anything, as Viktor and I crouched in a circle of our defenders.

Siofra made her way over to me, screaming over the noise. "Lisalya! How many are we fighting here? Should we retreat, or stand and fight?" I tried to focus on who this traitor with the bow was, and how many may be on their side.

"There are not many," I shouted back, drawing my weapon

to signal we should fight.

Siofra nodded, determined, and we both jumped into the fray together. Most of the crowd had been eager to join Vik's cause, and thus to jump to his defense as well. They seemed to have parsed out the group of loyalists, who had banded together and were almost completely surrounded. It felt as though my body had gone on autopilot, snippets of my training flashing through my mind at top speed as I slashed through my enemies. I tried not to feel too overwhelmed, but the rush of people actually trying to kill me was much different than sparing on a boat or in a camp with a single opponent. Jion fought beside me, protecting my rear from a man I hadn't even known was there until he was cut down by my comrade. I flushed, embarrassed to have been caught unawares when he and Siofra had always taught me to be on guard from all sides. I gave him a smile to signal my appreciation before raising Gaisgea to block a quickly oncoming attack.

The battle was over almost as quickly as it started. Though the Loyalists were grievously outnumbered, they had fought bitterly, refusing to surrender even to the very end. I assumed that was the sort of stubborn stupidity that we would be facing with Siglind and any who followed in his train of thought. Merek's men were able to restrain the few that had survived, and he had them marched off to Cessam's small prison.

As soon as the fight ended, Siofra rushed to the prince, ascertaining if he was alright.

"I'm fine," he replied, glancing up at me, gratitude bright in both his eyes and his smile. "Luckily Lisalya pulled me out of the way just in time." As soon as I was close enough, he lowered his voice to ensure his words didn't make it past mine and Siofra's ears. "Are we safe now?"

I nodded, feeling confident for the first time that day. "Yes, I believe all those loyal to Siglind in the area have all been defeated or imprisoned. Though I can't be too sure until I've met them individually. There's too many right now, the overall sense could mask those that disagree."

"I see," Vik replied. "Well, we've got the march home. Try to investigate as many as you can as we walk. Let Jion know of those you weren't able to get to, he'll take the others hunting or something and leave them at the camp so you will have the opportunity."

Once I signalled my understanding, he turned to Merek and raised his voice. "Merek, many thanks to you and your men for the protection you have just offered us. We greatly appreciate all of your assistance today."

Merek strolled up and held out his hand for a shake that Viktor accepted. "I hope that your mission succeeds. It will allow myself and everyone else in this town the opportunity for more freedom and a better life. Thank you for giving us the chance to fight for that." He glanced at the sky before continuing. "It's getting late. You best be heading back, or you won't beat the sun. I wouldn't recommend walking through these woods at night... or any woods in Bushand for that matter."

Bowing, Viktor showed his respect and thanks. Siofra, Jion, and I followed suit before saying our goodbyes to Merek and those of his men that were staying behind with him, so as not to leave the town without defense. Once we were ready to make our way back to the camp, Viktor spoke in a commanding, kingly voice that surprised me with its charisma.

"Soldiers!" he addressed the men and women grouped around him. "We are so happy to have you joining us. We have a few hours walk together as we make our way to the camp we have set up. During that time, we would like to get to know you as much as possible. Your background, your fighting experience, as much as we can learn so we can integrate you into our group as seamlessly as possible. If you can any questions or concerns, please bring them to Siofra, my guard." Siofra rose her hand to identify herself.

Viktor continued, "Now, are you all ready to fight for your freedom?" A roaring cheer burst forth, and I almost felt the need to cover my ears. The encouragement wrapped up in that cheer brought a smile to my face, one that was mirrored on the face of our leader. Viktor and Jion, the designated leaders of the troupe, then turned and walked into the forest, the group following suit.

Almost immediately I began the work that I had been tasked with. It took a minute or two to get my mind in the correct state, not fully open, for then I would hear every person making up this large company. Rather, I focused on keeping my mind mostly closed, only allowing a sliver to open up. My time training on the ship was well spent, this was something I would never have been able to attempt prior. This sliver allowed me to hone in on only the person nearest to me. I practised a bit on Vik, walking beside him and sensing his uneasiness at our attack wither, being replaced by appreciation and hope at the number of new followers we had gained and who had come to our aid. I noted with curiosity that it was getting increasingly difficult to get a read on him, though I felt too preoccupied with my task to dwell on it. Once I felt confident in this method, I began moving throughout the group. I tried to appear as casual as possible, making chit chat as often as I could to seem as though my movement through the group was natural.

I moved swiftly, trying to make sure I could get a reading on as many people as possible. The work was exhausting, and rather dull if I'm honest… nearly everyone had the same fire within them, stoked and ready to fight, burning with a hatred of Siglind. Until they didn't. There were two members who rose a red flag in my mind. Nothing overtly proved to me that they were loyalists, but the blaze igniting everyone else wasn't there. In fact, nothing was there. Rather, they seem filled with an iciness I had not experienced and couldn't explain. For the moment, I pushed it aside and continued on my mission, making a mental note of their names and faces to report to Jion and Viktor.

Surprisingly, I was able to make my way through everyone. I had grown more efficient in our exploits thus far, and hardly even felt the stirrings of a migraine, which was exciting. I closed my mind. We were quickly approaching camp, so I made my way back up to the front of the group to make my report to Vik.

"How close are we to camp?" I asked, sidling up between the prince and Jion.

Jion shrugged. "I'm starting to recognize the landscape; I think we're already approaching the edge. Probably only about another twenty minutes of walking until we're at the center."

"Have you finished canvasing the group?" Viktor asked.

Nodding, I made my reply after making sure we were far enough ahead to avoid prying ears. "Yes, and I have some information to report." As Vik and Jion listened solemnly, I explained to them the strange icy feeling I had gotten from the two particular members that concerned me.

"Have you felt this before, from anyone else?" Jion interjected.

"No, nothing like this before," I answered.

"And did you feel anything else from them? Or just this… nothing?" Viktor asked.

"Just the nothingness. An icy nothingness."

Jion and Viktor shared a glance, and both appeared to be deep in troubled thought. Finally Viktor turned to me. "Is it possible that maybe there are some people that are…" He seemed to be struggling to find the right word. "Some people that are immune to your abilities?"

I paused, taking a deep breath and considering the possibility. I'd never come across someone I couldn't read before, and though it seemed a likely explanation, something in my heart told me it was not accurate in this case. "To be honest, I had not thought of that, but-"

"Surely there are people in the world with unique minds you cannot read. It seems the most likely explanation for this nothingness you felt," Jion said.

"I-uh-" I stammered, trying to figure out how best to explain to them why I disagreed. "Something in my gut just tells me that is not the case. They could be spies. They could reveal our location or our plans to the enemy. They could do *anything*, and we would have no warning because I can't get a read on them."

Viktor stopped, and it suddenly dawned on me that we had reached the heart of the camp. He jerked his head towards his shelter, and Jion and I followed him inside. "I'm sorry Lis," he said, taking a seat at the small table in the corner. "What would you have me do, here? We're desperate for men. I can't send them away just because of a gut feeling."

"Plus," Jion chimed in. "They fought on our side in the skirmish in the town center. Don't you think if they were loyal to Siglind they would have fought against us back there?"

"Jion raises a strong point."

I sighed, leaning up against the wall. "I can't argue, I can only tell you what I felt from them and what I feel myself. And none of it feels right."

"I think the best we can do is try to keep a close eye on them. I'll assign one of the men from the first trip to watch over them. Does that seem fair?" Viktor replied.

"If that's the best that can be done, fine," I said, trying to ignore what felt like a boulder in my gut.

Chapter Eleven

Lisalya

The camp began to take on a lively, almost celebratory feeling when the new comrades joined. It was bustling with activity, and each person fell into their own unique role in contributing to camp life. Teams of hunters, builders, scouts, and training squads formed and took a fair share of the weight of subsistence off of our original crew. Multiple new shelters cropped up to avoid overcrowding in the original ones, but per Viktor's orders, none came within several yards of mine.

Just as before, we waited a few days before planning our next venture to allow the newest team members a bit of time to acclimate. During that time, I ventured out with my mind, trying to make sure I had our next target pin-pointed to ease our preparation time. It was getting more difficult, the noise of the camp grew louder as it grew in size, and blocking them out was becoming a problem, increasing with each raid. I also had to start reaching further- there were no other towns or villages in relative proximity to the camp. We were going to have to make our next trip an overnight one, at the very least. It took some time, and at one point I had strained so hard to try to locate someone that I gave myself a migraine, something I had not suffered since our arrival. But soon, just before Viktor called us for planning, I discovered a town ripe with unrest.

"I've found it," I said, closing the door behind me as I entered Viktor's shack. Siofra and Jion were already present, seated with Vik at a small table. One chair was left for me, in which I took my seat between the Prince and Siofra. "I've located the next town we should target, though it is not close by any means."

Viktor smiled a boxy, handsome grin. "Wonderful. I expected we'd have to start venturing out further. How far would you say it is?"

"I believe it should be approximately a day and a half walk from here. We could perhaps make it in a day."

"We should bring provisions enough for two nights away, one there, one back, to ensure we have enough supplies for the journey. I'd rather have too much than not enough," Siofra said, as always the practical one. "And how large is this town? How many soldiers shall we bring in addition to the four of us?"

"It seems smaller than Cessam, but it's hard to say for certain given the distance."

"It will be so much harder to travel with as many people as we brought with us last go round," Jion reasoned.

Siofra snapped back immediately. "Yes but they came in handy, didn't they?"

Jion rolled his eyes. "We could have handled that on our own. Merek's men jumped to our aid at once."

"We can't just rely on who we may meet along the road that may or may not help us!"

"Stop!" Vik didn't shout, but his voice had a commanding timber that made Jion and Siofra both clamp their mouths shut straight away. "We'll take a handful of soldiers, less than what we brought before due to the length of the trip. Jion, round up four soldiers tonight and have them prepare for departure tomorrow. That will bring our party to eight, which is manageable for traveling but formidable enough if need be. We'll leave before sun up. I don't want to spend two nights away unless we absolutely have to, so let's get going as early as possible."

As soon as the plans were decided, preparations began at once. Each individual was responsible for making their own pack for food and water, under the directive of bringing enough for two full days. We set everything in the center of camp near the fire, planning to meet there early tomorrow morning to have a quick meal before our departure. It was only a bit after sundown when I went to bed, wanting to get the maximum amount of rest possible before the journey ahead.

The trip the next day was fairly uneventful. We were accompanied by a sorted mix of soldiers, one of our original crew, two from the first village, and one from Cessam (though not one of the two I had cautioned Vik and Jion about). Small talk helped ease the boredom of the journey, though we'd only been on two full walkabouts thus far it was already starting to get a bit old, particularly for Viktor, Jion, Siofra, and me. We had surely spent far too much time together in the past two months. It was weighing on Jion and Siofra in particular, whose bickering had increased tenfold, if it can be imagined.

When it was nearing dusk we began to search for a place to camp for the night. We had made significant progress, and I sensed we were ahead of schedule, on track for an arrival early the next morning. After informing Viktor of this, he seemed overjoyed, and we quickly found an alcove surrounded by some thick trees that would serve as a decent spot to camp for the night. Once we stopped, I put up my walls to protect my head and Viktor directed us to clear an area for a fire. "I don't want to waste the time and energy it will take to build a shelter for just a night," he explained. We got to work right away, moving any brush or debris from an area large enough for a fire and eight sleepers.

"Lis, can you help me with the fire?" Jion asked, gathering as many dry sticks and leaves as possible. It wasn't too challenging a task, considering the semi-arid landscape we were approaching the further from camp we got. The temperature was dropping, so once the fire was roaring we all sat crowded closely around it.

Viktor took his seat beside me, and as the night went on and grew ever more chilly, we huddled closer and closer. His proximity made me shiver, and it wasn't due to the chill in the air.

"Are you alright?" he asked, and I glanced to find his face closer to mine than I expected, causing me to start. Concern was evident in his eyes, and he was close enough that I noticed dark stubble on his chin. *He must have lost his razor in the shipwreck. I should ask around and try to find another one for him,* I thought.

Shaking my head, I tried to remember what he had asked me, but failed. "What?" I asked, feeling somewhat dazed.

He smiled kindly. "You shivered. Are you alright, or are you cold? Do you need another blanket?" He stretched out his arm, opening the blanket that was surrounding him. I blushed and shook my head. I knew it was just a kind gesture, but the idea of nestling close enough to him to share a blanket made my cheeks feel hot.

"I'm fine, thank you though," I said, though I scooted slightly closer anyway. Before I knew it I was drifting off, my head falling to rest on his shoulder. The next morning I only briefly recalled him laying me down and spreading both blankets over my sleeping form.

***

Again we rose before the sun and were swiftly packed up and on our way. Just as I had predicted, we had reached our destination an hour or so after we set out on the second day. Siofra entered the town alone, and we watched eagerly for her signal. Seeing no one in the town square, she entered into a tavern. Shortly after, she exited the tavern, appearing to just need a breath of fresh air, but we recognised the signal.

"Alright," Viktor said, turning to the additional guards we brought with us. "We're going to go into town, please stay here and keep an eye out. We will be back as soon as possible."

"Yes sir," they replied, all assuming a watchful position.

"Ready?" Vik asked Jion and I. With his gaze, he implored me to give him a signal that we weren't walking into any hostility. I opened my mind quickly, getting a sense of everything around me. While I felt nothing of concern, I couldn't help but feel anxious in a way I had not felt before the other excursions, much more so than I had felt in Cessam. For a moment I wrestled with telling Viktor, but I worried he

140

would be dismissive. Just that moment was all Vik needed to sense something was wrong.

Gently grabbing my arm, he pulled me off to the side and out of earshot of our companions. "What is it? We have to be quick, we can't just leave Siofra out there alone."

"I know, I just-"

"Do you sense something?" he implored earnestly.

I shook my head. "Not exactly."

"What do you mean?"

Sighing, I tried to explain myself. "I don't sense anything specific to be concerned about. I just have this feeling. A foreboding feeling."

His frustration was clear in the hard set of his mouth. "Lis, we can't just stop everything we're doing or not accept people because of any stray feeling you may have."

"I-" I started, only for him to cut me off.

"If you feel hostility coming from someone, actual hostility, then please let me know. Otherwise, we're moving forward."

I clamped my lips shut, feeling furious at his condescending dismissal, and he took my silence as acquiescence.

"Come on, let's go," he said, heading out towards the town. Jion gave me a questioning look, which I returned with a scowl. Shrugging, and sure Vik or I would fill him in on the discussion later, he followed his prince.

I stood for a moment longer, seething, before heading out after them. As upset as I was that Viktor not only refused to listen to me but spoke to me like I was a child misbehaving, I knew that they would need me and my unique abilities with them. We rejoined Siofra, who brought us inside and introduced us to the individuals she had been conversing with. From here, things went much the same as they had the previous two times. Viktor, the 'envoy', explained our situation, our struggle, and our goal before imploring the small council for assistance. This town appeared much smaller than Cessam, in fact it was barely bigger than the first village we'd been to. A group of three town leaders listened to Viktor's spiel astutely before stepping aside to speak together privately. Opening my mind, I sensed their desire to join us, but hesitation at the guarantee of danger. When they came back to the table we were sharing, they justified their apprehension.

"We sympathize with your cause," an elderly man explained. "Our main concern here is our proximity to Nul. Though our village seems small and insignificant, we are a mere day's march away from Nul. Should Siglind win this war, his wrath against those who betrayed him will be mighty. Our whole village will suffer, and will likely be decimated. The closer to Nul, the greater the danger. I'm not entirely sure it's a risk we're able to take."

Viktor nodded solemnly, trying not to make his disappointment painfully obvious, though I could feel it pouring from him like sweat. "I understand. We appreciate the thought you've put into this. And we would also appreciate your discretion on this matter."

"Of course. Though we aren't able to join in your fight, we do very much dislike Siglind and his manner of ruling. Terror and violence is not the way to people's hearts. Our discretion is all that we can offer, but we give it gladly, and wish you the best of luck on your quest."

We followed Viktor's lead as he stood to bow. "Thank you kindly," he said, and we moved to exit the pub.

Suddenly the doors flew open and a large group of soldiers entered. Royal soldiers burst in, a much different sort than the fierce, but local Loyalists we'd run into previously. They were decked head to toe in armor black as night, as if it had been dipped in tar, and they surrounded us at once.

I was stunned, as we all are, but I couldn't understand how I hadn't seen this coming. I'd had my mind open the entire time. Why did I not sense anything?

"What is this?" Viktor's voice boomed from beside me. I turned to look at him to find that he had drawn his sword, as had Jion and Siofra. The question seemed to be directed towards no one in particular, and yet everyone. The men we'd been conversing with, the soldiers who had just burst in, and most of all me; he was asking why I had not warned him.

Tears stung my eyes as I saw the betrayed look on his face, but all I could do was utter a small but desperate, "I felt *nothing*."

A tall man stepped forward, an evil grin splitting his pale face. With horror I realized I had seen him before, telling soldiers to mutilate and murder a defenseless boy in front of his mother. "I am Captain Carthoc of the Nul army infantry. And you must be the envoy we've heard so much about."

"Who sent you?" Viktor seethed.

Captain Carthoc's twisted smile grew as he cocked his head. "Surely you know who... And don't look for saving from the pitiful soldiers you left on the edge of town. They have been destroyed." With those words he signalled his force to move. "Do not kill the strangers, please. We need their information." His voice had a bored lilt to it that boiled my blood, but I didn't have time to linger on it when the Nulian soldiers began charging at us from seemingly all sides.

They were overwhelming and terrifying in their attack. Summoning as much bravery as I could manage, I pulled Gaisgea from its sheath and tried my best to defend myself. I felled the first soldier that charged towards me with a side-step and a slash, but my luck ran out there.

The next was more agile, and predicted my movements. When I swung to block him, he grabbed my arm, twisting it until Gaisgea fell from my grasp and a scream was yanked from my lips. I fought to peel myself away from his grasp, but he was much too strong. He pushed me to the ground, and drove his knee into my back to hold me there as he roughly tied my hands together. I looked around in horror at the scene surrounding us. The small party we had been speaking with, who had had no weapons due to Siglind's law, had all been killed mercilessly regardless. We had been surrounded and we were grossly overpowered, despite the fearsome warriors we had among us.

Jion, in particular, was putting up a vicious fight. He was

surrounded by three men, his sword moving more swiftly than I'd ever seen. Finally one of his opponents sliced his sword arm open, causing him to drop his blade. Howling in pain, he collapsed on the ground and cradled his injured arm close to his broad chest. A soldier grabbed Gaisgea from the ground where I had dropped it, and Viktor growled watching his mother's blade get confiscated by the enemy.

"You didn't need to kill them. They weren't helping us," Viktor said, seeing the dead mean that had so recently declined to assist us in favor of keeping their town and themselves safe. Guilt twisted his face as he spoke. "They were loyal to the king."

"Ahh," The captain replied as his soldiers worked on restraining each of us with rope. "But you're wrong. They betrayed our king the second they let an envoy of Doctsland into their town without killing him. Although I am glad they didn't kill you. King Siglind will reward the man who brings such an enemy to his court. And what information I might glean from you to please him." He smiled wickedly, and I could feel my heart freeze over, for when I opened my mind to try to read them, I felt that same icy nothingness I had felt from the two men from Cessam. I knew at once who had doubled crossed us.

The Nul soldiers ruthlessly strung us together in a line with Vik and Jion at the helm, Siofra and I at the rear. It seems they thought of us as less of a threat due to our gender, which, knowing Siofra, I hoped would be a mistake. Then, we began to march.

Having no concept of the geography of Bushand, I couldn't be sure where they were leading us, but my best guess was Nul. If that proved true, and we were delivered to Siglind there, that would certainly prove to be a disastrous end to our quest. Whatever happened, we could not let it come to that.

I remembered the townspeople mentioning they were only a day's march from Nul. By this point it was already well past midday. In fact, dusk was fast approaching. Our best hope was that they would not march overnight and deliver us by morning, but that they would stop to camp. That would give us a bit more time, perhaps even the possibility of escape. I held on to that hope with all the strength I had in me. As if he could read *my* mind, Viktor turned to whisper to me as we were driven along with the troop, "Can you tell where they're taking us?" I tried once again to open my mind and get a reading on any of the soldiers around us, but I could only get a clear sense of my three comrades. I had to shut my mind at once. Viktor's panic, distress, and sense of failure was overpowering to the point where I physically flinched.

"No," I whispered back, shaking my head.

One of the guards must have heard me, for a whip cracked right by my ear, and I felt a sharp pain on my right cheek. "No talking!" he shouted, and I couldn't help but cower, though I hated the weakness it made me feel. Without the use of my power I felt completely helpless, not to mention useless.

They marched, dragging us behind them at a merciless pace, and it was well after dark before we finally stopped for a rest. Huddling close together against the cold of the night, we dared not speak for fear of repercussions, The need to scramble for an escape was evident in each other's eyes. Bound and without weapons or a clear manner of communication, someone was going to have to get very creative and stealthy in order to come up with a plan, and quickly. At this point we were probably only half a day from Nul, and if we made it there we would surely be doomed.

Siofra wasted not a second. Though stripped of her weapons, she was still adorned in her characteristic armour, which was sharp, albeit feminine. She jerked her head towards Jion, silently asking him to move slightly in front of her, shielding her a bit from view, though not enough to raise alarm. Jion understood immediately- for two people who bickered as though they hated each other, they worked remarkably well under pressure. *A fitting pair for a king's guard*, I thought. From there I couldn't tell what her plan was, or even if she had one in particular. Jion was partially blocking her from my point of view, but I thought I could make out her rubbing the rope against the edge of her armored breastplate.

My mind stayed racing. It was as dire of a situation as we'd been in so far; in fact, as I'd been in in my life thus far. They had wound the ropes so tightly around my hands that I could barely move them. The skin on my wrists burned and reddened as the rope scratched and twisted the flesh. One glance at the intricate knot told me it wouldn't be easy to undo, and the rope was far too dense to try to bite through or snap with any amount of force I could muster.

I glanced over at Viktor, wondering if our captors had any clue who he truly was. The idea made me feel sick. His head was hung, and though I couldn't see the expression on his face, I could tell by the clench in his sharp jaw that he was enraged and desperate. As Captain Carthoc approached, Vik looked up, a wild ferocity in his gaze.

"Now comes the time to gather that precious information you're holding, *envoy.*" Carthoc spit the word with malice, mocking it's typical peaceful meaning.

A smile so sinister that even I felt intimidated grew across Vik's face. "I will tell you nothing."

Carthoc response was a chilling laughter. "I love when people say that. It makes getting you to talk so much more fun." He summoned several soldiers and directed them to bring Viktor into a makeshift tent they had erected, and that's when it finally dawned on my naive mind that they intended to torture him.

I froze at his words, panicked and wondering what they were possibly going to do to him. Knowing Viktor's utmost importance to our mission, I knew that no matter what happened, he needed to be protected as the only hope standing between our amicable country and the barbarous dictator of Bushand. If any one of us were to make it out of this predicament alive and relatively unhurt, it needed to be the prince. The thought barely crossed into my mind before the exclamation came from my mouth. "I am an empath!"

Everyone, Carthoc, his minions, Viktor, all froze at once. "Ahh, so the rumors are true," Carthoc said, in a viciously happy lilt. "There *is* an empath in your midst."

"No! She's lying!" Viktor shouted in a desperate attempt to redirect Carthoc and save me from his wicked intentions, whatever they may be.

Carthoc, focused entirely on me now, ignoring him completely. Striding forward, he leaned over my small form menacingly, grabbing my chin and peering in to my eyes. "Are you lying?" he asked. Rather than answer, I summoned all my courage and fixed him with a defiant gaze, only to hear another one of his chilling laughs in response.

"Forget the envoy," he said to his men. "Take the empath." I watched Viktor's eyes widen in panic as he began to thrash, trying to escape his bounds and protesting. It mattered not. My mission had succeeded, and the prince was being left in relative peace, at least for the time being. I could only hope that whatever Siofra was up to would pay off in time.

I felt as though I was in a daze, nearly frozen in fear as three men grabbed me and dragged me into the tent a mere fifty feet from where my friends lay huddled near the fire. It was sparsely furnished. There was a makeshift bed, and a lone chair next to a small fire. The guards pushed me into the chair before securing me to it with more of the same thick rope. I barely had enough time to wonder what was to come of me before Captain Carthoc strolled inside. He was short, so short, in fact, that he barely had to crouch to fix me with his malicious gaze, black hair falling slightly over his eyes.

"I don't know why you're so keen on protecting that envoy of yours. Surely you have some idea of what is to happen." His dark brown eyes flickered back and forth, searching my face. Trying to keep my expression neutral, I shifted my gaze to the ground, refusing to look at him. "It doesn't have to be that way, though," he continued. "King Siglind could very well use an empath. Tell us what we need to know, and join our cause. Despite what these Doctsland rats have told you, our king is merely trying to fight for what is rightfully his. Is that so wrong?"

I kept my mouth tightly shut and after a few moments he seemed to realize I was not going to answer.

147

"Tell me, empath, do you wonder why you didn't sense our presence? Why you failed to warn your comrades of the approaching danger?"

Despite my desire to disengage, curiosity got the better of me and I glanced up, betraying my interest. "Ahh, so you *do* wonder. Let me clue you in to a little secret. Doctsland is not the only country to employ those with unique abilities."

"What do you mean?" I spat, wondering what could possibly dampen my powers to the extent that I missed an entire small force.

He smiled, clearly happy to be finally getting under my skin. "A sorcerer has recently joined the council of our king. He is a powerful sorcerer, with knowledge of many ancient spells, even an ancient spell that would hide one's mind from an empath."

I stiffened, fear growing inside my belly. It was one thing to tend a magic that was natural in your family and in your blood, such as my empathic abilities and my family's proclivity towards medicinal magic. It was another thing entirely to nourish an unnatural power, planted and tended only with spells and potions rather than a birthright. The word sorcerer implied someone self-made in the arts, and one capable of such magic as Carthoc is referring to would be someone truly dangerous.

Sensing my fear, and quite pleased with himself, he continued. "His magic is strong. So strong that he could cloak myself and my entire team, masking us from you. Imagine, if you joined us, what the two of you could accomplish together."

I imagine in his mind this was supposed to be an alluring idea, however it filled me only with terror and disgust. I would never want to mingle my family's wholesome magic with the corrupt power of a sorcerer. Carthoc was close now, his face hovering near mine, eagerly awaiting what he was sure would be an acceptance. Instead, I spat in his face, which immediately twisted with fury.

He stood and wiped his face at once, and shouted for a guard. "Bring this *witch outside.*" He spat the word with venom. "And secure her to a tree. If she won't join us or answer our questions willingly, I will whip the answers out of her."

Without hesitation, they did his bidding. I thrashed as they approached me, fighting back with every ounce of my strength despite the fact that I was bound and being restrained by several strong men. But before I knew it my arms were secured around a tree. I felt the cool edge of a knife as my jacket and tunic were both sliced open, exposing my back to the cold night air. I closed my eyes tightly, and tried to build up enough walls around my mind to protect myself from any pain I may feel. I'd never tried to shield myself from my own pain, but I prayed to the Kelps it would work.

"Why are you here?" Captain Carthoc asked.

I was determined not to speak, and after a moment I felt the lash against my back. My walls crumbled upon impact, and a scream loosed from my throat despite my will to keep quiet. The pain was worse than anything I could have imagined, and for a brief moment I wished he would just kill me instead.

"Did the Prince of Doctsland send you?"

Another lash, and I squeezed my eyes shut as tears spilled down my cheeks. Still, I held my ground and did not utter a word. Part of me rejoiced at this question though, because it revealed that they did not know that the Prince of Doctsland was among them.

He continued. "How many empaths does the prince have in his employ?"

Again, silence, and again, pain seared through my back as I howled in agony.

"What are you doing in Bushand? Have you come to attack? How strong is Doctsland's army?" his barrage of questions continued, a lash or more between each question. I always heard the crack of the whip right before I felt the impact, and that small moment of expectation was almost worse than the agony that followed. Almost.

I looked down to see blood streaming down the legs of my

pants and pooling on the dirt beneath my feet. The entirety of my back was aflame, and each time I thought it couldn't get any worse another lash would come and shatter that notion. With each strike it seemed a hundred knives were tearing into me. I kept waiting to pass out, or for my back to go numb. *There's only so much suffering I can take before my body gives out… right?* I willed an end, whether it was a rescue, sleep, numbness, or even death. An hour I endured, and it was the longest hour I will ever live. But finally, it stopped.

"It's late," Carthoc said, circling around the tree to look at me, arrogance and pride written on his white face as he surveyed his handiwork. "My arm is getting rather tired. Let's pick this up in the morning, shall we? You can stay here through the night, and think about how your participation tomorrow may improve your current predicament."

I rested my cheek against the rough bark of the tree and closed my eyes, relieved that my torment was ending, at least for a little while. I wondered how my friends were fairing, if Siofra was able to escape, and hoped that they would be left in peace while Carthoc fixed his cruel intentions on me. *Maybe*, I hoped desperately, *he was distracted enough with me to allow Siofra and the others to slip away unnoticed.* I tried to open my mind to reach out for them, but to my shock I found I could not. I was exhausted, more exhausted than I had ever been, and my mind would not allow me to stretch and touch anyone else's. Though I was alarmed, I couldn't do anything about it. Rather, I allowed my eyes to flutter shut, not having enough energy to stay awake for even a second longer.

I awoke to the sound of yelling. Disoriented, I blinked my bleary eyes open. My body screamed in pain, and I winced with every movement. It felt as though Carthoc's whip had been embedded in my back, and phantom lashes wracked through me. The sky was still dark, but a bloody sunrise was beginning to peak over the horizon, meaning I had been left out for hours, standing and tied. I couldn't feel my legs, only the searing pain in my back. My upper body shook violently, and I could not still myself. Still tightly bound to the tree, I couldn't turn to see what was happening, but in my limited field of vision I saw fire. I didn't know the source of the fire, or where Captain Carthoc was, but I hoped with all my heart that the flames would consume him entirely.

Suddenly, a deep, familiar voice rose above the chaos. "Where is Lisalya?" it boomed, echoing throughout the camp. "Where is the empath?"

"Back behind the tent, on the edge of camp, tied to a large oak," came the high lilt of Carthoc's voice in a whimper. Whatever had happened, he had lost his arrogance, and the thought brought a small smile to my face.

I don't know how much longer it was, every minute felt like an eternity, but eventually the face that came with that familiar voice appeared before me. "Viktor," I choked, finding my voice hoarse and speaking painful.

"Shh," he said in reply as he began cutting my bonds. "Save your energy."

"What has happened?"

Once he had freed me, he looped my arm over his shoulder. "I'll explain when we're safer, come on."

My legs wobbled as I tried to move with him, and the combination of the sudden movement, the aching pain coursing through my entire body, and the dry, bloody taste in my mouth suddenly overwhelmed me. Lurching forward, I emptied what little there was in my stomach onto the forest floor before our feet. In the back of my mind, part of me wanted to cower in embarrassment, but mostly I was just too tired to care. Viktor certainly seemed too determined to care, not even pausing to bat an eyelash, but rather moving forward as swiftly as he could manage with me as his burden.

I tried to keep up with him, but my legs couldn't move as quickly as I wanted them to, and I was growing increasingly frustrated with their failure. We'd barely made it to the perimeter of the initial enemy camp before they'd given up completely. Viktor noticed before I did; everything seemed to be fuzzy and in slow motion to me.

"Jion!" he barked. "Help to steady her. I'm going to carry her on my back."

Jion's arms replaced Viktor's while the former moved to place himself in front of me. With his guidance, I draped my arms over his neck so he could lift me onto his back.

"We've got a long walk," he murmured, soft enough that only I could hear with my head rested on his shoulder. I took a deep breath, breathing in his musky scent which had grown familiar to me, and allowed it to comfort me. "You should try to rest. Sleep, I've got you."

So many questions raced through my head and I yearned for answers, but my eyes betrayed me, feeling leaden with heavy burdens. Despite my efforts to stay awake I couldn't possibly keep them open. So, I followed his suggestion and gave in, letting my eyes fall shut and sinking into unconsciousness.

***

When I woke next I was confused. I found myself nearly face to face with a fire. I panicked, forgetting my rescue and expecting to be in Carthoc's tent once more. Glancing around, I saw Siofra poking at the fire with a stick and sighed, relieved to see a familiar face.

"Where is Viktor?" I asked, remembering his strong arms carrying me as I slept.

She gestured across the fire, and turning my head I saw him and Jion in a deep discussion, though about what I could not tell.

"They're discussing the way back to camp," Siofra said. "Jion thinks he can figure out a shortcut. Vik doesn't want to risk it with your condition, in case Jion is wrong and we find ourselves lost."

"My... condition?" I asked, my head feeling too foggy to comprehend much of what she was saying.

She seemed confused by my question, looking at me with her brow furrowed. "Yes, we don't want to move you any more than necessary, considering your injuries sustained during your time with Captain Carthoc," she spoke gently, as if reminding a child of a horrible nightmare.

I flinched, everything rushing back to me at once. Allowing my eyes to flutter closed, I tried to keep the memories and the pain at bay.

"Just try to rest," Siofra said.

Mustering my strength, I reopened my eyes. "What happened?" I asked, still wondering after Viktor's refusal to answer.

He took his chance now, having appeared close by once more. "Siofra rescued us."

"How?" I croaked.

"I used the edge of my armor to saw through the rope," she answered. "Once the captain and the guards took you away, they shifted their focus off of us. It was fairly easy to get away. Once I was free of my bonds, I sprinted back to camp as quickly as possible to get back-up. After rallying some troops, we marched back to perform the rescue mission. Unfortunately we didn't make it in time to save you from Carthoc's ministrations. The two camps were almost a full day's march apart, we barely made it back and forth between them in one night."

"How are you feeling?" Viktor asked. He had crossed over the fire and was kneeling beside me, blue eyes searching my face to assess my condition.

I squeezed my eyes shut. Speaking, thinking, just being awake and maintaining it was exhausting in my current state.

"Never better," I joked, hoping he would do me a favor and leave it at that.

Of course, he seemed to see right through me. Softly, so softly I could hardly feel it, he brushed a lock of hair from my face, which was damp from sweat. Sadness marred his handsome face before he stood.

"Let's go. No shortcuts, I'm putting my foot down. We can't afford any delays. We've got to get far away from Nul, and we've got to get Lis back to camp."

Shortly after, I began to drift in and out of consciousness again, my brain settling on one last thought before I finally fell asleep; how strangely warm it made me feel to hear my nickname cross his lips for the first time.

Chapter Twelve

Viktor

As much as I wanted to let Lisalya rest and sleep in relative peace, we had been in one place for far too long. I lifted her, helping her to stand so I could try to carry her on my back again. My heart ached when she groaned.

"Sorry…" I mumbled, trying to steady my movements so she wouldn't be jostled around too much. "I'm trying to be as gentle and swift as I can, but we've got to get going."

"Are you going to carry me?" she asked. I couldn't see her face, but she spoke slowly as if disoriented.

I smiled, glancing over my shoulder, hoping to reassure her in some way. "I've been carrying you up 'til now. So, yes, I'll continue."

"I'm sure I can walk," she replied.

I almost laughed at her stubborn inability to accept help without protest. "Don't be silly," I said, guilt over her condition gnawing at me with abandon. "You put yourself in my place. You saved me from the fate that you endured, though you shouldn't have. The least I can do, the absolute least, is to carry you for a bit so you can rest."

"I've been resting," she protested, trying to lift her head.

"Oh no you don't," I cried, maneuvering myself in front of her so she sloped forward and fell onto my back, her cheek resting between my shoulder blades. "Would you stop being so damn stubborn for once?"

"No…" she murmured, before drifting off once more as I began to move forward. *Of course not*, I thought. *Her stubborn nature is one of the things I lo- wait, what?* I pushed the thought aside, not ready to confront or accept the way I might feel.

The next few hours were a blur. We walked quickly and steadily, trying to reach camp as soon as possible. I kept Lisalya on my back, her tanned arms draped over my chest, walking with a hunch to keep her balanced and in place. I didn't lift my head or turn to look around, focusing on watching my feet to avoid tripping. A fall could prove disastrous in Lisalya's fragile state. Siofra walked in front of me, leading the way, and we kept quiet through the duration of our journey, trying to do anything possible to go undetected.

I have no idea how long it took. I was so determined to get Lisalya to safety that I focused only on her and on moving forward, but eventually we made it back to camp. When we finally arrived, I took Lis to her personal shelter, laying her gently down on her stomach on the bed.

"One of the men from Cessam is a healer. Should I grab him?" Siofra asked, staring down at Lisalya, concern and distress etched on her face.

"Yes please, send him at once," I replied.

The room was too small for a chair, so I sat at the end of her bed, afraid to leave her alone. I struggled to stay awake, watching the steady rise and fall of her breathing to make sure it never stopped. Her cheek was squished against the pillow, giving her face (or what I could make out of it through her knotted, wild hair) an air of youth and innocence. She seemed more at peace sleeping now than she had since before our capture, and the fact that that peace would disappear upon her waking torn at me, especially since I considered it to be my fault.

I was just beginning to drift off myself when a knock at the door jerked me awake. "Come in," I said, standing to open the door.

"Thank you," the young man said as he entered the room, crowded with just the three of us due to its small size. He stood tall, lanky, and awkward, but I could tell that he was eager to help. "I am Jaeboc, of Cessam. Lady Siofra sent for me."

"Yes, thank you," I replied. "You may remember Lisalya. She accompanied us in Cessam. We were captured by some Nulian soldiers, and she was questioned by Captain Carthoc."

The moment I said Carthoc's name the color drained from Jaeboc's face. "Captain Carthoc?" he whispered, terror clear in his large eyes. "She is lucky to be alive."

"Have you heard of him?" I asked, wanting to know how far his influence spread.

"Everyone has. He's a terror. He seems to delight in inflicting pain, even on his own countrymen. It is shameful. King Siglind sends him and his band of soldiers to towns and villages across Bushand, forcing people to return with them to Nul to join Siglind's growing army. Those that refuse him do not typically survive." He stopped speaking and began to examine the wounds on Lisalya's back.

I bit my cheek and tried to steady my hands, which had begun to shake with rage at the thought of Siglind forcing people to join his army under threat of death, and using what was clearly a sadistic madman to do it.

"Thank you for the information," I said, jaw clenched. "How is she?"

"Her injuries are beyond my skill," he said, and my heart sank. "I can, however, make a drink for her. There are several herbs in my kit I brought from home. I can mix up a tea for her to drink when she wakes. It may help her handle the pain."

"Please do," I said.

He exited with my thanks, and returned shortly afterwards with the herbs he had promised and instructions on their use; all I had to do was crunch them up and mix them in boiling water.

After his departure, I returned to my spot on the end of her bed, watching over her. A few hours passed of me drifting in and out of consciousness during my guard of her, but then she finally began to wake.

"Try not to move," I said, causing her to start. "Sorry, I didn't mean to scare you."

She turned her head to look at me. "How long have we

been back here?"

"We arrived late last night. It was a little slow going, it took a little over one day for us to make it back. Do you remember much from the journey?"

"No," she said, closing her eyes as she shifted and grimaced. "I mean, I remember bits and pieces, but I have no memory of coming home. I didn't realize we were traveling for that long. Did you carry me that entire time?"

"Jion and I traded you once or twice, but we tried to keep you as stable as possible, so I had you most of the time. How are you feeling?"

"Pretty rough," she said, her voice sounding hoarse.

"We had a healer take a look at you last night, but your injuries are a bit beyond his skill. He did give me some herbs to mix up a tea with when you awake," I explained. "I'm going to warm up some water for you. I'll be right back, try to stay awake for a bit so you can drink it while it's still warm. He said it will help with the pain."

With that, I stood and rushed out, trying to hurry in my fear that she would fall asleep again.

I returned as quickly as possible, carrying a steaming mug of a strong smelling herbal drink. "You'll have to try to sit up to drink this, if you can."

"Is there berryroot in it?" she asked. "Or dragonshearth?"

I paused, uncertain. "I'm not sure what's in it. What is dragonshearth?"

"It's an herb my grandmother uses in her healing tonics. Berryroot, sage, thimbleweed, and dragonshearth to numb the pain."

"I'll ask if any of those are in this. If not, we'll find them and make that tonic as well. For now, try to sit up to drink this. I'll help you."

I gently braced her arms with my own as she pushed herself upright. Her face was scrunched in agony, and it took several minutes before she was fully upright.

"Don't lean back against the wall," I warned, seeing her sway in that direction. "The moment your back makes contact it will feel even worse. Try to hunch forward if you need to, or lean sideways against me."

She must not have been listening to me, or her mind was clouded in her pain, for she allowed herself to sway backwards regardless. As soon as her body made contact with the wall, she cried out, immediately shooting forward as tears sprang to her eyes and spilled onto her cheeks.

"Lis!" I cried, putting my arm out and bracing her so I didn't fall forward onto the floor from the force of her lurch. "Are you okay? I *just* told you not to lean against the wall!" Immediately I felt regret at my tone, which due to my concern came across much more harshly than I intended.

"Well I'm *sorry*," she spat back, gritting her teeth.

I ignored her bitter reply, knowing I'd deserved it, and instead moved to look at her back.

"Do you mind?" I asked, reaching towards her shirt. She shook her head and I continued speaking as I examined the afflicted area. The tunic was sliced open in the back, but the material had clung and crusted to her wound regardless. "It probably wasn't in the best judgement, but we left the shirt you've had on this whole time. You weren't awake, and we didn't want to remove it in the forest just in case something could get in your wounds. Now that we're back in an environment we can at least semi-sterilize, I think we should take it off and try to let your back breathe. Here, take the blanket to cover yourself."

I held up the edge of the blanket, and she reached forward to grasp it and held it tightly under her chin and against her chest.

"The blood has dried, the shirt is crusted against you. I think I'll have to cut it to get it off. You should drink your tea first, hopefully that will help to dull the pain a bit. I'm sure this won't feel good."

She leaned against my side and I tried to ignore the warmth in my chest at her contact as she grabbed the steaming cup of tea I had brought in for her, bringing it under her long nose and smelling it.

"I don't know what this is, but it has berryroot in it," she murmured.

"That's good, right?" I replied with a small smile. "Go on, drink up."

Doing just as I suggested, she took a sip of the tea. After that first taste, she tipped the cup back and drained it.

"This acts fast," she said, gazing at the empty cup in wonder.

"Good. I'm going to start working on your shirt. Let me know if it becomes unbearable at any point and I'll stop. Though, I feel it may be better to try to just get it over with."

She nodded. "Please just get it over with. I feel numb at the moment."

"Alright. Try to focus on something else if you can," I said before readjusting myself so I was behind her. Then I set to work. It was slow work, peeling the fabric away from her flesh bit by bit.

A few moments passed and she huffed, but so I halted my ministrations to ask, "Are you okay?"

"Yes, yes, please continue. I'm just trying to remember my grandmother's healing methods, but I never paid much attention so I'm struggling."

"Aren't you supposed to take over for her when she passes?" I asked, resuming my work and trying to keep her engaged in conversation as a distraction.

"Well, yes, but I never liked to think about that. The fact that someday she wouldn't be there to guide me. I think part of me felt like the longer I put off learning, the longer she would have to stick around to teach me."

"There's no logic in that."

"You think I don't know that?" she snapped, turning back to look at me. She paused before grimacing. "Sorry, I shouldn't snarl at you like that," she said, turning back around.

"Probably not," I replied. "I am your king, after all. Though there's been no coronation, so maybe I'm just your prince. But I don't blame you."

"Why?" she asked.

"Because, it's entirely my fault that you're in the situation that you're in. I took you away from your home, I led us into a trap that got us caught by Siglind's men, I allowed you to be tortured in my stead."

"You didn't *allow* me, I volunteered."

"Ah, but if I had revealed my true identity, Carthoc would not have cared about you in the slightest. Empath or not."

"You're more important to the mission than I am."

"I would say that we are equally important." *It's probably time to accept that neither of us will win this squabble*, I thought. *We are both far too stubborn.*

"Regardless, I don't hold any resentment towards you. Maybe I did at one point-"

"Maybe?" I interjected, raising a skeptical eyebrow as I thought back on how cold and snarky she had been to me in Loch.

She grinned. *A beautiful grin,* I thought before I could help myself. "Okay I *definitely* did at one point, early on. But ultimately, it was my choice to accompany you on this mission. And it was the right choice. The only choice, really. I love Doctsland, and I love Loch. If there is anything I can do to protect our home, and it's leader, I will."

I smiled at her words before looking up. "I'm finished. Do you have the blanket? I got the shirt separated from your back, it's probably best to remove it completely to try to clean the wounds."

She gathered the blanket in her hands and held it close to her chest. "Alright, I'm ready." As gently as we could, we worked together to remove the garment. I helped her to lift each arm up and out of the sleeve, and though the fact that the shirt was cut made it much easier than it would have been, it still took several minutes because I was being so slow and particular, terrified to injure her further.

Once it was removed, I glanced away as I spoke, trying to avert my eyes from her. "I'm afraid I don't know much about healing. I'm assuming hot water will help?"

"We'll need to clean the wound, though I'm not entirely sure how to do that out here. Let me think for a minute. In the meantime, do you have any more of that tea? It's wearing off fast," she said.

"No, I'm afraid not. Stay here and rest a bit, and I'll go out and see if we can find any of those items you mentioned before, berryroot, dragonshearth, thimbleweed, and what else? Sage?"

She nodded as she moved to lay down on her stomach, and offered a brief description of each herb to help me in my search.

"Okay. I'll be back as soon as I'm able."

Feeling overwhelmed by the amount of foliage that needed to be searched within the boundaries of the camp, I decided to ask for help.

"Siofra," I called, heading towards the center of camp.

"Chopping firewood!" her voice called back. I rounded the edge of the fire pit and turned a corner to the wood pile.

"What do you need? Is Lisalya okay?" she asked, laying an axe down before wiping sweat from her brow.

"She seems as well as she can be given her condition. I need help finding a few herbs, though."

"I already have some scouts out checking on the safety of the camp and its boundaries. We'll have them look for these herbs as well. Do you have a list?"

"Yes," I replied. "Berryroot, dragonshearth, thimbleweed, and sage."

She nodded, committing it to memory before grabbing a passing scout and relaying the information.

"Also, Siofra, can you conduct a roll call? I want to make sure we account for anyone we lost during last night's events."

I didn't have to wait long before a few of the scouts returned, each with one of the herbs, until my bundle was complete. Siofra took it, promising to find Jaeboc and have him make and deliver some tea. I bowed in thanks, and was about to turn to leave when Siofra's voice stopped me.

"Vik, are you going to tell her?" she asked.

"Tell her what?" I replied, entirely confused by her question.

"That you're in love with her."

"What?" I blanched. "I'm not…" I choked off, the denial

sticking in my throat. And then, quietly I asked a question. "How did you know?"

She smiled. "I know you. I see the way you look at her. And the way you let her get under your skin as no one has before. You should tell her."

"I can't," I said resolutely. *She certainly doesn't return the feeling. And even if she did, my father married a commoner, and now my birthright is in question. How can I do the same?*

Siofra gazed at me, pity in her eyes. "You can. And you should. Just think on it. And hurry along now, I can see you're desperate to get back to her." I nodded, then rushed back to Lisalya's shelter, not wanting to leave her alone for long.

As soon as I arrived I burst through the door, only to find her sitting upright on the bed, without the blanket to cover her. Immediately I felt my cheeks grow hot as I whirled around to put my back to her.

"Lis!" I screeched. "I'm so sorry!"

"It's.. alright. I should have been covered. You said you'd be back. I'm fine now, you can turn around," she replied, her voice breaking slightly.

"Are you alright?" I asked, turning back around and looking at her critically. "You sound worse, somehow." I searched her face, which had a sheen of sweat over it despite the fact that she was shivering.

"The tea wore off," she said simply.

"Ah, right. Well, I have good news. We went a few scouts out and were able to round up the items needed for your grandmother's tonic. The healer from Cessam is working on making it at the moment. I just wanted to come in and check on you."

"Thanks," she replied. "I remembered, or rather it came to me, I suppose, what my grandmother used for sterilization. Snowleaf. She would crush the leaves and place them in a pot of boiling water, allowing them to steep. After a few minutes she would bathe the wound with said water. It's supposed to both clean and calm the afflicted area."

"Hmm, I'm not certain we'll be able to find that here. The climate is much warmer than in Doctsland, and snowleaf thrives in a cold environment, does it not?" she merely shrugged, seeming as though she didn't know.

I sighed. "Nevertheless, I'll send a few people out to search. We need to do something." I leaned to take another look at her back. "The wounds are still open. They're not bleeding anymore, not much at least, though pulling the shirt off opened a few scabs. I'd like to get it cleaned before it tries to heal any further." I stood and made ready to leave.

"Thank you," she said. "For everything you're doing for me."

Pausing, I turned to look at her before I left. "It's really the least I can do, Lisalya. Truly. I'm sorry to keep leaving you, I'll be back shortly. Hopefully this time with some more tonic for your pain."

I returned this time with my arms full of a mug and a large pot, both steaming with warmth.

"Just as I thought, there doesn't seem to be any snowleaf growing in Bushand, or at least not anywhere near us. However Siofra, the angel that she is, had brought some along from home because she enjoys snowleaf tea. She had no idea it would be used to clean wounds. By some miracle it was not damaged in the shipwreck. She'd had it in her pocket when she hopped into the lifeboat." I took a seat beside Lisalya on her bed and gently set my burdens on the floor. "We followed your instruction, crushing up the leaves and steeping them in a pot of water. I also brought a cup of the thimbleweed tonic. Do you want to drink that before or after we clean your wounds?"

She ignored my question in favor of asking one of her own. "Why didn't you listen to me?"

I gazed at her. "What do you mean? I listened to you, and had both of these made in accordance with your instruction."

She seemed frustrated. "No, that's not what I mean. I *told* you and Jion about those men in Cessam. I told you something wasn't right about them, but you didn't listen. I thought about it while you were gone making the tea. I ran through everything that happened since the moment we landed in Bushand, trying to pinpoint exactly when things went wrong and where things could have or should have gone differently. No matter how many times I assessed or what angle I came from, I kept arriving at the same obvious conclusion: the two men in Cessam with the same frozen minds as Carthoc and his men. And you and Jion accepted them into our party despite my warning and misgivings. " I held my tongue, knowing better than to interrupt her in the state she was in. "And you ignored me when I knew something was off about that town we were ambushed in. You didn't listen, you completely dismissed me, and look what happened."

As she spoke, my anger grew to match her own. *She's acting like I intended for all of this to happen. Plus, she's making assumptions and connecting events that don't necessarily need to be related.* "What makes you so sure that those events are even related?" I snapped back.

"I told you I felt nothing from those men, and ice cold nothing. Carthoc and his soldiers contained that very same nothingness."

"And? Maybe you just aren't as all powerful as you thought. Just because you could read the minds of everyone in *Loch*, which is a very small town, doesn't necessarily mean you can read the minds of everyone in the world!"

"Viktor," she said, filling the word with venom. I blanched, startled by the poison. "Carthoc told me Siglind has a sorcerer in his employ. A sorcerer with the power to hide someone's mind from an empath. When an empath attempts to get a read of someone under such a spell, all they feel is emptiness. A chilling void."

The color drained from my face as the realization of what her words meant hit me. So the rumors were true. "You mean to say that..." I trailed off, wrestling with the knowledge she had presented.

"That if you and Jion had listened to me instead of completely dismissing me, we most likely wouldn't have been captured, and this wouldn't have happened to me? Yes, I mean to say exactly that."

"How can you be so sure? It's possible that they were already on to us, that we would have been walking in to a trap regardless of whether or not they joined our company," I argued.

She glared daggers at me. What's that old saying…if looks could kill? If that were the case, I would certainly be dead. "You cannot stand there and look me in the eye and tell me you believe that. I found that village, they were true. Not willing to risk themselves for our cause, but not on Siglind's side either. Carthoc confirmed as much by slaughtering them. The village itself was not a trap, rather we were followed and waylaid there. Somehow those men were in contact with Captain Carthoc."

"How?"

"I don't know!" she screamed at me. "I can sense emotions, I can't read thoughts, and I certainly couldn't do either on those men because of the spell they were under!" She seethed as she sat, confined to the bed, back raw and bleeding. "Can't you just admit that you were wrong? You should have listened to me when I cautioned you against taking on those men when we were leaving Cessam. You should have listened to me two days ago when I told you I had a bad feeling before we went into that village."

I roared back to life. "Siofra was out there! So you think we should have abandoned her to face Carthoc and his men alone?"

"That's not what I'm saying and you know it," she said, gritting her teeth. A moment passed in tense silence.

She glanced around the small room, fighting back tears, and seemed to notice the items I had placed on the floor. "Will you just help me bathe my back and leave?" she murmured, her voice sounding so small in comparison to the uproar just a minute ago. "The water is going to get cold, and then we'll have wasted Siofra's snowleaf for nothing."

Rather than answer, I bent down and picked up the pot. I handed her the cup of tonic as I began to speak, "Drink your tea first, then meet me outside, if you can. I'll have to pour this over you, and I don't want to get everything all wet in here."

As soon as I was outside I sat on a log across from the door. My legs began to bounce anxiously, and I picked at my fingernails, thinking about how badly I wanted a drink. Lisalya's words raced through my mind, filling me with a bizarre combination of rage and guilt.

I was so wrapped up in my own head that I didn't notice Lisalya until she cleared her throat and spoke. "I'm ready."

I stood and called Jaeboc over. "This is Jaeboc, the healer I told you about," I said as he walked up. "He's going to help me so we can ensure this is done correctly."

Lisalya tried to give a bow in thanks, though her movement was limited. "Thank you, Jaeboc."

He seemed confused by the custom, but returned the bow nonetheless, his shaggy mop of blonde hair falling into his face as he did so. "You're welcome, miss. Now, the afflicted area covers the surface area of your back as well as a few scrapes and lashes on the backs of your arms. I think it will be best to have you sit with your back to us while we work on cleaning the wounds. Can you sit on this?" He gestured to the log I had just been using.

She nodded before moving to do as he requested. Wobbling a bit, she almost lost my balance trying to lower myself to a seated position, but I grabbed her arm to save her from disaster.

As soon as I was sure she was secure, I murmured, "I hope it's not, but this may be painful. Are you ready?"

"Yes," she whispered back, squeezing her eyes shut.

The process took a while. First we poured the warm water over the length of her back and arms where it was needed. Then we soaked a clean cloth in it and used that to do a more thorough and specific job of cleaning each wound individually. Lisalya was strong, wincing or whimpering only every once in a while. She squeezed her eyes shut and bit her lip as we went over a particularly deep slash.

"We're almost done," I said softly. At long last, we were finished and I breathed a sigh of relief. Or at least I was about

166

to, until Siofra came running up.

"Viktor!" she shouted. "I'm sorry. I know I shouldn't be bothering you right now, but I completed the roll call you requested. It took all day due to the number of people out hunting, fishing, gathering water, etcetera, but we're done. And we have a problem. We're missing two people."

I winced and swallowed, chewing my lip before making my reply. "Let me guess, two people from Cessam?"

Siofra cocked her head. "Yes. How did you know?"

I turned to look at Lisalya, who fixed me with a pointed glare. Of course the two people she had suspected as spies were gone now that they had sold us to Carthoc and Siglind. I was not surprised in the least.

I sighed. "I'll explain in a bit. Lis, do you need help getting back to bed? This is the longest you've been up in days, you could probably do with some more rest."

"No," she said. "I'll be fine. It's a short way, and grandmother's tonic has not worn off yet."

"Okay," I replied, turning back to Siofra. "Meet me in my cabin in a few minutes, and tell Jion. We have quite a bit to discuss about what's happened, and Lisalya informed me of a few things that I'll need to pass to you."

"Yes sir," Siofra said, turning to hurry back to the main area of camp.

"Are you sure you'll be alright if I leave you for a bit?" I asked, looking back at Lis. I hated the idea of leaving her alone, even if my duty to inform my companions required it.

"I'm just going to be sleeping. You don't need to be there for that," she said, pushing myself up off the log and heading in to bed without another word.

Chapter Thirteen

Lisalya

I dreamt of magic, not the twisted magic I'd encountered in Bushand, but rather the wholesome magic of my family. Passed down through countless generations, our magic was as natural to us as breathing, as pure as fresh white snow. Sure it was harder for some of us to tap into than others, and some were much stronger in certain areas, but the gift flowed in the blood of each woman of the Manyeo line. The gift of magic, and the gift of healing.

As soon as I opened my eyes, a spell was on my lips. One I did not recall Grandmother teaching me- it felt as though I knew it based on instinct rather than memory. Pushing myself up off my bed, I was saddened to find the effects of the tea had worn off overnight. It was to be expected, but still it pained me.

I moved slowly, crawling out of my bed at a snail's pace. *I need to get to Viktor,* I thought, and let that notion propel me when my physical strength wanted to fail. The spell required the assistance of someone I loved. I wasn't sure yet *what* my feelings towards Viktor were, but I knew I cared for him deeply, and that his presence was a comfort. As angry as I was with him after our fight and for dismissing my warnings, it did not change how I felt for him.

I knew I would need to dress, I didn't want to walk around the camp topless with naught but a blanket to cover my front, so I made my way over to my pack in the corner. To my surprise, I found that there was a large tunic laid on top of it. Much too large for me, but upon closer inspection I realized I recognized it as a shirt I had seen Viktor wear on occasion. I pulled it on, relieved to have something baggy available that would allow my wounds to breathe. I noted that it smelled of him, though I wasn't sure why I cared.

Once dressed, I pushed open the door and made my way out into the world. It was dawn. It seemed as though I had slept all through the day and night after Viktor and Jaeboc helped to clean my back for me. A slight chill was in the air, though the balmy climate here meant it wasn't even close to the cold that Doctsland has during the winter months. Silence blanketed the camp and it appeared I was the only one up at this hour, though I suspected that appearances may be deceiving.

Moving gently and deliberately, I walked over to Viktor's cabin. I was careful to avoid tree branches or roots, not wanting to scrap my back on anything or fall and worsen my injuries. It took time, and I was quite tired by the time I arrived, this being the most I had moved in days. I knocked quietly, not wanting to wake him up on the off chance he was sleeping. However, just as I had suspected, the door opened only a moment after I had knocked. His hair was tousled and he tried to rub the sleep out of his eyes. "Lis?"

"I'm sorry, were you asleep?" I said, moving to turn back around and leave him to sleep in peace if so.

"No, not at all. I was trying to, but there always seems to be too much on my mind as of late," he replied before opening the door wider. "Please, come in."

As I entered I noticed a candle burning on the center of his small table illuminating the map we'd received from Ailee. I glanced around the room, taking note of how disorganized it seemed in comparison to how it had looked just a few days ago when our four original crew had met here. "Are you... alright?" I asked, stopping when I reached the center of the room.

"Uh, yeah," he said, though he seemed distracted as he sat down in front of the map. "I'm fine. How are you?"

"I'm okay, considering," I replied. "I think I may have remembered, or found, a spell. A healing spell. It might help to speed up the healing process. I'm not certain, but I thought it may be worth a try."

Viktor nodded eagerly. "Absolutely. Whatever could possibly lessen your pain or help you to heal is worth a try. What do you need to perform this spell?"

"Well, you see, that's the issue. I'll need a few herbs, all of which I know we have or can find here, so that's fine. But also a lock of hair from a relative."

He sighed. "I see. That does pose a problem. I don't suppose you brought a lock of hair from someone in your family as a keepsake?"

"No, I did not. I wonder, however, if it would work with someone I care deeply about. I don't know if it will work, but I feel as though I have to try at least."

He stared at me, looking the epitome of tired and confused, dark bags under his eyes.. "Someone you care deeply about?"

I forced a smile through my nerves. "Um, yes. I'm hoping perhaps that will work in the absence of family."

Viktor cleared his throat, seeming a bit uncomfortable. "Okay, so shall I wake Siofra? I know you two have grown to become close friends on this trip."

"No," I said, shaking my head. "I, um, I think a piece of hair from you should do."

"From me?" he repeated, looking quite startled. It was nerve-wracking enough to admit I didn't hate him the first time round, I didn't have the gumption to say it again, so instead I nodded my affirmation.

He appeared to process the information for a moment, a range of emotions flickering across his face that I couldn't quite discern. Part of me wanted to open my mind to get a read on him, but I chastised myself for the temptation as it would be a gross invasion of privacy. Finally, he offered a tender smile.

"Of course, I can willingly give you such a token." He stood and moved about the cabin. To my surprise, he pulled Gaisgea from under his bed. I had assumed the blade had been lost in our capture and the ensuing struggle.

Guessing my confusion, he explained. "While I was

interrogating Carthoc, looking for you, I found Gaisgea in his tent. He must have kept it when they stripped us all of our weapons. I've been holding on to it for safekeeping until you're well enough to wield it once more." He set this down on the table before grabbing a quill and a piece of paper. "Write down the other herbs you need here. I'll send someone out to retrieve them."

I did as he requested, and waited while he went outside to find someone to complete the assigned task.

He returned shortly. "Alright. I have someone working on it. Hopefully she will be able to find everything quickly. She's going to collect them all in one bowl. Will that work?"

"Yes. We can cut the lock of hair and add it with the other items once they're here."

"And then what?"

I sighed. "I'm not entirely sure to be honest. I don't remember Grandmother ever doing this spell. It...came to me somehow in a dream, and I've just been listening to what my gut tells me to do as it comes, so I'm hoping once the ingredients are all in front of me I'll know what to do. I'm not sure it will even work."

"Well, healing magic is in your blood, right? Perhaps you don't remember because your grandmother never taught you this spell. Maybe it is coming to you because it is your birthright to know such things."

I looked at him, doubting his words even though they made sense and Grandmother had said such things had happened to her in the past. Somehow I just couldn't picture myself to be that powerful yet, at least not in the art of healing.

He laughed at the look on my face. "You don't seem so sure, but after everything we've been through, I have faith in you. It will come to you. And it will work. Now, how much of my hair do you need? And will you help me cut it?"

"Absolutely," I said, standing and picking up Gaisgea. Viktor had his long silver hair tied back, though strands had fallen out and were framing his lean face. I reached up to his hair tie, asking, "May I?"

"Of cour-" he began, though he turned to look at me and our eyes met, faces close and the word died on his lips. We stared at each other, both startled, and the strangest feeling was whirling around in my gut, like a thousand butterflies. And then, an unexpected knock brought silence.

Viktor immediately jerked back, looking as startled as I felt. Without a word he stood and went to the door, opening it and greeting the knocker. They shared a few words that I couldn't quite hear and before long Viktor was returning to his seat, now carrying a small bowl with plants sticking out over the top.

"Here are your ingredients," he said, seeming a bit sheepish and with a pink hue to his cheeks.

"Thank you," I said, bowing my head slightly. He reached back and pulled the hair tie from his hair, allowing it to fall freely to his shoulders. Gently I wielded Gaisgea with my right hand and picked up a small lock of hair no wider than my little finger. "I'll take a piece near the nape of your neck. Hopefully it will be less noticeable."

"Okay," Viktor murmured.

"Be careful not to move," I said as I lifted the blade, placing it against the soft string of hair. The hard cut sliced through effortlessly, and the strands fell into the awaiting bowl. "Done," I whispered, afraid to break the fragile silence that had filled the cabin.

"Now what?" he asked, turning to face me.

I slumped sideways into my chair, dejected. "I don't know. I thought I would know by now."

"Try not to panic. You won't be able to think clearly. It's more likely to come to you if you remain calm."

"That's easy for you to say!" I wailed, desperation taking over me. "You haven't been in pain for days!"

Viktor's eyes were downcast, and he seemed overcome with a sadness that made me regret my words. "I know," he sighed. "I'm sorry."

"Sorry?" I repeated, not expecting that response.

"I'm sorry that we didn't listen to you... all those times that we should have. I'm sorry I brushed you off and in turn caused you to go through all of this. And I'm sorry I didn't apologize yesterday. You were right, and deep down I knew it though I tried to deny it because the truth is so hard to bear. I'm just…. So sorry." A tear streamed down his cheek, and I was surprised at how much the sight of it pained me.

"I'm sorry too," I replied. "I lashed out at you yesterday, and it was unfair. I'm upset, yes, but I'm upset at the situation, and at Carthoc, but not at you. Not anymore. I know that obviously if you had known what was to happen you wouldn't have chosen the course of action that you chose. You had no idea, you couldn't have."

He lifted his eyes to mine, and there was a tenderness in them I had not witnessed before. "Truce?"

"Truce," I said, smiling softly. "Now, back to the task at hand." I reached forward and gathered all the items in the bowl into my hand, molding them together in my fist.

"Have you figured out what to do?" he asked, eagerly leaning forward.

"Not exactly…" I said, gazing down at my hand. "I'm basically just operating on instinct right now, it's anyone's guess what will happen." I shut my eyes, squeezing my hands around the gathered items, and words began to flow from my lips that I had never heard before.

'All that is and all that was
Healers of my blood from past
Hear me now and forever last
Body, soul, and spirit harmed
But not forever as was warned
Help me now with these tools
That with my love I may be whole'

My eyes flickered open just as my hands did, and to my shock the herbs and hair in my grasp had transformed, making a rudimentary brush with Viktor's silver locks as bristles. Looking up, I found that Viktor's mouth had dropped open and he was staring at me in awe.

"I have no idea where that came from," I said, feeling just as shocked as he looked, if not more. I lifted the brush, turning it over in my hands and examining it. It appeared to be a hand-crafted tool, and if I had not witnessed it as a bunch of herbs and hair I wouldn't even believe it had been so only a minute ago.

I handed it to Viktor and instructed him. "Brush this over my wounds."

He stood and nodded before speaking. "You'll need to remove the shirt. Perhaps it will be more comfortable if you lie down on the bed. There will be less of a chance of you being accidentally exposed that way."

Viktor assisted by helping to strip the fabric of me without it touching the wounds on my back. Once the shirt was removed I laid face down on the bed. "I'm ready."

He hesitated. "Are you sure this won't hurt you?"

"No, I'm not sure. I can't be. But we have to try. Just… be gentle, please."

A look of determination passed over his face as he knelt on the bed beside me. I hardly even noticed when he began sweeping the brush over me, he was being so delicate that it felt as though the bristles were barely touching me. However, I knew where he had been because a calm numbing effect settled over the skin wherever he moved the brush.

A few minutes passed before he spoke. "Is it working? It seems as though the redness is dying down a bit."

"Yes," I sighed, basking in the comfort of it and feeling my eyes grow heavy. He continued working, covering every inch of afflicted flesh, and before he was finished I drifted off to sleep.

***

This became somewhat of a routine. The magic of the brush helped to take away a lot of the pain, and helped to soothe the wounds, but it was not able to heal them immediately after only one session. Therefore, each morning I awoke and made my way to Viktor's cabin, and he brushed over my back. Doing this continually helped to speed up the healing process, and what should have taken several weeks or even months to heal was nearly there after only three weeks.

However, even three weeks was too long for our mission to be stalled.

It was after one of these morning sessions that Viktor finally brought up the inevitable. "The wounds have closed, and the scabs are nearly gone. All that remains is a bit of redness and scars. Do they still pain you?"

I shook my head. "Not really. Sometimes the area seems tender, but for the most part it is back to normal. I have my full range of motion back as well."

"Good. I suppose that means we should begin moving once more then. We didn't want to risk it while you were recovering, but I'm afraid we've been idle too long."

"Do you want me to reach out, try to find another town of sympathizers?"

"No," he replied, sitting down at the table across from where I was seated on the bed. "There will be nowhere closer than the last town, which was a two day journey round trip. I'm not sure yet what we will do." He gazed down at his hands, and I knew it was hard for him to admit that he was at a loss. He took his role as prince so seriously, and anytime he was unsure or the path was unclear to him, he felt as if he was failing in that role.

"Have you spoken to Jion or Siofra? Perhaps they have an idea," I suggested.

"Yes," he replied. "We've had quite a few discussions throughout your recovery, and though they haven't helped me come to a decision their input is invaluable to me. Jion wants to make straight for Nul. He says we don't have time to go out and rally more people before our fleet arrives, and he is correct there. Siofra calls for the opposite. She says it's too dangerous to attack Nul with the amount of people we currently have. She wants to try to go on one more excursion to add at least a bit to our numbers before we make our way to the city."

I bit my lip and ran over the options in my head, realising that neither one seemed to offer an ideal outcome.

Viktor continued. "I'll have to make a decision soon. We can't linger here much longer now that we know Siglind is on to us. By now he probably even has a rough idea of where our camp is, considering Carthoc would have known Siofra escaped, made it back to camp, and back for a rescue all in one night."

"Wait," I said, stuck on his words. "Carthoc would have known… how would that knowledge get to Siglind? Was Carthoc not killed in the rescue?"

Viktor grimaced, and I braced myself for whatever unhappy news he was about to break. "Alas, unfortunately he was not."

I ran through what little memories I had of that night. "I thought I heard you threatening him. I assumed…"

"It's my fault that he got away. I questioned him, asked where you were. As soon as he told me, I bolted off in your direction. I wasn't thinking clearly, I should have killed him as soon as I got the information I needed. But instead, while I was focused on getting to you, he slipped away."

Horror rocked through my body. This entire time, I had thought my torturer dead, and had found at least some comfort in that fact. Now, though, the knowledge that he was still out there made me feel sick. I rushed out of Vik's front door and emptied my stomach onto the ground beneath my feet.

"Lisalya!" he exclaimed, racing to my aid and helping to pull my long hair away from my face. "Are you okay? What's wrong?"

"I-" I choked out, wiping my mouth with the back of my hand. "I had assumed he was dead. To know that he is still out there. That I could have to face him is…" I trailed off, wrestling with the terror that came with that thought.

Viktor gathered me into a comforting hug. "I will do everything in my power to protect you from him. He won't get his hands on you a second time."

I sniffled against his tunic and closed my eyes, enjoying the warmth of his embrace. That is, until someone cleared their throat. "Am I interrupting something?" Siofra asked.

Viktor and I broke apart, immediately putting distance between us. "No," I said. "I just found out Carthoc escaped the raid, I was upset. Viktor was merely offering me a bit of comfort."

"Ahh," Siofra said. "I understand. Well, I'm sorry to barge in unlooked for. But I've completed the calculations to find out when our fleet should be landing at Nul. They should be arriving next week."

Grimacing at the news, Viktor gestured for us to follow him inside. "Is Jion coming?"

"Yes, he's on his way. He was just finishing his breakfast when I left, so he should be arriving shortly."

"Good. I don't want to make any plans without his input."

Siofra raised an eyebrow. "You know what his input will be."

"All the same," he replied, shrugging, and just as he spoke there was a knock on the door, followed by a shout of 'IT'S ME' that made the three of us chuckle. "Come in!" Viktor hollered back.

Once Jion entered the cabin, we all sat around Viktor's small table and began planning. Well, *they* began planning. Knowing nothing about battle, warfare, espionage, or any of the like, I sat back and kept my mouth shut.

Viktor began by rolling the map of Bushand out on the table and pointing toward Nul on the south western coast. "Siofra informs me that the fleet should be arriving in Nul next week. Jion, you know how to read a map and judge distance better than I, so correct me if I'm wrong, but I believe we are a five day's march from the city."

Jion brushed his hair back out of his eyes and sighed. "Yeah, give or take a day. If we move quickly enough, and don't run into any obstacles, we should be able to make it in five days."

"We can't guarantee we won't run into any obstacles. It's best to assume it will take at least six days. In that case, Siofra, I'm sorry, but I'm afraid we just don't have time to go on another rallying mission. If we don't arrive in conjunction with our ships, it will put the entire fleet at risk. That's not a risk I can afford to take. Without the fleet, we have no hope."

Siofra agreed solemnly. "I understand. And I agree, it's not a risk we can afford. However, I do have a suggestion that may suit everyone." We waited eagerly for her to continue. She pointed at the map. "Green Marsh is just along the route between us and Nul. We can still make one more attempt to gather more people to our banners, but we won't be going terribly out of our way to do so. Perhaps only delaying ourselves a day, or even less."

Jion's eyes widened. "I think that would work. We could afford a delay that slight, especially if it means growing our numbers. What do you think, Vik?"

"I don't want to force Lisalya to use her powers already. She's still healing, and the march will be hard enough."

"Vik," I said, effectively cutting him off. "I appreciate your concern. However, I can manage. I've gotten much better at controlling my abilities since I left Loch. Finding and locating one town while we're on the move should not be too taxing, especially if it will be fairly near to us. I already know from past attempts that there is nothing within a day's march of camp, so I will open my mind and make an attempt after our first day's march."

"Are you sure?" His eyes searched my face, scanning for any sign of uncertainty. "I don't want to push you."

"I'm positive."

He sighed. "Alright. We do need more men, we're woefully behind on numbers. I had anticipated having many more opportunities to gather more to our cause than we were able to attempt due to the... unforeseen circumstances that occurred."

"Then it's settled," Siofra said, finality in her strong voice. "When will we be leaving? I suggest as soon as possible."

"Yes, absolutely. At first light, I'll send out an order to pack up as quickly as possible. Hopefully we'll be able to make off as early as tomorrow afternoon. Lis, are you going to be able to head out that soon?" Vik asked.

"I'm feeling much better. My back feels stiff on occasion, but the wounds have healed thanks to your help, and the spell. I'm confident I can handle the journey, though it may be a bit more difficult than previous jaunts."

"Then it's settled," Jion said, grinning, repeating Siofra's words. "We leave tomorrow."

Each one of us felt a bit lighter, a bit more at ease, now that we had a definitive plan that suited everyone. The rest of the evening was spent avoiding the heavy topic of the future, but rather enjoying each other's company. We played a few card games, laughed, and tried to appreciate this time of relative peace before we began to march towards what could very well be our doom.

***

The next morning was a scramble. Viktor had given the departure order at first light, saying "We leave as soon as we're all packed and ready to depart. It is a long march, and I don't know how much time we will have to stop and hunt, so try to bring as many food items as you can carry. King Siglind has most likely been made aware of our presence by now, so there's no point in taking the time to dismantle the camp to hide our tracks. We will face him and will no longer be operating in secret. The time has come, we march to face our enemy, and to defeat him!" He raised his sword high in the air as he finished his speech, earning a resounding cheer from the camp.

Shortly after he finished, everyone broke apart to begin frantically getting ready. I myself made my way to my small cabin. My hands shook as I folded each item of clothing (most of which had been purchased or gifted from new Bushanian members of our camp), placing them gently into my pack, and I realized how nervous I was. This would begin the last leg of our journey, arguably the most crucial leg. The options were simple, limited; if we did not succeed, we died. Faced with this reality, I took a seat on my bed and tried to steady my breathing. There also the possibility of meeting Carthoc in battle. If he had made his way back to Nul, surely he would be fighting alongside Siglind's troops. I felt torn, part of me wanted to face him and destroy him, getting revenge for my ill treatment. The other part of me

179

wished to never see his face or hear his voice again, even to kill him.

I took a few moments to myself, letting my mind breathe for a bit and reveling in the silence before I'd have to either have my walls up or feel everyone around me for the duration of the march and the battle. Once my hands had calmed, I resumed my packing. I didn't have much, so it didn't take terribly long. Merely a few items of clothing, a blanket, my water skin, and Gaisgea, which I was now able to strap to my back. During my recovery, Jion had fashioned a strap for me to wear to hold the blade. My height made it difficult to wear on my hip without the sword bumping into the ground, so he devised a way for me to carry it on my back, where I could still easily reach it's handle and pull it loose in a fight.

Taking one last deep breath, I put my walls up, stretched my shoulders and my back, and strolled out the door. I said a small goodbye to the little cottage that had been my home for the past month and a half or so before heading back to the center of camp.

The whole area buzzed with activity, people dashing to and fro trying to get ready to leave as quickly as possible. All apart from Jion, who sat perched on a log near the still blazing central fire. His nonchalance made me laugh as I approached. "Well you don't seem too busy," I said, taking a seat beside him.

He glanced my way, raising an eyebrow, "Nor do you. Siofra's giving orders, keeping everyone on track, in her element. I got myself ready so I'm set."

"And Viktor? Is he ready?"

A knowing smirk grew on his face that made me blush, though I wasn't sure why. "He's in his cabin still, probably worrying over something or other. He tends to take a while to get ready, though I imagine he should be in a rush this morning. He certainly won't want us to have to wait on his account. You can go assist him, if you'd like."

I turned away from his smile, "No, that's alright. I'm sure he has everything under control."

At that moment, Siofra strolled up to the fire, just in time to change the subject to my relief. "We're almost ready. Just a few more people need to finish packing up, but we should be able to make off within an hour. I take it the two of you are prepared to leave?"

"We could head off at once. We're the most prepared of the entire camp," Jion answered.

"Great. I've told everyone to rally here when they're ready, I don't imagine it will be terribly long. We might end up waiting on Vik, as usual."

"Come on, Siofra, give me some more credit," Viktor said, approaching the fire with his pack slung on his back, and his sword at his hip. "I've left my old ways behind me, including the perpetual tardiness."

She grinned, "So you have."

"Are we all here? Ready to make off?" Viktor glanced up at the sky. "It's not even noon yet, we're ahead of schedule."

"We're waiting on a few stragglers, they should be here soon" Siofra answered. Jion stood and grabbed a bucket of water, dousing the fire to snuff it out.

Just as Siofra had predicted, we only had to wait about fifteen minutes before every one of our large party was grouped around the fire.

Viktor raised his voice to address the crowd. "Thank you, everyone, for your haste in preparing to depart. We're ahead of schedule, which means we'll have some additional time to try to gather more people to our party, rather than rushing. Our plan is as follows: We will begin our journey now, heading steadily towards Nul, where we will meet a Doctsland fleet and combine forces to attack the city and, after capturing it, remove Siglind from his seat of power. Timing is of the utmost importance. We must arrive at the city at approximately the same time as the fleet. We have allowed a day in our marching schedule to rally more troops while we are on our way. Our plan is to approach Green Marsh, but if any of you know of another town or city along our route that is averse to Siglind's rule and more likely to join us, please inform Siofra, Jion, or myself. We've only time for one stop, one raid, so we must choose wisely and select the location that will likely bring us the most volunteers. We will march from dawn til dusk each day, with only a stop to rest at midday and have lunch. Let the thought of victory drive you. We march towards freedom from the oppression that Siglind has bestowed on you, and wills to bestow on Doctsland." A cheer rose up from the crowd, and Viktor finished his speech with one last announcement. "And now, we depart!"

Chapter Fourteen

Viktor

We set out at once in the direction of the river. After spending a significant amount of time examining the map of Bushand, Jion and I agreed the smoothest path would be along Waterford River. We would keep the river on our right, staying close enough that we could hear the roaring water, but far enough in the woods that we could avoid being seen by any passing boats. I wanted to attempt to keep our journey secret, feeling it would be better to try to catch King Siglind unawares.

"He knows there are a handful of us, and thinks the party consists of an envoy. He may know we're here, but he doesn't know why, nor does he know the extent of our plan. Even if the two spies reported our number after Cessam, they would not know of the fleet approaching Nul. I'd like to keep that under wraps until we arrive, if possible. We will need every advantage that we can possibly get."

Though we tried to move as quickly as possible, it was difficult to move swiftly through the forest with a large number of people. Our efforts had amassed six hundred soldiers to our cause, which meant the going was slow though steady.

The core four of us that had initially set out lead the march. As we walked I took the time to admire the countryside of Bushand. I hadn't been to another country; I hadn't even spent much time out of Capital City, and though we'd been in Bushand for a long time at this point I hadn't really taken the time to take note of the landscape. It was a tad warmer, and the small difference in the climate meant that the foliage varied to that at home in Doctsland. The forest was thick and poignantly green, and I felt a little sad that we were leading a force of six hundred men and women to stomp through it, wrecking any areas that Siglind had not yet gotten to. I could only hope we would not snuff out too much of the beauty of the landscape. I had hoped that we would see some wildlife, but animals had hidden themselves as soon as they could hear us coming, though I could hardly blame them. I worried it may be difficult for Jion and the others to find food to hunt, unless we managed to find a way to be a lot more quiet as we moved.

We made it several hours before the sky grew dark around us. I pushed us to keep going until the night's visibility made it impossible, then I called for a halt. "We'll stop here. I don't think we can go much further tonight without risking injuries we can't afford- the ground is too unstable. Find a spot and try to get comfortable. We'll leave at first light."

"Sir?" a voice rose from the crowd in question. "Can we risk fires?"

I glanced at Lisalya, silently asking if there were any people nearby that could possibly see the flames. She met my eyes, giving me a small nod in response. I raised my voice in answer, addressing as much of the camp as possible. "Yes, we can afford fires tonight. I suggest making groups of ten or fifteen, possibly even less, and each group making a fire for dinner and for warmth overnight. We'll be making our's near this area," I gestured to a flat area around me and smiled. "If you're unsure what group to join, you're welcome to join us."

As soon as I finished speaking the army began to break off into small groups. Shortly thereafter, flames began to spring up as far as the eye could see, indicating that they were following my instructions. Jion set to work at once and before long our fire was roaring as well. I pulled a blanket out of my pack and set it on the ground, as close to the flames as safely possible.

Lisalya arranged her blanket nearby, laying her pack and Gaisgea by her side before laying herself down as well, stomach to the ground.

"Are you alright?" I asked.

"Yes, I'm fine. My back is a bit sore, that's all," she replied, laying her head in the crook of her arm, facing the fire. Orange flickers danced across her skin, which had grown pale during the confinement of her recovery.

"Was it too much? Do you think you'll fare okay tomorrow?" I asked, concern gnawing at me. *I hope I didn't push her too hard. Although, what choice did I have?*

She smiled reassuringly, "Of course, I'll be fine."

"If you feel like you're being pushed too far, please let me know. I've carried you before. I don't have a problem doing it again."

Her grin grew at my offer, "Thank you, truly. I believe I should be alright." Her stomach growled audibly. "That is if I don't starve to death before tomorrow's march. I need some dinner."

I threw my head back, laughing. "Yes, of course. We all do. I was so excited to finally get on the road that I completely forgot to eat something for lunch. Now I'm famished. Let's get some meat on the fire."

"Yes, please, before I fall asleep and miss another meal," she joked, snuggling in under her blanket.

Jion and I worked together to cook a small meal for us and the few others who had joined at our fire. By the time we were finished, I noticed Lisalya's eyelids beginning to droop. "Don't fall asleep just yet," I said, making a plate for her. "Dinner is ready."

She sat up, reinvigorated at the prospect of eating. "Just in time," she said, taking the plate from my hands "Many thanks."

I gave her a kind smile and a nod before dishing up a plate for myself and devouring my dinner rapidly. As soon as the food was gone, weariness crept into my eyes. I put my hand over my mouth as I yawned and laid back down, covering myself with a thin blanket. The last thing I saw before drifting off to sleep was Gaisgea glinting in the firelight beside Lis.

***

When I awoke, it was to a gentle hand shaking my shoulder, and Siofra's voice murmuring my name. I rubbed my eyes in confusion. "What's going on?" I asked, sitting upright.

"Sorry to wake you," she said. "I was up for my guard shift when one of the women in the camp approached me. She confirmed Green Marsh's location, and the possibility of them being easily swayed to our cause. She said they're possibly only a half a day from our current location. She also confirmed that Lura is their leader."

My eyes widened at the mention of my step-sister's name, "Lura? Is she sure?"

I could just make out the shape of her head nodding through the darkness. "She seems very sure."

"Please take me to her," I said, getting up and pulling on my jacket. Siofra led me a short distance to a small group of people who stood and bowed upon my arrival.

"Good morning," I sat among them, near to their minute fire. "I've heard you know of Green marsh. Please, tell me everything you know about this place, especially concerning Lura of Nul."

A young woman moved forward to sit beside me. "Yes, it is my home city. I left several years ago to be with my husband in Cessam, we wanted more distance between us and Nul," she said, glancing to a man beside her I assumed was the aforementioned husband. "But Lura has been governess there since her brother became king."

My eyebrows shot up at this new knowledge. "She has?"

"Indeed. Shortly after Siglind's coronation, it became clear what kind of king he would be. He was too young, too selfish to have that kind of power. He began at once to increase taxes to have more military funds, and to grow his army. The people of Nul spoke out, called for Lura to be crowned as the eldest, despite her gender. In response, Siglind sent her away. He probably would have had her killed if he thought he could get away with it unnoticed, but the people of Nul, and of all

186

of Bushand, have always loved Lura. He would undoubtedly have lost any favor that he had. She took refuge in Green Marsh, and was immediately made governess, and has been ruling there ever since."

"And do you think she will be sympathetic to our cause?" I asked earnestly.

She glanced around at her companions, who all shrugged. "It's hard to say" she answered. "Lura does not agree with her brother's ways, and has not upheld some of his more recent, ridiculous laws. She sees the error in his ways, and surely, deep down, knows he is not fit for rule. Saying that she will openly defy him, though. That is an entirely different story."

I chewed my lip, pondering her words. It was encouraging to know that Lura was so close. After all, our hope in a Bushanean leader lay in her. "Thank you so much for this information, it has been most helpful," I said, standing. I pulled Siofra away from the fire and spoke quietly. "We need to go there. This is our best opportunity yet. If we can get Lura on our side, it will speak volumes to the people of Bushand."

"Are you entirely sure they will join us?" she asked.

"No, of course not. But I believe it's worth a try. And it's definitely worth having Lis locate it and try to get a sense of them. I'll go wake her and ask her to do that now."

"Okay," she replied. "I agree. Let me know what she finds out. In the meantime I'm going to start getting everyone up and ready to go."

I made my way back to where Lisalya was sleeping soundly. While I'd been away with Siofra, Jion had risen and was cooking breakfast over the fire. Lisalya looked so peaceful, I hated having to wake her even as I reached out to do so. I brushed a few strands of black hair which had fallen over her eye behind her ear and murmured her name.

She blinked her eyes open. "The sky is still dark," she mumbled.

"I know, I'm sorry. We think we know where Green Marsh is, only a half day from here. I'm hoping you can try to locate it, perhaps get a read on their location and their allegiance."

"What time is it?" she asked drowsily, rubbing her eyes with the back of her hands.

"It's just before dawn. Again, I'm sorry to wake you up, but we'll be getting everyone up and on the road before the sun has fully risen anyway, so I haven't robbed you of a terrible amount of sleep."

"Okay," she said, pushing hair out of her face.

I grabbed a steaming plate of eggs from Jion and handed it to her. "Here. Jion made you some breakfast. We still had some eggs left from the chickens we had to leave at the base camp. We need to use them before they go bad."

"Thanks." Once she finished eating, she closed her eyes as I'd seen her do whenever she was focusing on locating someone or something with her powers. After a while, she said, "I've found it."

"Good," I answered. "And their allegiance?"

"They are ripe with hatred for the king. I believe they will join us. Though, there are very many. It's quite possible that not all of them will feel as such."

"Of course, but as long as we have a large enough majority, we have to take the risk."

"The majority is definitely in our favor," she said, blinking her eyes open. She looked at me for a moment. "Did you get any sleep last night?" she asked.

"I got enough," I answered, gazing into the fire with tired eyes before turning to look at her. I averted the subject back to the topic at hand. "How close are they? As close as expected?"

"A little closer. Slightly less than a half day's march, I would guess, straight ahead in the direction we were walking yesterday. Does the river run straight from here?"

"For a bit, yes. It begins to wind and curve as we move closer to Nul, but I'd say for the duration of today's journey it should be fairly straight. Are you saying it will be right along the riverside?"

She nodded. "We won't be able to miss it."

I stood and began poking the fire with a long stick.

"Wonderful. I'm sorry, again, for waking you. You can go back to sleep if you want, or start getting ready for our departure. I'm hoping to leave within the hour."

Throwing her blanket back, she stood and began to pack up what few belongings she had taken out for the night. Shortly after, she turned to me. "How can I help get the camp ready to move onward? I'm not going to be able to go back to sleep anyway, I might as well be of some use."

"Siofra is already waking people up. Jion and I will probably start helping shortly. If you could join us that would be of great help," I said with a smile. Standing, we both began the task. The size of the camp meant that it was not a quick job. In fact, making our rounds took the better part of the hour in which I had hoped to leave.

By the time everyone was awake and ready to go, the sun was painting the sky a variety of purples and pinks.

"Are we going with everyone?" Lisalya asked as Jion, Siofra, and I regrouped by our fire. "Before we only went with a small crew."

"Yes, we're going with everyone this time. The need for secrecy is not as urgent as it was previously. Siglind knows we're here. Obviously it's better if our whereabouts are unknown, but it's more of a risk to go to a large town with only a small group of us. I'm not about to take the chance that what happened before could happen again," I explained, pouring water on the fire and stomping it out.

Siofra, who had been gathering as much information about our destination as possible, began to speak. "According to the individual that suggested Green Marsh, and it has a large wall around it. It's only accessible via two gates, one on the west side of the wall, one on the east. The town is large enough it may be considered a small city. You were able to verify the size as well, correct Lis?" Lisalya verified her statement silently with a nod, and Siofra smiled before continuing. "If we're successful here, it will greatly increase our shot at defeating King Siglind. This mission is critical, more than any other up to this point."

"Then we'll make sure we succeed. There is no other

option." Jion spoke with a confidence that I found it difficult to muster after our last attempt at gathering soldiers. Lisalya seemed to share my sentiment, and shivered. Jion noticed. "Are you alright?"

"Yes, of course. I'm fine. Let's get a move on."

And with that, we were off. The walk was just about as uneventful as the previous day's had been, and after a few hours' march, Lis stopped, signalling to alert us of our proximity. "From what I can tell, we're only a half mile away," she said.

"We're coming from the northeast, so hopefully we'll be able to easily identify the eastern gate as we approach," Jion added. "I'm not sure how we're going to make it appear as though we come in peace with this force behind us. They're probably going to assume we're there to attack, which could prove disastrous."

I tapped my foot, deep in thought, before I spoke. "Yes, I've been mulling that over all morning as well. It's not going to be easy, but I think I have an idea of what may work. It's no guarantee, of course, but it may be our best shot. Let's stop here for lunch and we'll lay out the plan."

I waited until everyone was done eating to announce my plan to the rest of the company. Then we began to move forward once more. Lisalya kept her mind open and trained on our destination, searching for any hint of loyalty to Siglind, or the chilling feeling she had felt from Carthoc and his men. So far, thankfully, she said she had none.

We had only been walking a few minutes when the forest began to thin around us, and before long we could make out the unmistakable brick and stone of a large wall. Just shy of fifteen feet in height, it loomed intimidatingly over the surrounding woods.

I held a hand up, signaling for the bulk of the party to wait there as Siofra, Lis, and I continued forward. Uneasiness absorbed me, and I felt my hands begin to tremble as I thought about how much rested on this one mission.

Lisalya, sensing my anxiety, rested her hand on my arm. "I sense nothing that should alarm us here. As long as we can convince them our cause is true, I believe they will join us."

I took a shuddering breath and nodded, my lips quirking nervously.

I heard them before I saw them, a loud clear voice calling from above. "Who are you, and why have you come?"

I suddenly realized there were countless sentinels perched along the top of the wall. Briefly, I wondered how I had not noticed them before, but as we grew closer I could make out rivets in the wall that they could hide behind, shielding themselves from view completely if they desired it.

"Hello!" I called back, a pleasant lilt to my voice, trying to convey that our presence was not a threat. "Myself and my companions have traveled a long way in the hopes of speaking with the leader of this great city, Green Marsh."

"Traveled a long way? From where? And how many of you are there? I see only three."

"From Doctsland," I announced, and we all held our breath after the word was spoken. This would be the moment of truth. They could shoot us from the high point of the wall, or welcome us into the city. Purposely, I did not answer the sentinel's second question, which certainly would increase the likelihood of our getting shot.

"Wait here," the voice called, and several of the archers disappeared. Those that were left stayed standing on the edge of the walls, arrows at the ready and trained at our heads.

"I hate waiting," Siofra mumbled, shifting impatiently from foot to foot.

"I know," I replied, a nervous smile on my lips. "It won't be long. I hope."

We stood in tense silence for what was probably only ten minutes at the longest, but felt like several hours. As each second went by, the tension in our party grew. I pitied Lisalya, who must have felt the agitation rolling off of at least Siofra. I had been getting better at hiding my mind from her, not to mention dealing with her own unease.

Just when it was beginning to become unbearable, the speaker returned. "We do not permit strangers into our city, but the governess of Green Marsh has agreed to speak with you. She'll be coming out shortly, and you must not move from your current places. You're in our sights. Should anything appear to go amiss, you'll be dead before you know it."

Although I was excited to have an audience with Lura, a shiver went through me at the sincerity of the threat. I replied, trying to install a confidence in my voice that I certainly didn't feel. "Yes, of course. We understand. We greatly appreciate her willingness to meet us."

There was no verbal reply, but the gate before us began to slowly pull open. A tall woman, dressed head to toe in armor, strode out to meet us. Though she appeared intimidating, when she took her helmet off she wore a kind smile. I immediately recognized the signature orange hair both my step siblings shared, and Lura's round rosy cheeks. She had hardly aged a day. "Visitors from Doctsland? And three of them, at least." She glanced back at the forest, raising a knowing eyebrow. "To what do we owe this honor, step-brother?"

I bowed, and my companions followed suit. "Thank you for receiving us, Lura. I have two close companions of mine accompanying me, Siofra and Lisalya."

"I am Lura, governess of Green Marsh. But you have not yet answered my question. Why are you here, Viktor?"

"We come seeking your help. As you seem to have guessed, we are not alone here. In fact, we come with a force of foot soldiers, made up primarily of Bushanian citizens that have joined our cause. I'm sure you're well aware of the threat King Siglind has made against my home country. We have come to protect ourselves, and to protect Bushand from his harsh rule."

"Our help?" Lura inquired. At the mention of the foot soldiers she had grown tense, and Lisalya bumped my hand lightly with her own in warning. "And how can we help to protect Doctsland? Not to mention why?"

As so began the speech, the same one I had given three times hence, though at this telling there was a newfound sense of urgency and desperation in me. I explained the plan in detail, emphasizing the fact that the naval fleet would be arriving soon, and when we join forces with the Doctsland fleet, our likelihood of defeating Siglind greatly would greatly.

Silence fell over our small group when I had finished speaking. We held our breath.

After a while, Lura spoke. "How do I know this is not some trap? Siglind has been trying to overrun Green Marsh with his brutish soldiers and his sorcerer for months. My brother is very eager to remove me from power now that he has more of a firm hold on this country. We keep our doors closed without any outright attack, but we won't be able to hold out for long. What is there to say you have not been sent by him, to trick me into saying I would join with his enemies? Surely that would give him enough cause to openly attack my city, under the guise of thwarting terrorism?"

Drawing my sword, I drew a gasp from Lisalya and Siofra as I placed it on the ground at Lura's feet. "Siglind has been tormenting you and your city, along with the rest of his kingdom for long enough. Now he threatens to do the same to mine, but I cannot stand by and allow that to happen."

Awe dropped Lura's jaw open as she gazed at the sword at her feet, an ultimate sign of humility and respect, especially from one royal to another.

I spoke again, my voice sounding more like my father's than my own- a royal edge that came from somewhere within me I was slowly learning existed. "We are marching to Nul. We will remove King Siglind from rule, for the betterment of my people, and the people of this country. You can choose to join us, or you can choose to let us pass in peace." Conviction was strong in my voice, though I could only hope it was strong enough to convince Lura.

"If it were entirely up to me, we would join you. I believe you, and the young boy I remember at my mother's coronation certainly wouldn't trick me into ruin. But alas, I cannot make this decision for my whole city alone. I must consult with the council. Pray tell, who else from Bushand has joined you? This may help to convince the others of the worthiness of your cause, and the likelihood of success."

I explained the sources of our allies, and when I mentioned Cessam, Lura lit up. "Cessam! So Merek is with you then? This is wonderful news, he is well known, as well as trusted and respected."

I opened my mouth, about to explain that Merek had remained behind to protect the citizens in Cessam, but a voice stopped me. "Yes, Merek is with them."

We whirled to find the man in question sauntering up to our small party.

"Merek!" I exclaimed, overjoyed at his sudden appearance at exactly the perfect time. "I had not expected to see you, though I could not be more pleased."

"It's hard to march an army alongside the river without being noticed. When I heard whispers that a force was moving this way, I decided it was time for me and my small guard to leave Cessam. It leaves Cessam all but defenseless, but I suspect Siglind will shortly have more to worry about than my inconsequential little town."

"Merek, will you come speak to the council with me? I believe our combined voices will likely sway them," Lura implored.

Bowing, Merek replied. "Of course, my lady."

Lura turned back to us. "Please wait here until we're inside the city gates. Then we will let the sentinels know you can rejoin your camp while you wait for our response."

"If we're going to make it to Nul in time, we need to get back on the road by this evening at the latest. We need to get at least a few miles in before nightfall," I said.

Merek nodded. "Understood. We will return with an answer as quickly as possible. Regardless of whether or not Green Marsh will join you, I will."

"Many thanks, my friend."

Just as Lura instructed, we waited and watched until they disappeared behind the city walls. Then, we turned and made our way back to the forest where our camp waited. As soon as we broached the border of the trees, Jion greeted us eagerly. "Back already? Merek passed through, I directed him to you. Did he help to sway them to our cause?"

"We don't have an answer yet. Merek and Lura have gone back inside the city to speak to their council. We were told to wait here until they have an answer for us," I replied.

"I see. Well, would you like something to eat to pass the time? We prepared lunch while you were gone."

"Yes, please. I'm starved," Siofra said, plopping down on the ground beside the fire. Lisalya and I followed suit, and we ate the rabbit Jion had caught and prepared in stressed silence. I tried not to let the anxious anticipation coursing through me occupy my every thought, but was finding it difficult. Again, I yearned for a drink to steady my nerves. Glancing up, I met Lisalya's eyes, and was grateful for the kind, encouraging smile she sent me.

It was only shortly after we had finished eating that Merek and Lura appeared together through the trees. I scrunched my eyebrows as I stood; we had all anticipated a much longer wait. "Back already?"

Merek grinned widely. "I'm quite convincing."

"Green Marsh is close to Nul," Lura said, appearing more somber than her companion. "We experience my brother's tyranny more often than not. Our people are eager to fight back. It did not take much convincing. We will march with you. Our army is currently preparing to leave. We have a fairly large force of foot soldiers and cavalry that I've managed to keep secret from my brother in the event that he attacks. Approximately five-thousand men and women make up our ranks. It will take some time to prepare, the soldiers need to say goodbye to their families and gather their belongings. I don't expect we will be ready to leave before nightfall."

"Understood," I said, trying to remain calm though excitement was coursing through my veins like adrenaline. "We will begin to move forward. When the Green Marsh army is ready, you can follow us, and hit Nul as a second wave."

"We will depart tomorrow morning at the latest," Lura promised, before turning and heading back to the city.

195

"I'll be joining your ranks if you don't mind," Merek said after Lura left.

"Of course! We are happy to have you. And the men and women of Cessam will surely be overjoyed to be reunited with their leader." I smiled, my heart warming at the friendship blossoming between us.

As soon as the plan was settled, we packed up and were on our way again. "How much farther are we set to march?" Lisalya asked.

"Well, we'll go a few hours tonight, like Vik said. Then it should only be another two days, if we stay on track," Jion answered.

A shiver passed through her body at his reply. I knew the possible confrontation she faced with Carthoc terrified her and, hoping to offer some comfort, I brushed my hand over her arm lightly, and so quickly that no one else would have noticed. When she glanced up, I met her eyes with a reassuring smile and a whisper of "It will be okay. We'll win." She took a shuddering breath, flashing a nervous smile in response.

***

We marched until we felt on the brink of collapse. The darkness was so deep I could hardly see my companions beside me, and I felt as though I was going to fall asleep standing up. As soon as I called for a halt, Lisalya dropped her stuff to the ground and sat down heavily.

"How are you faring?" I asked.

"Fine," she grumbled, and I knew she was annoyed at how long I'd pushed everyone without allowing a rest. *I just hope she understands that I don't really have a choice,* I thought.

I chose my next words carefully, not wanting to spoil her mood any further. "Are you sure? Is your back giving you any trouble?"

She hesitated before quietly saying, "It's bothering me, yes."

I draped a curtain over my mind as I stretched my arm out,

offering her my hand and trying to ignore the butterflies that erupted in my stomach as she took it without question, and hoping my attempt at masking my emotions from her was working. "Come with me," I said. "We'll go to the river away from everyone and perform your healing spell one more. Perhaps that will give you some relief."

"Fine," she replied. "But I might fall asleep as you paint my back."

I chuckled, leading her through the woods to the riverside. "That's alright. I can carry you back to camp… *again*."

A loud laugh boomed from her chest, "Would you stop making that joke?"

"Not while it still makes you laugh," I replied, a softness to my voice that I didn't catch until it happened, though I hoped she wouldn't notice or read into it. The noise of the rushing water suddenly boomed over every other sound.

After finding a patch of soft grass, I sat down. Lisalya paused. "Could you look away? I'll have to take off my shirt before I lay down."

"Of course," I replied, thankful for the darkness of the evening that could hide the blush that was surely painting my cheeks. I gazed out on the rushing water of the river as I waited. "This area is quite beautiful. I imagine we won't see anything like this for much longer. The closer we get to Nul, the more decimated land we will see," I said, remembering the scorched earth we had witnessed outside Cessam.

"Siglind does not seem to care for nature much," she replied.

"No," I said. "I don't remember him caring much when we were kids either. The people of Doctsland as a whole have more regard for nature than Bushand, I think it's merely a cultural difference, but Siglind takes it a step further."

"Why is he so… angry?" she asked, laying on the ground beside me and handing me the brush she had made with her spell.

I set to work at once. "I can't say for certain. Only he can. And, perhaps Lura. But I can tell you my guess. From what I remember, Siglind was very attached to his mother. He didn't take kindly to it when she left Bushand to marry my father. He hated my father, hated Doctsland, for taking her away. But he also hated her. He felt it was her duty to stay in Bushand and care for him, the male heir. He was young, petulant, and had no one to tell him so. The regents he was left with catered to his every whim, and fed into the hatred blooming from him. Growing up unchecked like that... well, he never did grow up. He's an adult, older than me, but he is still acting like a power-hungry child. He wants and wants and wants, and nothing is enough. He is going to devour his own country and then, if we don't stop him, ours."

She trembled under my hands before speaking. "Then we must stop him."

"Yes, we must," I said. "Is this helping?" I asked after a beat.

"Mmm," she hummed in response. "It is. I feel so relaxed I could just melt into the earth."

I chuckled. "Please don't. I could still use your help out here."

"Hmm, I suppose I'll stick around. For you," she replied.

For the rest of the spell we sat in peaceful silence. I continued until she signalled for me to stop. "Thank you. My back feels more at east than it has since... Well, since this all happened." I turned as she moved to put her shirt back on. I grabbed her hand and helped her to her feet when she was finished.

"Any time," I replied as we made our way back to camp, using Jion's small fire as a guide.

As we approached the fire and our companions she dropped my hand, and I realized all at once that we'd been holding hands since we left the riverside. I ran the tips of my fingers together as I lay down by the fire, missing her warmth.

Chapter Fifteen

Lisalya

An order of silence blanketed any sound as our army marched for the next two days. Siofra and Jion raised the concern that if the noise of an army was heard, Siglind would be aware of our march and have extra time to prepare. Therefore, we were forbidden to speak above a whisper as we moved.

Merek, who had been to Nul on a few occasions, familiarized us with the city's layout. We wanted to join forces with the incoming Doctsland fleet, so as soon as we were within a day's march we moved away from the river and towards the beach so as to approach Nul from the water. There were four main gates opening the large city of Nul to the world, but even though they faced no major threat, Siglind's paranoia kept them all under lock and guard. We were going to be coming to the east gate, which stretched over the water to allow Nulian trade ships in and out. According to Merek, and verified by several other of our companions who were familiar with the city, a small patch of land on either side of the bay stretched under the gate. It was barely enough to notice, but a slight man could slide under on his belly. It was one weak point in the fifty foot stone wall; one weak point in Nul. Between the great military minds of Jion and Siofra and with Merek's knowledge of Nul, a whispered plan was devised.

Near the end of the second march we halted for the last time, and Viktor took the opportunity to offer words of encouragement to all of us. "We're very near to our destination," he said, speaking softly but with power in his deep voice. "Tomorrow morning Captain Merek will enter Nul unnoticed, where he will wait for the telltale sound of the horn of the Doctsland fleet. That sound will be our rousing. We will rush the Southern Gate of Nul, taking the city by surprise and overwhelming them with both forces.

"Yes, Nul is a strong city, a powerful city with a ruthless leader, but we are also strong. And we have passion, purpose, and a desire for freedom on our side. That makes us stronger, and no matter how many men Siglind on his side they cannot take that from us." If it weren't for our known need for silence, surely a loud cheer would have rung out as he finished his speech. His words lit a fire within me, and I strongly desired to take Gaisgea and storm the city at once.

"Now," he continued. "Unfortunately, we're too near the city to risk lighting any fires, but we have a tradition in Doctsland- a hearty meal the eve before a battle. Please, enjoy yourselves tonight. Eat to your fill, drink any wine you've carried with. Tomorrow brings victory." He ended with a smile, and I turned to the crowd to see that many faces mirrored it. Rather than Vik, my friend, I saw before me the future king of Doctsland. And he wore leadership well.

That evening was everything Viktor had encouraged. Laughter, games, food, and drink filled the camp and the quiet, yet joyous energy was so strong it almost boiled up and over my walls. And though by the end of the night I was exhausted and my body yearned to sleep, I didn't want to lie down for fear of what the morrow may bring.

Finally, the prince gave me no choice. Most of the camp had gone to sleep, but I remained awake, sitting near the emerald beach and watching the moonlight dance on the waves. Viktor sat beside me, and I could just make out his face in the light of the full moon and stars.

"You should get some rest," he said.

I raised an eyebrow. "As should you."

"Right you are," he replied, chuckling. "It's hard to rest the night before a battle, I know. But it's all the more reason to sleep. If you're exhausted, it will be harder to wield your sword. Gaisgea will feel heavier in your hands, burdensome.

It will be easier to make a mistake, and in the heat of battle you can't afford a mistake, great or small."

"I understand," I murmured, looking down at my feet in the sand and mulling over his words. "I just want a few more minutes of peace before..." I trailed off, not wanting to think about tomorrow quite yet.

Viktor nodded beside me. "A few more minutes of peace then."

His presence beside me was comforting enough that I soon felt my eyes begin to flutter shut. With a sigh, I decided it was time to stop delaying the inevitable, and I moved to lay myself down to sleep. The last thing I saw before drifting away was the outline of Viktor's broad shoulders against the waves as he sat staring out into the sea.

***

Noise and clatter woke me the next morning. The sun was high in the sky so I knew I must have been allowed to sleep in.

I sat up, rubbing the sleep from my eyes and trying to discern what was happening. A buzzing surrounded me, the air filled with voices and the ringing of steel and armor. "You'd better hurry to get dressed." Siofra's voice startled me. I hadn't even realized she was close. "We're nearly ready to march towards the south gate."

"Has Merek already..." I started.

"Yes," she answered before I could finish. "He left early this morning, still under the cover of darkness."

"Oh," I murmured, saddened by the lack of goodbye from our newfound friend. The bustling of everyone around reminded me of Siofra's words to hurry, so I stood and began frantically getting dressed. While much of our armor had been lost in the shipwreck, we had gained some pieces from Cessam and the other towns that had joined us. While it was somewhat ill fitting and extremely uncomfortable, it worked. I wore a shirt of mail with a large plate over top to protect my chest, and a helmet. For ease of maneuvering, I wore fitted leather trousers, the same I had been marching in the past days. In a matter of minutes, I was ready.

"Here," Siofra said, handing me a piece of bread and a strip of salted steak. "Eat this."

"I'm not hungry," I replied, feeling like there was already a rock in my stomach, vibrating with anxiety.

She would not take no for an answer. "We don't know when we'll have another meal. It will help sustain you throughout the battle."

"She's right," Viktor said, appearing out of a crowd of soldiers. He was already dressed, his hair pulled back into a low bun against his neck, his sword at his side. "I know it's difficult to eat, I struggled this morning as well. But you must."

Nodding, I took the offered items from Siofra and tried to stomach them. It was difficult, my mouth felt dry and it seemed nearly impossible to chew and swallow, but with Vik and Siofra's words running through my mind, I forced it down.

"How far is it to the gate?" I asked as I finished my small meal.

"Only about an hour's march," Viktor answered. "But we need to leave now, and to move quickly. The ships will be here at any moment. But before we leave, I need you to do something for me. Could you check the city? See if you can pinpoint Merek and ascertain his safety. If not, could you at least try to sense suspicion from the city? Or knowledge of our presence and the threat?"

"Of course," I replied. Closing my eyes, I opened my mind and began to probe at the city walls, searching for Merek. It was rather easy to find him, for a multitude of reasons. First, it's usually easier for me to find the mind of someone I know in a sea of strangers. Secondly, most others in the city must have been under the sorcerer's spell. As soon as I sought the city, I was hit with a wave of chills radiating from its inhabitants. I recoiled from the icy blast, causing a startled "Lis? What happened? Are you alright?" from Viktor.

"Fine. I'm fine," I said, quickly regaining my composure

and pushing past the icy blast. "The sorcerer is there. He's masking almost everyone." The only people I could sense aside from Merek must have been lower class civilians with no part in this war, for all I felt from them was terror at the mass quantities of soldiers that had taken control of their city since Siglind began his rule. I turned my complete focus to Merek until I sensed his confidence in the plan, and then pulled away, retreating back within my own mind and throwing up barricades.

"He's safe," I assured Vik. "He's confident in our plan, in our role. Waiting for the time to come."

Viktor set his jaw, and a light came into his eyes that I had not seen since our battle at Cessam. A fearsome light that haunted the gaze of a warrior. "Good. Let's go."

He raised his voice a little to address the camp. "We march to the gate. And then, to war!" A cheer rang out, quiet enough to not raise alarm, but full of power and conviction. And then we were off.

The march was short and silent. Staying within the shelter of the few trees remaining around Nul, we kept the city's walls in sight while we all listened eagerly for the sound of the ship's call. It came when we had only just arrived within view of the gate. Up rose the unquestionable lilt of a Doctsland battle cry, which always began with a high pitch, sunk low, and then rose again before sharply cutting off.

Everything happened at once, and I was swept away in the rush. A great noise rose from the city, voices screaming in fear as the gate just visible beyond the trees began to swing open.

"NOW!" Viktor roared, raising his sword high above his head and charging forward with a snarl like a beast. I hesitated for half a moment, my feet glued to the earth, before I remembered Viktor's request that I remain by his side for protection. I knew he meant for my own protection, and yet the only thing that pushed me forward was the desire to protect him. He needed someone to watch his back, and were he to be separated from Jion or Siofra, I needed to be there for him. With that in mind, I pulled my feet from the ground despite my fear and joined the rushing crowd, hurrying to catch up to my prince.

As I surged forward with the crowd, we broke free from the frail protection of the trees. We were now laid bare, hurtling towards Nul on a wide plain. The city seemed to grow larger as we approached, and the closer we got the clearer it became.

By the time I noticed the archers stationed atop the wall it was too late, they were already letting loose their arrows. Terror washed over everyone strong enough that I could sense it through my walls as a volley of arrows rained down. Those with shields held them above their heads for protection. Those without ducked their heads as they ran, and prayed, to the Kelps or to whatever gods the Bushanian worshiped.

Together we moved forward, regardless of those who were struck and had fallen, careful not to lose sight of the destination. Three more torrents struck us before we reached the city's walls, and we left a sea of dead on the field in our wake. Emotions bubbled up inside me, tears threatening, but I buried them deep. Such weakness in the midst of a war could prove deadly.

Our army roared even as we ran, and I found myself yelling along, propelling myself forward with the sound of my voice. Before we reached the gates I had regained my position at Viktor's side, running alongside him with Jion. As soon as we breached the wall, chaos erupted. A sea of Nulian soldiers stood waiting for us, and we crashed into them like a barricade as a clatter of steel rang out, occupying nearly every sense.

In a strange way I felt thankful for our skirmish in Cessam. It allowed me to draw from that experience as I swung Gaisgea, striking down any one that came near me in the signature black armor of Nul. All the fear and anxiety I had been harboring all week was swept from my body by a flood of adrenaline.

"Move forward!" I heard Viktor yell. "Towards the keep!"

The keep. I looked up, searching through the slit in my

helmet for our target. It was not difficult to find, looming large over the city as a black-stoned tyrant. It was made up of a series of round towers grouped together haphazardly, as if, at one point, it had been several different buildings that had since been forced together. Each tower was topped with a tall spire, giving the already threatening building an even more sinister look. It seemed as though it was in the center of the city, perched atop a tall hill, and I knew we had a long way to fight before we could arrive there.

Cutting our way forward, we made significant strides before hitting another wave of soldiers rushing from the direction of the keep. I found myself fighting side by side with Viktor and was so wrapped up in the excitement of battle, I didn't even notice the large Nulian soldier running up behind me until it was too late. He fell to the side, dead before I had even known he existed, Viktor's sword sticking out from his gut.

Shocked, I looked up at Vik as he pulled his sword from the man. "Thanks," I shouted over the loud cacophony of battle.

"Anytime!" he called back with a smile on his face before it turned back into the hardened grimace he wore when in the throes of battle.

Following his lead, I turned my focus back to action, and just in time for as soon as I raised Gaisgea I blocked a long sword only a foot or so from my face. It was wielded by a gruff man, close enough that I could see the hatred in his onyx eyes as he raised his blade and struck again. I parried the blow, and remembered Jion's instruction. When the opponent is bigger than you, stronger, use speed. Use agility.

With that in mind, I ducked under his next swing and whirled, placing myself in his blind spot before thrusting out with Gaisgea, striking him in the side. He fell to his knees before toppling to the ground, and I took a heaving breath before continuing forward.

To my dismay, I had lost Viktor. Siofra, however, was still in my line of sight. I fought my way over to her until we were side by side. "Where is Viktor?" I called over the noise.

"Further ahead," she replied. "His sights are set on the keep. He's fighting his way there like a madman, trying to get there as quickly as he can. Jion is with him, but we need to catch up. Make sure he's protected on all sides."

"Agreed." I set my jaw, determination coursing through my veins as Siofra and I hurried forward.

Chaos ruled the narrow streets of Nul. Cobblestones swam in blood, and I couldn't help but notice that it all looked the same, whether it came from us or our enemies. Just as I ran past a Nulian soldier burst forth from a shop window and slashed the throat of a woman I recognized from Cessam, who had been running alongside me, with a dagger. He targeted me next, but I was able to block his blow with Gaisgea at the last second. I knew from my training it would be difficult to fight a man wielding such a small blade with my long sword, so I backed away from him quickly, giving myself enough time to pull free from my boot the dagger Jion had given me. Still wielding Gaisgea in my right hand, I brandished the dagger in my left and sneered at him. "Well?"

With a wicked grin he lunged forward, but again I was able to parry his thrusts. This continued for several minutes until finally I was able to twist around to his side before thrusting my dagger into him, right where I suspected his kidney to be. My suspicion was confirmed when I felt a searing pain in my own kidney. He dropped to his knees, and I finished him off with a quick slash to his throat, easing both his pain and my own. *I need to strengthen my walls*, I thought desperately. *Feeling the pain of others is not going to be conducive to surviving this fight.*

Moving quickly, I ducked into a nearby shop to escape the tumult just long enough to harden the blockade I had set up in my mind. I shut the door behind me and turned to find that I was in a small bakery. I took a shuddering breath and leaned against the counter, closing my eyes to focus.

A small whimper forced them back open, and turning I peeked over the counter. A woman and a small child sat cowering behind the counter, clutching each other, eyes wide with terror. I was horrified to know the fear they held in their eyes was of me.

The child opened his mouth to scream, and acting fast I reached out and clamped my hand over his mouth, whispering "Shhh... I'm not going to hurt you." I moved my hand before continuing to speak. "Most of the fighting is taking place in the streets. Is there a basement here? Or a hidden storage area of some sort?" The woman nodded nervously. "Hide yourself there. Don't make a sound. The Doctsland army is not the enemy, we seek to free you from Siglind's rule. Once we reach the keep and remove the king, the battle will be over and the city will be safe. You must remain hidden until then. Terrible things can happen in the heat of battle."

Taking my advice to heart, they quietly shuffled around the counter and into a back room. Once I felt they were safe, I returned to the task at hand. Closing my eyes, I reinforced the existing walls as best I could. I finished with a sigh and a prayer that it would be good enough, I couldn't afford to waste any more time here; I still needed to catch up to Viktor and Jion.

With that in mind, I burst forth from the shop, ready to rejoin the fray. "Lis!" I heard a familiar voice shout. "Thank Kelps, there you are." Jion came running up to me from further down the street. "How did you fall so far behind? When Vik realized you were no longer near us he sent me back to find you. We feared the worst."

"I'm sorry," I explained. "I had to strengthen my walls. Look out!" A soldier rushed up behind Jion, who swung around swiftly and dropped them with a single blow before they were close enough to be a real threat.

"Thanks. Now let's go. I don't like being separated from Vik."

I nodded, dropping my dagger back into my boot in order to wield Gaisgea with both hands for better precision. We took off together, heading once more in the direction of the menacing keep.

The city of Nul seemed to be laid out on a large hill, with the keep at its center. The streets were steep and were often broken up with large sections of stairs. Jion was moving swiftly, and it wasn't long before I was struggling to keep up with his pace. Not only was I generally more out of shape than he was (not in the practice of running long distances whilst fighting dressed in heavy armor and wielding a sword nearly my same size) but I had had very little movement in a month due to my injuries and recovery time. Breathless, I propelled myself forward knowing that Jion would not want to halt, and Viktor could have need of his strength. Jion paused to take out a Nulian soldier that got in his way, and it gave me the opportunity to catch up.

"Are you alright?" he asked, eyes scanning my face, though I wasn't sure what he was searching for given my helmet concealed most of it.

"A little out of breath, that's all," I said. "I'll be fine. Let's keep going."

"Take your helmet off. I know Siofra insists on everyone wearing one, but it's so heavy, it makes everything hotter and more difficult."

"Are you sure?" I asked.

"Yes, just make sure to stay behind me. I'll take out anyone coming towards us. You'll be less likely to be hit. But I also have faith in your ability to protect yourself, helmet or no. After all, you had a damn good teacher," he winked in pure Jion fashion, and it somehow pulled a grin out of me despite our circumstances.

I pulled my helmet off and immediately felt lighter. "That thing must weigh ten pounds. Alright let's move."

Jion barked a laugh before turning and rushing ahead once more. It's hard to say how long we were running for. The city felt vast, and it took longer to cover the distance due to the interruptions of battle. We focused solely on moving forward, only fighting when we were directly threatened, in order to make up the distance and find Viktor. Finally, after what felt like hours of running and fighting, I could make out his distinct silver hair in the distance.

"There he is!" I shouted to Jion, pointing ahead. Vik was fast approaching the steps of the keep. Jion and I glanced at each other, knowing we would need to catch him before he got there. We couldn't let him face Siglind alone.

"Vik!" Jion bellowed, trying to get the attention of his friend. We felt a new surge of energy as we picked up speed, keeping him in our sights.

I called out to him once more when we were a bit closer, and this time we heard and turned at the sound of my voice.

"Lis!" he exclaimed as I ran up. "Thank God. What happened? You're bleeding!"

"Huh?" I replied, confused and unaware of what he was referring to. I followed his gaze down to my right leg and found a large gash which was soaking my trousers in blood. "Oh." I was unsure of when or where it had happened, but the adrenaline coursing through my body made it so I couldn't even feel the wound. "I'm okay. It's not deep."

"Alright. Now come. We're almost there." He grabbed my hand, pulling me forward as we began to run up the steps.

After dashing up several dozen steps, we found ourselves before the towering keep. Armored guards rushed towards us, a last defense of the stone structure, and we met them with a clash of steel.

I swung Gaisgea high over my head, striking the guard who had approached me, though the sword bounced back against his thick armor. Now that he was close enough for me to see his face, I realized with horror that I recognized him. "Carthoc," I whispered, trying to gather my frantic thoughts. My hands began to shake, trembling that soon overtook my body.

A smile grew on his face, one that sent chills down my back. "The empath. How lovely it is to see you again."

I clamped my lips shut, not wanting to give him the satisfaction of a response. Burying the initial panic and dread I felt at the sight of him, I let hatred and rage replace it. Letting those emotions fuel me, and gripping Gaisgea so hard my knuckles went white, I lunged at him.

He raised his blade to block my strike. "Did you miss me?" he asked, fingering the whip rolled up on his hip with his free hand. "You seem to have recovered quickly."

Curiosity swirled in his black gaze, and I knew he was desperate to know how I wasn't still laid up with the injuries he inflicted. It was driving him mad, and I smiled wickedly at the knowledge that he would never have the satisfaction of knowing how I had been healed. Frustrated with my silence, he attacked with renewed vigor, slashing at me viciously. I was able to deflect each of his blows, but not able to land any of my own. His armor was thick and sturdy, and despite how strong and sharp of a blade Gaisgea, I couldn't even knick it. I knew I needed a different strategy.

Thinking quickly, I scanned his body, searching for gaps in his armor. I moved quickly, dodging his blows and hoping to tire him out as he tried to hit me, and used the time to try to remember more of my training. Briefly I recalled a note from Siofra. *The neck is almost always vulnerable.* I needed to get close enough for a blow, and focus my aim there.

Whirling, I tried to get out of the way of another blow but was too slow. His sword sliced my leg. My legs buckled, dropping me to my knees as I howled in pain, and the smug smile I remembered from my night at his mercy returned to his face. He thought he had me; he was underestimating.

Gritting my teeth, I tried to keep my own smile from my face as I reached into my boot with my left hand, grabbing the dagger and hiding it behind my back. Not able to resist the opportunity to gloat, he sauntered into my range, and held the tip of his sword under my throat. "We could have done great things together in King Siglind's name. What a shame," he said.

Moving more swiftly than I knew I could, I slipped to the side of his blade and launched upwards, driving my dagger right into a small gap between his helmet and his chest plate.

The blade sunk deep into the side of his neck, and blood began to bubble up out of his mouth as his eyes went wide with shock. He dropped to his knees, his sword falling from his grasp and clattering on the stone.

"I would never have joined you," I sneered, yanking my blade from his throat. He fell forward, face smashing on the pavement, dead. Immediately feeling an enormous weight

210

lifted from my shoulders, I turned my attention back to the larger battle.

As we battled before the gates, more and more of our army joined us at the keep. Several men and women I didn't recognize appeared with a thick battering ram. Vik visibly brightened when he saw them.

"Ah! The troops from the ships have arrived!" he exclaimed, running over to them at once. They recognized him on sight, and immediately bowed as well as they could whilst hoisting the large ram, addressing him as 'Prince Viktor' to the shock and awe of any of the Bushand army that was in earshot.

"It's time to take the keep!" Viktor's low voice rose over the cries of battle, and a resounding cheer followed his proclamation.

Viktor joined my side as the troops moved the battering ram towards the large wooden doors of the structure and began to thrust against it with all their might. "This is the last step. We're almost there," he said. He was breathless, a sheen of sweat on his face and his hair was wet and stuck to his cheeks, but there was a fire in his eyes that I wouldn't have wanted to be on the receiving end of.

The doors proved very thick and sturdy, but the troops never wavered in their relentless bashing. All the while, the Nulian soldiers we had sprinted past were catching up to us, appearing on the crest of the hilltop. We formed a barrier around the ram, protecting them from the new threat so they could focus. Finally, we heard the tell-tale sound of wood splintering and it was like music to our ears. Viktor barked out more orders. "Hold the hill! Myself and my guards are going inside to find Siglind."

"I'm coming with you!" a voice called above the uproar, and Lura fought passed several soldiers to catch up to us.

"Princess Lura, I can't tell you how glad I am to see you," Viktor replied, grinning.

She bowed. "Thank you, Prince Viktor. Now, let's head inside. You'll need my help navigating the keep, and maybe I can talk some sense into my brother."

Our team and a few others handpicked by the prince slipped beyond the barrier of soldiers and past the doors of the Nul keep.

Behind us, the doors swung shut with a bang and silence fell. The sounds of battle were closed outside and the new silence was deafening. But more eerie, or concerning, to me was the iciness that was beginning to creep into my mind, seeping through my walls.

"Where is everyone?" I asked quietly, feeling uncomfortable breaking the silence. We were in a large, empty room, which looked to be some sort of entry hall, though I was not at all familiar with the typical layout of a castle having never before been in one.

"We need to find the throne room. They'll probably be barricaded in there." Viktor's eyes were scanning our surroundings rapidly as he spoke.

"This way," Lura whispered back, leading us down a dark hallway on the left. Moving forward slowly, we all kept our blades and our guards up.

"Lis," Viktor said. "Can you sense them? Maybe verify we're going in the right direction."

I flinched, dreading the thought of opening myself up in this creepy place. With a steadying breath, I began to lower my walls. At once I felt flooded with a chill that went straight to my bones. The poignancy of the feeling had me physically shivering, and Siofra draped a comforting arm around me. At first the feeling swallowed me whole, but after a bit I was able to hone in and determine the direction of its source. As soon as I figured that out, I raised my walls back up, not able to bear it any longer.

"Follow me," I rasped, marching towards a staircase on the right.

Despite the vastness of the castle, its corridors were narrow. Winding and twisting to the point of confusion. We were moving downwards, and had to walk in single file due to the size constraint.

"Where are we headed?" Viktor directed the question to both Lura and myself.

"I'm following the source of that chilling feeling. It will lead me to the sorcerer and hopefully Siglind will be with him," I answered.

Lura's response followed shortly after mine. "This is the direction of a secret shelter room. There is an escape from the castle there. If they sense we are coming, they may try to escape."

"We must hurry," Viktor replied. We continued forward, and just when I felt I was going to go insane the corridor ended and we reached a wooden door.

"In here," I said, doing my best not to cower before the force of what was on the other side.

Viktor set his jaw, determination clear on his handsome face. "We need to be careful when we go in. This could easily be an ambush, and the position of this door makes it so we can't all get inside at once. Lis, I want you near the back of the group. Jion and I will go in first, Siofra you follow, and then the rest of you. Be on your guard." Then, he pushed the door open and all hell broke loose.

Just as Viktor suspected, an ambush lay in wait. From my position near the end of the group, I couldn't see what was happening, but the clatter of steel was enough to tell me a fight was ensuing. By the time I made it inside, all was made clear. A large force had been gathered in the small room, and an active battle was taking place, but the real danger was the archer. An arrow whizzed past my head as soon as I stepped into the room, and I knew at once the archer needed to be taken out.

I immediately scanned the room, searching and found two, one on each side of the room across from the door. "Take out the archers!" I shouted to my companions, a few of which had their own bows slung against their backs, and pointed in the direction of the enemy. I knew I needed to direct my focus to the source of the icy chill that was slowly taking over my body.

Pushing past the scuffle, I moved stealthily along the wall. In the back left corner of the room, I saw two men frantically trying to open what appeared to be a trap door. One was striking, with orange hair that matched Lura's, squinting brown eyes, and full lips. He was thin and muscular, and the crown around his head signified to me that he was the dreaded King Siglind. The other was hard for me to even look at, for the coldness emanated from him and I knew at once that he was the sorcerer Carthoc spoke of.

Suddenly Viktor was at my side, bellowing, "Siglind! You think you can escape, coward?!" He rushed forward just as his target looked up in alarm, fear and raged painted onto his face.

Just before Viktor was about to reach them, the sorcerer whipped a long staff out from under his cloak. I called Viktor's name to warn him, for his attention was focused solely on Siglind, but I was too late. With a sharp twist of the staff and the word "Aggressio." A dagger that was in Siglind's hand flew from him and straight into Viktor's side.

"Viktor!" I screamed, trying to rush to his side but finding my feet too heavy to move. I glanced down at them, trying to figure out what was wrong and when I looked up, I saw the sorcerer grinning at me, pleased with his spell.

Gritting my teeth in rage, I focused my attention solely on my feet. *If he can do this with magic, I can undo it with magic.* My body felt like it was vibrating with energy, and I imagined all of that energy pooling at the bottom of my feet, and peeling them up from the ground. As I pictured this in my head, I physically attempted to lift my feet as well. While it didn't work completely, I felt myself move slightly, and that was enough to encourage me. I had the sorcerer's attention, he was focused solely trying to keep me in one place and clearly growing frustrated that I was fighting back somewhat successfully. I tried several more times, and each time moved slightly more, until I was fully in control of my body once more.

In the meantime, Viktor had continued towards Siglind despite his injury. While I had the sorcerer's attention, the two had begun sparing.

"I thought you were just an empath!" the sorcerer sneered as I approached. "How did you escape my spell?"

"Light magic always overcomes dark," I replied. "And I am of the Manyeo bloodline." I said, dropping my family's name as the symbol of natural, pure magic.

His face paled and his eyes went wide, and I knew my family's powerful reputation had somehow crossed borders to become legend in not just Doctsland. I raised Gaisgea, and imagined the sword lifting a clear protective barrier over myself to shield me from his spells.

But he was too powerful. Just as I was in range to strike him, a spell snaked through my magic and around my neck. I was forcefully raised and then slammed into the ground by an invisible force and held there, as I felt the air being squeezed from my lungs.

I knew by the time I was able to conjure up a counter spell I would be dead, so it was up to a physical attack. Gaisgea, which had clattered to the ground in my struggle, was laying off to the side, just barely out of reach. Remembering the dagger, I quickly reached down and yanked it from my boot, slicing my own leg in the process, though I cared not. Once it was free, I slashed at the sorcerer's ankle, cutting into the back of his heel. The spell was broken at once and I gasped for air.

I grabbed Gaisgea and scrambled to my feet, preparing for another attack. The sorcerer had dropped to his knees, appearing weak, but I had been hunting enough with Jion by this point to know that a wounded animal was often the most dangerous.

He flung another spell at me, and this time I felt tendrils wrap around my sword arm, turning it until the point of the blade was facing me. I gripped the hilt with both hands, fighting against it with all my strength, physical and mental. I was panicked, failing, the blade was inching closer and closer to my chest as sweat was dripping from my eyes. Gritting my teeth, I closed my eyes and mustered up everything I possibly could, shooting it from me like a blast. He fell back, and my arms were released just as the blade was beginning to scratch my armor.

"If you're going to kill me, use your magic. I refuse to die like a common *soldier*." He spat the word.

I stood over him, and held Gaisgea to his throat. "As I said, I am of the Manyeo bloodline. And we do not use magic to harm." He was dangerous, and I knew I needed to kill him before he did more damage, but it was difficult to kill a man on his knees before me who seemed defenseless, though I knew he was anything but.

His eyes darted to the side and my dagger, which I had dropped after cutting his heel, lifted from the ground and came hurtling towards me. The attack forced me to act quickly, putting aside my thoughts and feelings I stuck him with Gaisgea, killing him instantly. The dagger clattered to the ground. Frozen, I tried to comprehend what had happened and catch my breath from the fight.

"Vik!" Siofra's agonized wail thawed me, and I jerked my head in her direction. She was rushing across the room, and I followed her direction with my eyes and was horrified by what I saw.

Our Prince had sunk to his knees, and Siglind was pulling his sword from a bloody wound in Viktor's chest, and smiling. He turned. "You may have taken my city, but now I have taken you 'Prince.'" The word was venomous, and anger unlike any I had ever felt welled inside me like a blaze.

Jion, who had a long deep cut across his cheek, had joined Siofra in her mad dash towards Siglind. The two of them together were horrifying in their anger, and I couldn't imagine being on the receiving end of it. They crashed into Siglind with force, and the battle between the three of them was like a tornado, whipping around the room.

Captivated, I stood in shock and watched as Siglind was somehow staving off blows from the two fiercest warriors I had ever seen. They danced a deadly jig, no one able to make contact with their opponents.

And once it did happen, it was if in slow motion. Siglind was the first to connect, with a hard strike to Siofra's stomach that sunk his blade deep into her. Blood bubbled up from her mouth, spilling onto her chin as Jion roared and attacked Siglind with renewed force and even more aggression, if possible.

I glanced around, trying frantically to find Lura and hoping that she could help to control her wild-eyed younger brother. She was locked in a heated battle with two Nulian guards, despite the fact that she was frantically looking over at Vik and Siglind every chance she got. Seeing Jion and Siofra rush at Siglind seemed to enforce her with renewed effort, and she quickly dispatched her opponents and rushed over into the fray swirling around her brother.

"Siglind! Stop this! You cannot win. Surrender. The people of Bushand, and of Doctsland, merely want their freedom. They will be kind," she pleaded, trying to reason with him as he fought against Jion desperately.

He roared back at his sister, moving to attack her as well as Jion. "You're just saying that because you want my crown. You always have. Everyone is after what is rightfully mine: Bushand *and* Doctsland!"

Knowing I could not help them, I turned my attention to Viktor and found that despite his injuries, he was crawling over to where Jion and Siglind continued to fight. His sword was held tightly in his grasp and once he was close to the battle, he pushed himself up on his feet as I gaped in amazement at his fortitude.

Siglind must have sensed his presence, for he turned suddenly, orange hair whipping around, and shock was written on his features as he found himself face to face with the Prince. Viktor used his moment of shock to his advantage, and without hesitation he stabbed our enemy. "We have taken your city, and you will *not* take Doctsland, or its king," Viktor sneered venomously, pulling the sword from Siglind's abdomen and swiping across his neck, killing him before collapsing himself.

Lura collapsed next to her brother, sobbing and pulling him into her lap. My heart went out to her, sensing her agony and loss even through my walls, but I was overwhelmed myself with panic for Viktor.

Scrambling over to him, I frantically checked his wounds and tried to get him to wake up, to no avail. A million things passed through my mind as Prince Viktor lay dying before me, but one thought was more powerful than the others. "Vik, you cannot die," I whispered, cradling his blood and sweat smeared face in my hands. "I love you."

Chapter Sixteen

Lisalya

It was difficult to feel much joy, despite our success. Doctsland was free of its threat, Bushand was free from tyranny. But the cost was so great, and I felt it heavy in my soul as I watched the wrapped body of my friend slip into the sea, to an everlasting and honorable grave with the Kelps.

Sniffling, I wiped at my tears and turned to Jion. "Could we not have brought her home? To bury her on Doctsland soil? Does she not deserve that much? To be laid to rest in the country she died for?"

His face was covered with the track marks of his own tears. "Her body would not keep for the long journey home. You're right, she deserves to be buried at home. We could not and would not lay her to rest here on foreign soil. The sea is a fitting end for a soldier of Doctsland. Siofra would be happy to have it as her final resting place."

I looked to Viktor for reassurance. He had been inconsolable when he was finally well enough to understand our loss. By that point Jion and I had had some time to process, as well as being preoccupied with the prince and his recovery. For Viktor, the pain was still a bit more fresh. Rather than give me a verbal reply, he simply nodded before stalking back to his cabin.

After our victory, a long council had been held by the people of Bushand, attended by leaders from nearly every town and village in the country to decide a course of action for their future. Having had enough of a dictatorship, they decided to elect their next leader, and in a wonderful twist of fate Merek and Lura tied in the vote and they decided to rule

Bushand together as a team. One of their first orders of business as new rulers was to order a ship made as a gift to Viktor, their way of saying thank you for our efforts in securing freedom for their country.

It was on that very ship that we made our bittersweet journey home. Thankfully it was much less eventful than our way to Bushand, though what it lacked in adventure it made up for in melancholy. It was merely a few weeks before we were once more approaching Loch, and although I'd only been away from home for a couple of months, it felt like an eternity.

One evening as we were closing in on my home Viktor called me into his cabin.

"How are you?" I asked as I entered and he closed the door behind me. He'd kept to himself for most of the journey, and I hadn't really had a chance to speak with him, especially not one on one. And for the sake of his privacy, I kept my mind from probing into his, despite my concern for his well-being. His recovery had been difficult, despite my best efforts. Not only did I lack experience in performing healing magic on my own, but I had never seen grandmother deal with wounds as great as his- the arrow wound in his side which wanted to fester, and the stab in his chest which definitely should have killed him. It was a miracle he survived, and he wore the scars to prove it.

"Physically? I'm fine. You're a very skilled healer, Lis," he said with a small smile as he sat down at his table.

I followed suit. "That's great, but you know that's not what I meant." He chuckled humorlessly, "Yes, I know." He looked down at his hands which were fiddling nervously before meeting my eyes. "I'm okay. It's hard coming home without one of my best friends. It's also hard not knowing what I'm going home to. I left in secret, snuck off against the wishes of my advisors to fight a war. I-" he hesitated, searching for the right words. "I just don't know. During this trip home I've been working on a manuscript, documenting all that has happened. I'm hoping it will be enough for the counsellors in Capital City to understand my departure was necessary. I'll need your help, though." He handed me a stack of papers and a pen. "Will you document all that has happened, starting from our arrival in Loch?"

I nodded, took the paper and set it aside. "You're going home a hero, Viktor. The man- the King- that saved Doctsland from guaranteed invasion. And every man and woman that returns to Capital City with you will defend that claim."

He nodded, still deep in thought, and biting the inside of his cheek to stave off the tears that were welling in his eyes. I hesitated before bringing up what I guessed was truly bothering him. "Vik, what happened to Siofra isn't your fault. There's nothing you could have done."

"I could've fought harder."

"No, you couldn't have. You fought valiantly. In no way were you lacking, though you should have been considering your injuries. Listen to me- *believe me*- when I tell you that it wasn't your fault."

A tear spilled onto his cheek and he looked away, gathering himself for several minutes before he spoke again. "I heard you," he said.

"Heard me? What do you mean?"

"That day. When you thought I was dead."

My mind raced back to the day of the battle, which was weeks ago by now, and frantically tried to recall what I had said. When it dawned on me, I felt the color drain from my face. "You weren't meant to hear that," I whispered.

"Why not?" he replied. "Why shouldn't I know how you feel?"

"Because you're the prince and it's, I'm-""I feel the same way, Lisalya," he spoke gently and waited until I met his eyes to continue. "I love you, Lis." I sat gaping at him, my brain firing in all directions and trying to understand what he had said and how I hadn't felt it from him before.

Seeming to read my thoughts, he smirked. "We've been around each other a long while- I've learned how to mask certain thoughts and feelings, even from you. "My eyes widened. I didn't even know someone could do that.

Reaching across the table, he grabbed my hand. "I want you to come home with me. To Capital City."

"Vik, I-" I began, my thoughts scrambled and racing, still reeling from his confession. "I haven't seen my family in months. I need to go home to Loch."

"Of course, I'm not asking you to come right away. We are nearly to Loch, and we planned to stop there for several days regardless. But when it does come time to return to the city, I would like you to be by my side." Sensing my hesitation, he quickly continued. "I know this is a lot all at once. We aren't arriving until tomorrow, and then we won't be leaving before the end of the week. Please, just... think about it?" he implored, watery eyes searching my face.

"I- yes, I'll think about it. Of course," I replied, gazing down at my hand in his before meeting his eyes. "You love me? Really?"

Leaning forward, he brushed a strand of my hair back, tucking it behind my ear as he smiled gently. "I do. I have for a while actually. Probably since shortly after the shipwreck, though it took me a while to fully realize it."

"Why didn't you tell me?"

"I never imagined you would feel the same. To be honest, that day after I saw Siofra," he choked off. "After the fight with Siglind, I was ready to give up. As you've said, those wounds should have killed me. I was so tired, in so much pain, and had just watched my best friend die. I just wanted to go to sleep, and would have. But your voice, what you said... it called me back. It gave me a reason to fight for my life. You saved me, in more ways than one."

Suddenly the distance between us, though fairly small, seemed far too great. Leaning forward, I pressed my lips to his. The gesture seemed to take him by surprise, though he recovered quickly and melted into the kiss. "I love you," he whispered again, this time against my lips.

"I love you too, Viktor."

***

222

When I left Viktor's cabin the next morning, I found that we were approaching Loch a bit sooner than expected. In fact, the small town was visible on the horizon.

"Ah ha ha." Jion's voice startled me. "There you are. How was it, spending the night in the captain's suite?" I laughed, hiding my face in my hands as he continued. "I'm just teasing you. I was looking for you a few minutes ago to let you know you're nearly home. Although... did he finally ask you?"

"Ask me what? To come to the city? He told you about that?"

"Of course. He's been a nervous wreck about asking you. He meant to ask you before we even left Bushand, but he's been putting it off."

I glanced back to the cabin, where I had left Vik in bed to run out and grab some food to bring back when I was interrupted by Jion.

"So are you coming back to Capital City?"

Sighing, I struggled through my reply. "I-I don't know. I would like to. But... I need to see my family. I need to speak with my grandmother. The Manyeo heir has never left the family on a, well, on a permanent basis before."

"You can still maintain your family's legacy in Capital City. In fact, you can probably heal and help even more people. Loch is such a small town, and not easy to find without a boat. There are many people in the city that could use someone of your abilities that would not or could not make the journey here."

I didn't reply, but mulled over his words as I grabbed the food I'd promised Viktor. He hadn't wanted me to leave, in fact it was only the promise of my swift return with bread that convinced him.

"How long would you say it is until our arrival?" I asked, turning with my arms full to head back to the cabin.

"Two hours at the most."

"I'll be ready," I said before swinging the door shut. Viktor had not moved from his place in bed, where he sat shirtless and waiting for my return.

"There you are. What took you so long?" He reached for a piece of bread only to have me slap his hand away.

"Don't eat it in the bed. Gross. You'll get crumbs all over the sheets." I laughed and set the spread out on the table before sitting down. "I was talking to Jion. We're only about two hours from Loch."

"Are we?" he asked as he crawled out of bed. "Are you excited to see your family again?"

"Deliriously. I've never been away from them this long. It's been difficult."

He kissed the top of my head before taking a seat beside me, "I can imagine."

I watched him cut a piece of bread for himself before speaking. "Can I ask you something?"

"Anything," he replied, settling back into his chair and taking a bite.

"Say I take you up on your offer, and accompany you back to the city. What then? Where will I stay? How will I make my living?"

Viktor shrugged. "You could continue to do what you and your family do here, healing people."

"Surely if someone of my capabilities were to take up residence in the city and became known they would be swamped, overwhelmed, with people asking for assistance. One of the reasons I love Loch is it is a small place. We have time to help everyone that needs it, and don't have to turn anyone away. And you didn't answer my first question—where will I live? I don't imagine I can move right into the palace with you. I'm no princess, or queen. You'll be king soon."

"No, not right away. You're right. But my father married a commoner."

I raised an eyebrow. "Yes, and look at what that led to. Your rule was questioned due to your lineage."

"Well that wasn't exactly standard circumstance. I've given it a lot of thought, and once I'm king I want to adjust the laws. I don't see the point in forcing a royal to marry another royal, the law is outdated and my father should have changed it before he married my mother. Once we marry, you'll live with me. In the meantime, you can stay with Jion and Hope. They've got an extra room."

"Don't you think it will cause ill favor if you are crowned and immediately start repealing ancient laws?" He sighed and dropped his food onto the table, clearly getting irritated with my questioning. "Look, Vik, I'm sorry, but I don't think you've properly thought this through. There's so many if's and but's, and-"

"I don't *care* about the ifs and the buts. I love you, Lis. Isn't that enough? Isn't loving me enough? The love is there, we can work around everything else together. Plus, you promised you'd think about it *after* we arrive in Loch and visit your family. We aren't there yet, so you can't say no yet."

"I'm not *saying* that I'm saying no yet," I sighed, exasperated by his stubborn way of refusing to look at anything from a different perspective than his own. I reached for his hand, rubbing my thumb over his knuckles reassuringly. "I'm not saying no, yet. I just want you to understand that there's a lot for me to think about. It isn't as simple as you make it sound. But you're right. I'm not making a decision until after I see my family, and am able to talk it over with them."

"Good," he said, turning his attention back to the meal in front of him.

I stood. "I'm going to go pack my things and get ready since we're arriving soon. I'll see you in a bit." After one quick parting kiss, I made my way back to my room to prepare to leave the ship.

I had only just finished when a knock sounded at my door. Swinging the door open, I found myself face to face with Viktor. "We're here," he said, smiling softly though it didn't quite reach his eyes.

Nervous energy rolled off him, and I stood on my tip toes to press my lips to his, trying to reassure him. "Let's go see my family."

Oddly enough, the walk through Loch to my home felt

like one of the longest parts of the journey. Viktor was the only person to accompany me; Jion had hung back to direct the majority of the fleet in the towards Capital City, and to stay with the few that were choosing to remain in Loch with us and make sure they didn't get into too much trouble.

We were so close to home I could almost taste it, and the last stretch seemed to drag on and on. When we could finally make out the smoke coming from the chimney of my home, I couldn't stop myself from sprinting the rest of the way, unable to contain my excitement any longer. Viktor hung back, moving forward at his own pace to allow me some time to greet my family before his arrival.

As soon as I burst through the door I smelled my mother's cooking and felt that all was right in the world again. But that feeling only lasted for a moment. Despite the walls I now maintained without much thought, I could sense a deep melancholy blanketing our house.

"Mother!" I called, heading towards the kitchen. "Grandmother! Father!"

"Lisalya?" my mother's voice came from the kitchen moments before she stepped out, a shocked look on her face. As soon as her eyes fell on me a grin spread across her face, and she immediately rushed forward, enveloping me in her arms. "Oh, my sweet daughter, you're home!" she exclaimed, clutching me tightly.

"I'm home." I tried to hold back the tears welling up in my eyes. "We won. We defeated the King of Bushand. Or rather, Vik did."

"Vik?" she said with a wrinkle in her brow, unfamiliar with the nickname I had grown accustomed to hearing and using.

"Prince Viktor," I explained.

"Ahh, you must be close friends with the prince now to use such informalities when speaking of him. I don't think it's proper."

"Well, you see, we…" I broke off at the sight of my father coming in from the atrium. "Papa!" I cried, running into his embrace at once.

"Oh, I missed you both so much, and Grandmother. Where is she?" I asked. Papa just smiled down at me wistfully, and just as I was about to ask what was wrong a knock sounded at the door, signalling Vik's arrival.

"Honey, will you tell her? I'll go get the door." My mother left to go get the door and I moved to follow her, but my father stopped me.

"There's something I have to tell you, Lis."

"One moment, Pa. The Prince has arrived," I said as mother rounded the corner, Viktor following close behind. Rushing forward, I pulled Viktor into my arms. "Now," I said, turning back to my parents. "Where is Grandmother?"

The looks on their faces coupled with the sadness that seemed to be seeping from the very walls made me feel like I was going to throw up. "What is it?" I asked. "What's wrong?"

I felt myself pale as my father began to speak. Viktor wrapped a comforting arm around me. "Grandmother passed a month ago. She went peacefully in her sleep."

My knees buckled, and if it weren't for Viktor's arm around me, I would have fallen to the floor. There had been too much loss, too many ups and downs, and I couldn't process any of it anymore. I wanted to weep, I wanted to scream, but nothing was happening. I could only stand, frozen in shock as I felt a single tear drip my cheek.

"Lis? Are you okay?" Viktor asked frantically, panic in his voice as he wiped hair from my face, brushing a tear away with a soft swipe of his thumb. His face was blurry before me, and I was unable to focus, or find my voice. All I could manage was a shake of my head. *No*, I thought desperately, *I'm not okay.*

Viktor immediately went into prince mode, straightening and addressing my parents. "Lisalya is not well. Can you show us to her room?" My parents stood gaping at him, shocked at our apparent familiarity. Shortly after Viktor spoke my mother snapped out of her daze and directed us to my bedroom.

After helping me into bed, Viktor spoke once more. "I'd

like to stay with her, if that's alright."

My mother's eyes shot to me, silently asking permission. I nodded. "Yes, you're welcome to stay here as long as you would like, my liege," she replied, doing an awkward curtsy before leaving and shutting the door behind her.

"I'm so sorry, my love," he whispered, sitting beside me. Reaching out from under the covers, I grabbed his hand, and finally the tears came in full force. He crawled into bed beside me and folded me into his arms, allowing me to sob into his chest without judgement. I'm not sure how long we laid there, I cried until I had nothing left within me. In times like these, I relied on my grandmother's guidance and soothing nature. Being without her left a void in my life, and in my heart, and I didn't know where to turn.

"Vik," I croaked, my throat hoarse. "I'm going to stay here, with my parents tonight. I'll explain everything to them tomorrow, but I think it's best that I do it alone. They may not give me their honest advice if the prince-" He opened his mouth to object, and I knew he was going to say. 'I'm just Vik.' So I stopped him. "I know you're just you, but my parents don't yet. They still see you as the Prince of Doctsland, someone to be respected and esteemed."

"I understand," he said, pressing his lips to mine. "I'll give you time, and space. I'll head back to the inn and stay with Jion. When you're ready, come find me."

"I will," I said, kissing him once more. "I love you." I whispered the words forcefully against his lips.

He nodded, getting out of bed and heading out the door.

Shortly after Viktor left my mother came into my room. She climbed into bed with me, holding me in her arms.

"You love him, don't you?" she asked. Sniffling, I nodded. "I'm sorry you had to come home to this. She knew her time was coming, and she went peacefully and happily in her bed."

"I know," I replied. "But that hardly makes it easier."

"I know, dear. Just try to go to sleep, we'll catch up in the morning." Emotionally exhausted, I slipped into unconsciousness immediately.

Light streaming through my window woke me up the next morning. For a moment, everything seemed okay, but then the knowledge that had been dropped on me the previous day hit me and a pit formed in my stomach. Mother had already risen, and I could hear her banging around in the kitchen, most likely preparing breakfast. Rubbing my eyes, I yawned and peeled the covers away from my body. I felt a pang in my chest, missing Viktor, and realized it was the first time since we had left Loch all those months ago that I'd spent more than a few hours away from him.

"Are you awake, Lis?" My father's voice sounded from the other side of my door.

"Yes, come in," I called back.

"How are you?" he asked as he pushed open the door and came inside.

I laughed humorlessly. "I've been better."

"Aye I can imagine. You and Ma were dearly close," he said, sitting down on the bed beside me. I merely nodded, not able to find the right words to express the sense of loss I felt. "And I get the sense that you're at somewhat of a crossroads and were looking for her guidance."

I looked up sharply. "How did you know?"

He chuckled. "Please, I've known you for twenty-three years. I can read you like a book. So, will you tell us what's happened? We can sit down with your mother and have breakfast."

"Yes, please," I said, getting up out of bed despite the strong desire to stay in it for the rest of my life.

By the time we reached the atrium mother had laid out a large spread of food and was patiently awaiting our arrival. "Why so much food?" I asked. "It's just the three of us."

"To celebrate your homecoming. We've been waiting, and worried sick. It's been so long, Lis, we feared the worst."

"I know. It has been a long time. It was so hard being away for so long. So much has changed since I left…" I decided to start from the beginning, explaining everything

229

that had happened since I departed all those months ago. Getting through the torture at Carthoc's hands was difficult, especially when seeing the look of horror on my parents' faces. Also difficult was telling them of Siofra's death. She and I had become close friends, and revisiting her death was not easy. Lastly, I told them how I had fallen in love with the prince, and how he had confessed his love for me as well. They listened without interrupting, though I know some of it was as hard for them to hear as it was for me to tell. I finished with Viktor's request. "He asked me to go to Capital City with him. I wanted to talk it over with grandmother. I know how many people need our family here in Loch, I don't want to abandon them. Now that she's gone and I don't have her guidance, I don't know what to do. If I leave, our people will have no one to turn to. They'll have lost both of us."

"'Our people' does not just mean Loch," my mother said. "But all of Doctsland. It is not only in Loch that there are people that need help."

"I know. But our family has been here for generations. And you're both here."

"Lisalya, you love the prince, do you not?"

My father's question confused me, and I furrowed my brow as I replied. "Of course, I just told you."

"So why would you stay here, without him?"

"I-" I was stunned beyond words. "I don't-"

"You're scared, and it's understandable. You've always lived in Loch. And yes, our family has been in Loch for generations. But each generation a family should grow and improve. If you stay here in Loch, you'll just be living the same life your grandmother lived. Think of how many people you could help in the City. Much more than you could help staying here in Loch."

"But the people here need me."

"There are people everywhere that need you. And Loch is not easy to get to. People are much more likely to travel to the city for assistance when they need it than Loch." The similarities between his words and Jion's were not lost on me, and I chewed my lip in thought, looking to my mother to see if she seemed to feel the same way.

She reached out and grabbed my hand. "We will miss you. But we will come visit. You need to go to Capital City. The power of the Manyeo family line is strong in you. Stronger than it has been for a long time. Stronger than Loch. You have the ability and the opportunity to help so many more people. And to be with the man you love. You must go."

I took a deep shuddering breath, their words flying through my mind, and I knew that they were right. I stood immediately. "I need to tell Viktor. I'll be back."

"Please bring him back with you. I want to get to know the man who has stolen our daughter's heart," my mother said.

"I will," I said, smiling as I closed the door behind me.

Racing as fast as I could, I made it back to the center of Loch in record time. I burst through the door of the inn right away, and found Viktor and Jion's faces, clearly startled by my abrupt entrance. "I need to speak to you," I said, locking eyes with the Prince.

He nodded as he stood. "Of course. My room is this way."

I followed him to his room. "What are you doing here?" he asked. "I thought you needed time with your family."

"I do, and I intend to go back to spend more time with them, but I needed to talk to you right away," I explained. When he closed the door behind him he shifted nervously, and I felt bad for keeping him in suspense for even one night.

"I will come with you," I said, not wanting to keep him in the dark for a second longer. "I'll go to Capital City."

A grin spread over his face as he pulled me into his arms. "You have no idea how happy you've just made me, Lisalya," he mumbled into my hair. "And thank you for coming back to tell me. I was dying a little."

Laughing, I leaned up to give him a kiss. "I know, I'm sorry. I needed to speak with my family about it, but they were very encouraging, and made it clear that they think this is what I must do. If I stayed here, I'd be living my grandmother's life. I need to forge my own path. One I hope to share with you."

"Forever," he said with a dazzling smile. I had no idea

what the future may hold; what life in the city may be like, what a relationship with a king would hold, or how to be a queen one day, but although the unknown is typically a frightening thing, I wasn't scared.

THE END

Fantastic Books
Great Authors

darkstroke is
an imprint of
Crooked Cat Books

- Gripping Thrillers
- Cosy Mysteries
- Romantic Chick-Lit
- Fascinating Historicals
- Exciting Fantasy
- Young Adult
- Non-Fiction

Discover us online
www.darkstroke.com

Find us on instagram:
www.instagram.com/darkstrokebooks